BLOOD·BOUND·BOOKS

Presents

D0840873

NIGHT TERRORS
II

An Anthology of Horror

Edited by Theresa Dillon & Marc Ciccarone

You can destroy an army,
You can kill a man,
But you can't kill Terror,
And Terror is what I am!

- GWAR, 2004

CONTENTS

√ Habemus Papam
Desmond Warzel
1

√ A Mother's Love
John Peters
4

√ The Prophet
John Morgan
12

The Dark Room
Madhvi Ramani
18

Forbidden Fruit
Amber Keller
30

√ All Cry
Patricia Russo
32

√ Darkly Dreaming in Black Waters
Jason Andrew
44

Untouchable
Amanda C. Davis
57

The Wager √
Matthew Fryer
60

At Winter's End √
Brad C. Hodson
72

Revivified
Maria Alexander
79

One For The Road √
Jason V Brock
92

A Cat Named Mittens
Bob Macumber
102

Old Nick's Game Town
Dominic E. Lacasse
116

Origin Story √
Christopher Hawkins
122

√ All For You, Sara Sue
Ken Goldman
132

Hi Ted
David Bischoff
143

Child and Guardian
Michael B. Tager
148

Connection
Richard Barber
153

√ The Balancing Act
Lawrence Conquest
167

√ Somebody's Daughter
Angela Bodine
175

√ Now I Lay Me Down to Sleep
Matthew S. Dent
181

Worms in the Walls of My Mind
G.K. Hayes
193

In The Shadows They Hide √
AJ Brown
196

Until I Come Again √
Justin Gustainis
207

The Boy in the Well √
Danny Rhodes
214

Letting Out the Heat
Nicky Peacock
223

Tap Tap √
Gregory Bastianelli
228

Habemus Papam

Desmond Warzel

The crowd in Saint Peter's Square had begun to form just after dawn, and though its composition varied from hour to hour, it eventually assumed a mood of its own, equal parts melancholy and hope.

Within the confines of the Sistine Chapel, the attitude of the assemblage—a hundred Cardinals and twice again as many attendants—mirrored in large part that of the throng outside, though there was also an overlay of nervous tension. This was understandable; they had gathered here for the express purpose of committing a historical act. And though each Cardinal easily maintained his necessary air of contemplative peace, as a body the College of Cardinals shared an unspoken trepidation all their own. This, too, was forgivable; their souls bore a weight that was not shared with their subordinates.

It was well into the afternoon of the conclave's first—and likely final—day. Oaths had been taken, lunch served, prayers recited, and ballots distributed. At the back of the chamber sat Cardinal Taglieri, nervously fingering his ballot paper. His two attendants stood to one side, engaged in whispered conversation, which tapered off as the door was locked and the voting began.

In the days leading up to the conclave, there had occurred among the Cardinals numerous clandestine discussions suggesting—half-seriously—that each should vote for himself, to force a tie and prolong the proceedings. These mutterings carried no weight, of course; leaving aside the oath each Cardinal would swear as he presented his ballot to the Scrutineer, promising that he had voted his conscience, such a tactic would only delay the inevitable unpleasantness.

That which had to be done, would be done.

In the empty white space beneath the declaration *Eligo in Summum Pontificem*, Cardinal Taglieri filled in the name of Cardinal Manzano. Most of the others would do likewise; Manzano was

1

loved and respected throughout the Church, and the late Pope, on his deathbed, had all but named him successor.

And so it was done. The ballots were collected, counted, tabulated. Cardinal Manzano stood and accepted his election, smiling a sad smile, meeting no one's gaze. The ballots were taken to be burned; Manzano was whisked away to pray, select his vestments, and address the waiting crowd. The chamber emptied rapidly. Only the College of Cardinals—now numbering ninety-nine—remained behind, on the pretext of a final prayer.

No one spoke; the single sound within the chamber was the labored breathing of some of the older men.

The second election of the day was imminent, but this time there would be only one elector. They could only wait.

Taglieri wiped a single bead of sweat from his forehead. Though the walls were of cold stone and admitted almost no sunlight, the air in the chamber felt warm and thick.

Some of the others had begun silent prayer. Taglieri followed suit.

He prayed that the new Pope would enjoy good health and long life; long enough that he, himself, would be safely at rest when the next conclave took place.

He prayed that somehow, in some way, the centuries-old bargain would be forgotten or forgiven this time.

Knowing the hopelessness of this, he prayed for absolution, for though he had not made the bargain, he was as culpable as those who had done so, all those years ago. It stained his soul.

And furtively, almost reflexively, he prayed that it would not be he who was selected.

Ashamed, he ceased his entreaties and ventured a glance around the chamber. A few of the Cardinals stared resolutely at the floor; most clamped their eyes tightly shut. Nearly all were soaked with perspiration; the air was barely breathable and the furniture and walls were hot to the touch.

Any time, now.

Taglieri closed his eyes, tried to ready his soul in case his lot was drawn.

He was calm.

What was one soul weighed against six billion? What price too dear to stave off the end of the world for another few years?

Centuries ago, the Adversary had decreed that a single, righ-

2

teous soul, freely given, was inducement enough to delay his return to Earth.

At each conclave, the pact was renewed: the Cardinals selected from among their number the new servant of the Lord; the Adversary, as befitted his station, chose second.

As a blistering wind rushed through the chamber, Taglieri prayed for the souls of all those Cardinals who had been taken over the centuries. There was no knowing what torment they suffered in their diabolical prison, what unspeakable power the Adversary drew from their presence in his realm.

The floor burned his feet. The wind grew stronger, bringing with it foul vapors and the faint screams of the damned.

Something brushed his cheek; a stray ballot paper, perhaps. Or the caress of the Adversary himself as he moved among the candidates, judging them by his unknowable standard.

Let it even be me, prayed Taglieri, *only let it be soon.*

Some minutes later, the wind died away, the deathly heat began to fade.

When the Cardinals opened their eyes again, they were ninety-eight.

It had been Cardinal Mulroney. A good man; indeed, the best of them, or the Adversary would not have selected him as his prize.

Mulroney's attendants would have to be found and sworn to secrecy. His Archdiocese would be told that he had died peacefully in his sleep.

Outside, the crowd in Saint Peter's Square cheered as one, the sound of their merriment reverberating across all of Rome; they had witnessed the column of white smoke that heralded the successful election of a new Pope. Soon the former Cardinal Manzano would appear and give his inaugural address, and a new era of Church history would commence.

The Cardinals retired to their individual quarters, their duties now discharged. As they filed out, a faint, sulfurous odor wafted from the chamber but quickly dissipated and was gone.

Taglieri lay upon his thin mattress, listening to the wild ovation that greeted the new Pontiff.

Long may he reign.

A Mother's Love

John Peters

Amy Jennings stands on her front lawn, staring into the empty street. Fog-shrouded street lamps cast a ghostly pallor over the neighborhood. Amy shivers. She is clad only in a nightgown and her husband's trench coat, which gives scant warmth. Memories—pushing Adam on the swing, playing tag with her little boy and her husband, picnicking on the back deck—swirl through her mind like leaves stirred by the late night breeze. Recollections of a time now gone, taken under cover of night.

Behind her, activity fills the lawn, the house. Men in uniforms search, those in suits and ties talk with her husband, with neighbors. She hears them, noises meant to show activity, attention, though the results will be nil.

Amy knows this. She's been there, in her own detective clothes. *We will do everything possible. We have every available person working this case. We have a nationwide alert out, his description sent to every law enforcement agency in the country. We've had good success. We are hopeful.*

She has recited the statements a hundred times over—Amy's worked half the childhood kidnappings in the Midwest over the past decade. Empty words that leave the promise of hope while making no commitments, no hints at the truth.

Your child is gone. Unless we're lucky, you'll never see him again. His fate is sealed. Tonight, maybe next week, perhaps in a month, he will die. And it won't go easy.

That's what Amy thinks every time she mouths the words of cautioned hope. Those are the thoughts behind the practiced, noncommittal statements the men and women give tonight.

Amy walks across the wet grass. Fear flashes through her. Terror. Panic. *He was here, on this spot.* Amy falls to the ground, her hands tracing the path of horror, Adam's emotions still alive, traceable, as clear to her as a trail of blood. She's felt this before. Her 'gift' everyone calls it. The ability has made her a kidnapping

4

specialist, not because of her powers of observation or ability to out-think criminals, but simply because Amy can feel the emotions of those who have been taken, track their movements.

Tonight is different. Her stomach knots, the taste of bile seeps into her mouth. No professional detachment, just a battle to hold her emotions in check.

Amy climbs to her feet and marches by the men and women in uniform, the detectives in the living room, ignoring the "Mrs. Jennings" and "Are you okay?" Fifteen minutes later Amy pulls from her garage, stopping only because one of the uniforms stands in her way. She recognizes him as the shift captain.

"Amy, where are you going?"

"Out."

"I don't think that's a good idea."

"Am I under suspicion?"

"Should you be?"

"Captain, step away from the car. I'm leaving."

"The FBI response team will be here momentaril—"

"I'm a member of the goddamned response team, remember? I'm the one who leads them to the . . . " She cannot finish the sentence. "Get away from the car." Amy smashes the accelerator. On the street, even with the car between her and the pavement, she still feels it, like an ache in bones. *Terror. Dread.*

* * *

Amy turns the steering wheel sharply to the right, then to the left, and back again. She is not sure how far the car has climbed, though her ears pop continually with the change in altitude. The road is new to Amy, yet she takes the curves with speed and without thought, some deep instinct driving her forward, as if she has traversed this stretch of asphalt a thousand times.

To Amy's right, the mountain climbs above the road, steep banks covered in oak and pine, mountain laurel and vines creeping across the ground, occasionally peeling back to expose sheer rock. To her left, the mountain falls away to reveal an expansive valley of alternating forests and open farmland, ringed by bluish mountain ranges rising in the distance touching the white cumulus clouds. Born and bred on the flat nothingness of Iowa, where fields of corn stretch until they meet the horizon, Amy has never wanted to live

5

anywhere else, content with the open plains and broad, expansive sky.

Until a week ago . . . Adam gone . . . hopelessness . . . nighttime stops at cheap motels . . . calls home, her Ted worried, lost, alone in their home. Amy feels for him, but she can offer no comfort, no explanation. She's following Adam with an instinct borne only to those who have carried a child, a love and obsession only a mother can know. She will find him. At any cost.

As the road ascends, fog thickens into a swirling wall of white. Trees rise in the mist like rotting bones, then fall away as she drives by. *He is close.* Amy picks up her cell phone to call Ted. No service. Doesn't matter. *Adam is nearby.* Amy doesn't know how she understands this. She doesn't even think this to herself so much as some force places the idea in her mind, just as some impulse told her to leave home, to drive across the plains, through the cities, across the Mississippi and now into the mountains of Virginia, following an invisible trail only she can perceive.

The narrow pavement straightens, she crests the top, and the fog gives way to blue skies and bright sunlight. Before her unfolds rolling, rocky hills and meadows. Fences offer protection to sheep and goats, hold cattle and horses from escaping some unseen owner's possession. Other fields give life to crops. She passes long stretches of corn, not the elephant eye high stalks of her native Iowa, but corn nonetheless. Other times she sees the bushy spread of soybeans. Here and there are small plots of land growing plants she doesn't recognize, tall stalks with giant leaves opening outward, as if in supplication to the sky. *Tobacco.* Amy has no idea how she understands this, for she has never seen a tobacco plant. Still, she knows. She is aware of this land's history, its power to give and take, to bestow pleasure and grief, to convey life and harbor death.

Up and down she drives, over hills and into hollows. To her left the sun dips toward the horizon, casting the landscape in golden streams of light, the trees brilliant orange, yellow and velvety red.

Up ahead, on the left, Amy spies the ramshackle building, a series of darkened doors, little neon sign out front proclaiming vacancy at the Sky View Inn. Amy pulls into the parking lot. Ten minutes later, room key in hand, she opens a door and shudders. Inside is his spirit. *Adam. He died in this room.* She smells his blood, his horror.

Yet he is still nearby. Within her grasp. She feels this.

6

* * *

Amy turns from one side to another, her mind between sleep and wakefulness. She hears Adam crying softly, sees him, curled up, wet, inside . . .

She sits, awake, feet on the floor. A hotel clock flashes a fluorescent green four-fifteen. At the window, Amy peers through the blinds, the outside landscape cast in pale moonlight. She dresses and leaves, once again cresting hills, dipping into valleys, taking sharp curves.

There it is. A rolling field, leafy vines covering the ground. In the moonlight Amy makes out the large, misshapen pumpkins growing among the plants. Beside the road a dozen cars are parked, their occupants next to the fence, waiting, the head of the line standing at a large wooden gate.

They know. They all know. They all have someone here. A loved one, snatched away by a drunk driver, or a robbery gone bad, or a child molester.

Amy takes her place in line and waits. She hugs herself, fending off the biting chill of the night air. Inside her car, just a few dozen yards away, is her coat and gloves. Others behind her now, Amy refuses to give up her place in line. *Only so many can be saved.* She knows this, though she hasn't a clue how. *Some won't have the stomach for it, the price too high. Others will simply be too late.*

Not Amy. She will do whatever has to be done, wait however long she must.

A whippoorwill calls in the distance, its cry echoing over the land. The only other sound is the occasional crunch of gravel when another vehicle arrives, pulling from the road onto the shoulder. In the east, faint hints of purple, then orange, color the sky. To the west the round, yellow moon touches the far-off mountain tops. Dawn colors in the east deepen into a fiery mix of red and pumpkin orange, then fade to yellow. Amy watches, breath clouding around her face as the sun breaks the horizon.

She turns her attention toward a barn when its door opens. A man emerges—he wears plain blue overalls and a long-sleeved, red and black flannel shirt, with a simple straw hat atop his head. Frozen grass crackles under his feet as he reaches the gate, takes in the first family—a man and woman, probably early 20s, Amy guesses. Hand-in-hand they follow the farmer, disappearing into the barn.

7

Later—perhaps five minutes, maybe ten—a wail rings from inside. The door swings open and the couple return, she with her head on his shoulder, sobbing, he with his arms around her, supporting his wife. *This is the end for them.* Amy doesn't know how or why she understands this, but she does. Images flash in her head—baby carriage, car backing over it, screams, death of a young one, tension, blame, too much to overcome. The mother will be dead within a year, father an alcoholic.

Amy shakes the images from her mind. She waits. The sun climbs into the sky as the line grows shorter. Some return from the barn quietly, now understanding that loss is an inevitable part of life. Others cannot accept, crying, sobbing, begging for another chance. The man standing before her in line trembles. *A widower.* Amy can feel the hopelessness emanating from him before he takes unsteady steps toward the barn when his turn comes.

No. There is no price too great. Amy will not leave without Adam.

She is next, leaning on the gate. Others weep quietly as their turn nears. Some grow animated. One faints. Amy remains calm. She measures her breaths, keeps her heart rate under control, holds her emotions deep.

The barn door opens. Two men emerge, each dressed in jeans and red long-sleeved shirts. They carry the lifeless body of the widower. He has given all, willing to pay any price asked, and it was not enough.

It will be enough. I will bring him back. I will tear down the walls of Hell from the inside, but I will bring Adam back.

The first man, the farmer wearing overalls, steps to Amy. His face is drawn and tight. Wrinkles fan his eyes, line his forehead, his neck is leathery. The man smiles without humor. His gray eyes are dull. Amy recognizes the expression—the same she sees on those with whom she works, every time they find a body, or report a death. Hopelessness. Resignation.

"I will bring him back," Amy says. "Adam will live. He will walk with me from your farm."

The man opens the gate. They walk to the barn, pull the door shut and wait.

"Whatever the cost?" the man asks, as if he's read Amy's thoughts.

She nods. Even in the darkened building she understands the

man can see her, read her emotions.

He pulls a pouch from his overalls, scoops a handful of to-bacco and slips it into his mouth. "He's suffered terribly," the man says. His voice is soft and muffled.

Amy nods.

"Most folks come here, they'd be better off to have stayed home. It's like losing their loved one all over again. Worse, even, 'cause they come face to face with what happened. The suffering, the horror. And there's nothing can be done about it most times."

Amy looks at the man. "Whatever the cost." Her voice is even and flat.

"You understand you're going to have to watch, see every-thing that happened to him."

No reaction.

"If you do, we might be able to pull'm back. He'll be your son, but won't be your little Adam again. The things that happened to him . . . he will pay a terrible emotional toll. He will never be the same. There could be life-long consequences for him. And for oth-ers."

"You have children?" Amy asked.

The man nods. "Those two you saw carrying the body, they're my boys."

Amy stares at the man. "You carry those children, inside you?"

He shakes his head.

"A mother . . . " for the first time Amy falters. Words fail as a sob rises in her throat. She chokes it off, inhales deeply. "A mother's love is unlike any other on the planet. We carry our young, give birth, nurture them. There is no stronger bond."

"Plenty of mothers come here and leave empty-handed."

"Some are stronger than others."

The man nods. "Maybe you're right. We'll see."

Images flash through Amy's head. She sees what the men did to Adam, how they violated him, abused his body, destroyed his spirit. A week's worth of torture plays through her mind. Amy cries. She curses. She falls to her hands and knees, retches on the barn floor. Twice. Amy never once asks for relief, for the vision to cease.

The images do end. Her last vision is that of Adam, his head wrapped in plastic, eyes wide, mouth open, silently struggling for breath. Then darkness.

Amy is on the ground, tears and snot on her face, vomit on her clothes. She stands.

"Adam will remember," the farmer says. "He'll never recover from this, you understand?"

Amy nods.

"This way."

The man leads her through a door at the other end of the barn, into the pumpkin field. There, one of the giant orange gourds trembles. A crack snakes its way from top to bottom, bright light emanating from the fissure. The pumpkin ruptures to the cries of what sounds to Amy like a thousand demons, weeping and moaning and she understands they do not want to give him up.

Amy steps forward and thrusts her hands into the opening. Inside her hands burn, muck and slime coat her skin, waves of shock crawl up her arms. She does not pull away. Amy tries to tear apart the opening, ready to step inside. She feels the farmer's hand on her shoulder.

"You cannot enter," he whispers.

She screams in rage, her hands groping frantically. Her fingers brush something solid, and she clamps onto hair. Amy pulls, but nothing happens. She holds with her left hand, slips her right hand further in and feels the outline of her Adam's body. She grabs his arm, puts her foot against the outside of the giant pumpkin and heaves. Adam, his lifeless body coated in orange liquid, strands of the pumpkin's interior clinging to his body, slips through the opening.

Amy falls to the ground, pulling her baby to her. She squeezes him, crying, calling his name over and over. She feels his body shudder, then he gasps and cries out.

"It's okay, baby, it's okay. Mommy has you." She looks into his eyes as he turns his face toward hers. They are blank, his face expressionless, covered in guts from the pumpkin's interior. Then Adam cries and Amy pulls his face toward her breasts and holds him, rocking.

After a while—ten minutes, an hour?—she feels hands on her shoulder. It is the farmer and his sons. "We can take him inside, clean him up now."

"He's back?"

The farmer nods.

Amy stands and helps her son to his feet, still holding him

tightly against her body, and follows the farmer toward the old white house set off the road. An hour later, cleaned and bathed and dressed in blue jeans, red t-shirt and a jacket, Adam sits next to his mother on a bench in the front hallway of the home. His head is down, eyes staring at the floor.

"Your love is strong," the farmer says. "Remember, there will be consequences. He has suffered. Later, when he is older, there will be complications."

"Doesn't matter. I have him back now. We will get him the help he needs."

The farmer opens the top drawer of an antique washstand and withdraws a camera. "May we take your picture?"

"Why?"

"What we grow here, few ever see. Fewer understand. It's rare to see someone reap anything but death from our fields. Maybe it sounds silly, but we like to keep the ones who come back, their picture that is, and their names. A way to remember. Can we?" He lifts the camera and Amy nods.

"May I see them?"

"The pictures?"

She nods.

"I don't know if that's a good thing."

"Please?"

The man shrugs.

He snaps the boy's picture, then leads them through a door, into a long, darkened hallway. A light flips on, and she sees pictures, some yellowed, others fresher. A few are black and white, the rest color. Under the pictures, printed in plain black lettering are names: Richard Speck, Kirkwood, Ill.; John Wayne Gacey, Chicago, Ill.; Richard Ramirez, El Paso, Tex.; Ted Bundy, Burlington, Ver.; Aileen Carol Wuornos, Rochester, Mich.; Gary Leon Ridgeway Salt Lake City, Utah; Jeffrey Dahmer, West Allis, Wisc.

She looks from the pictures to the farmer. "These people..." She remembers his earlier words. *There could be lifelong consequences. For him, and for others.*

"Like I said," the farmer says. "The sort of person only a mother could love."

The Prophet

John Morgan

A silence descended over the room. A thick, awkward, funeral-parlor kind of silence that stretched out for long moments before the stranger spoke:

"I'm not going anywhere," he said. "Not until I've seen your brother."

The elderly couple had retreated to the kitchen. The woman, who looked as if she was about to break down in tears, collapsed into a chair while her husband had to lay a hand out on the worktop just to keep himself upright. As if to prove a point, the uninvited guest dragged a chair from under the table and casually lowered himself onto it.

"Who told you?" the old man croaked.

The stranger leaned forward and spread his hands. "I'm not here to cause you any trouble, Mr. Johnson. All I'm asking for is a short interview with Billy. Ten, fifteen minutes, tops. Then I'm out the door and gone for good; you'll never hear from me again."

Johnson narrowed his eyes and cocked his head. "What do you want with Billy?" he asked. In the small, dingy space his voice sounded like a bundle of dry sticks rubbing together.

"My name is Kane Curtis and I'm doing some research for a book." Grinning sheepishly, he waited for a response but didn't get one. "I'm a writer," he added, somewhat pointlessly. "I'm working on a project about life after death."

The Johnsons exchanged a look that was impossible to interpret so Curtis said: "It was Blackwood who told me about Billy."

Mrs. Johnson flinched.

Her husband, who stared at Curtis through deep pools of shadow, took a shuffling step forward. There was nothing threatening in the move itself—the man must have been pushing seventy—but there was something about the scene, the room, and the increasing darkness, that put the writer on edge.

"What did Blackwood tell you, Mr. Curtis?" asked the old

man.

Curtis fidgeted. "Not a lot," he admitted. "Just enough to get me curious. He was falling-down drunk at the time and a lot of what he told me was gibberish. But he did suggest that I pay your brother a visit . . . said Billy had the ability to talk with the dead. The 'real deal,' he called him. Reckoned Billy could tell me a thing or two about life after death."

Mrs. Johnson made a curious little noise at the back of her throat and Curtis let his eyes drift in her direction. She looked like something that could have been left outside to scare the crows.

"Listen," he said, "do you mind if we turn on the light? It's getting pretty dark . . . "

"Did Blackwood tell you about the night he came here?"

Curtis looked at the old man and laughed. It was a mirthless sound that fooled no one, least of all himself. "Oh yeah," he said. "He told me something all right."

Johnson took another step around the table, his fingernails dragging along its surface. "What did he tell you, Mr. Curtis?"

Curtis shifted in his seat and cleared his throat. "He told me you had your brother tied to a chair in the attic. Said he'd been there so long that his ass had fused to the seat and the ropes had sliced into his cheese-like flesh. He told me that after speaking to your brother for twenty minutes he suggested you do the world a favor and, to quote Blackwood, butcher the sick bastard's throat."

Curtis shrugged his shoulders and chuckled nervously. He waited for the old couple to break down with laughter, to wipe the tears from their eyes and

(turn on the freaking light)

dismiss the accusation as the funniest thing they had ever heard.

But they didn't, and that's when Curtis suspected that Blackwood might have been telling the truth after all.

Johnson shuffled closer, his slippered feet whispering along the linoleum. "Have you ever been to a séance, Mr. Curtis?" he asked.

Curtis blinked. "Could we have the light on, please?"

"Have you *ever been* to a séance?"

"No," said Curtis. "Not yet, but I intend to, for the book."

"Billy used to hold séances. Claimed the dead could speak through him. People used to come from miles around just to hear

13

him—made quite a name for himself. Did you ever wonder why it is that the dead talk nonsense, Mr. Curtis?"

"Nonsense?"

The old man's face twisted into a funeral mask, the creases made gray by the last, fading ghost of dusk. "Tell Bessie," he mimicked in a high, girlish—and quite disturbing—voice, "she should take that holiday . . . Tell Danny that I never thought the color blue suited him . . . Tell the kids that everything is peaches and cream over here . . . "

Curtis frowned and said with a shrug, "Because it's all a fake?"

Johnson moved closer, the smell of piss and old tobacco swirling around him like an aura of sickness. "It's because the dead lie, Mr. Curtis. Most of them don't want to burden us with the truth. So they yap about a bunch of shit that really don't matter."

"What truth would that be?"

"The truth about death; about the fate that awaits us all. There is no light. There is no joy. There's only . . . " Johnson let the sentence hang and in the inky darkness tilted his head towards the ceiling.

Curtis raised his own head, knowing that the gesture was aimed, not at the ceiling, but at the attic three floors above where, according to Blackwood, he would find Billy Johnson strapped to a chair—his face a wretched knot of agony, mouth yanked wide in a silent, never-ending scream. *Look into his eyes*, he recalled Blackwood saying, *and then try telling me there's no such place as hell.*

"But then, one night, something happened," Johnson continued. "Something else got into Billy. Something that didn't lie. I saw it happen, Mr. Curtis. I saw it with my own eyes. One moment he was giving his usual honey-coated spiel, and then he kinda jumped back in his seat—like he was shoved—and started to twitch all over. He started to lick his lips and grimace like he'd tasted something nasty; then he was thrashing his head and yelling stuff that made me cold all over. '*Get out of my head!*' he kept shrieking. '*I won't tell them that, I won't tell them that, I WON'T TELL THEM THAT!*'

"And then, well . . . he went insane. The light went out in his eyes, only to be replaced by a look so wicked that it damn near emptied the room. I tied him up, trying to keep him safe until the thing left him, but it never did." Johnson chuckled and his teeth shone like bone in the darkness. "We asked your friend, Blackwood, around

14

because we thought he might be able to help. He actually shat himself though, up there in the attic—did he tell you that? Well, I can't say I blame him. He knows what's waiting for him on the other side now; he knows what's waiting for all of us. The thing inside of Billy told him. The thing inside of Billy told him everything."

Curtis licked his lips. "Do you *really* believe your brother is possessed?"

Johnson nodded, his flesh creaking like old rope twisting on the gallows. "I don't know what it is, I hope to Christ I never find out, but I do know that it enjoys what it does . . . and that's telling us things, Mister Curtis. Dreadful things . . . dreadful, awful things . . . And it won't go away; it won't stop no matter what we do."

Curtis was silent for a moment, listening to the wind as it rattled the window in its flaky, rotting frame. "Take me to your brother, Mister Johnson," he said.

"No."

"I don't like making threats, but I'm pretty sure the police would take a dim view of your little ghost story, and the way you've been treating Billy."

Johnson was silent a while. The room had grown darker still and his features were now almost completely hidden by the shadows.

"If I take you to see him," the old man said, "do I have your word that you'll never come back?"

"Absolutely."

Johnson sighed and Curtis heard, but could barely see, the old man step away. "I'll get you a flashlight. You'll need one up there."

Curtis felt the relief wash over him in a dizzying flood. "Great," he said. "Is it all right if I turn the light on in here? I can barely see my hand in front of my face."

The old man's voice drifted back through the darkness. "The lights don't work," he said, the words cold and emotionless. "The lights haven't worked since the night we put Billy in the attic."

* * *

After his meeting with Billy Johnson, Curtis descended the stairs on legs so weak they felt like they'd been pumped full of anaesthetic.

15

Reaching the bottom, he floated dreamlike along the darkened hallway—he vaguely recalled dropping, or maybe hurling, the flashlight in the attic—and prodded the kitchen door open with the palm of a ghostly hand. There was a woefully inadequate candle burning on the kitchen table. It turned the dingy room into a flickering cave of shadow and half-light.

Mr. and Mrs. Johnson stood at the sink with their backs turned to him. They appeared to be washing and drying crockery. Curtis blinked and looked at them for a moment, and then his eyes fell upon the bottle of whiskey on the kitchen table. A tumbler was set out beside it. It was full to the brim.

"I thought you might need a drink," said Johnson, not bothering to turn around.

Curtis approached the table and brought the glass to his lips with a hand that was far from steady. Mrs. Johnson sneaked a glance over her shoulder and started whimpering again.

"He needs help," said Curtis, shakily. "You do know that, right? You do know that your brother is well and truly out of his fucking mind?"

And that was when Mrs. Johnson couldn't contain herself any longer, and when Curtis realized she hadn't been whimpering at all. She'd been chuckling. Chuckling like a mischievous little schoolgirl who has a secret no one else knows. The old woman rocked her head back on scrawny, almost non-existent shoulders and exploded into a whirlwind of howling laughter. Curtis stared at her withered frame, the candle light making her look like something dug up out of the ground; her husband who continued to dry the crockery as if everything was peachy perfect. It suddenly occurred to Curtis that—at some point in time, and no doubt within this very house— Mr. and Mrs. Johnson had descended into madness.

"It's a little too late for Billy, I'm afraid," said Johnson with his back still to Curtis and barely audible over his wife's laughing.

Curtis opened his mouth. Shut it again. He started to back away towards the door.

"You see," Johnson continued, casually wiping at a yellowing plate with the cloth, "we knew we had to do something to help Billy—something to make him better. But nothing worked. We couldn't just leave him tied to a chair forever, now could we?" He turned around, and there was something about the grin on his face that made Curtis want to lunge for the candle and snub it out. John-

16

son shot a glance up at the ceiling. "At the time, we thought there was only one way to set him free . . . death. I haven't been up to the attic in about five years or so, Mister Curtis. Neither has my wife, for that matter . . . "

Curtis was backing out of the room—retreating down the hallway—but still he couldn't tear his eyes away from the old man's dead-pan stare, or from his wormy, gray lips in the awful, flickering light

"We starved him to death. Five . . . years . . . ago."

Curtis' back hit the front door. He whirled around to open the latch and the last thing he heard before sprinting out into the cold night air was the shrieking of an old woman's insane laughter.

That, and the ranting of a crazy, old man. A crazy, old man screaming: "Mister Curtis! Oh, Mister *Currtiss!* I don't know what you were talking to up there, but its been dead a *looong* time, now!"

The Dark Room

Madhvi Ramani

Laura never dreamed. Or, at least, she never remembered her dreams. As a film editor, she relied on some intuition of how dreams worked to mold material into stories that worked on a subconscious as well as a conscious level, but it was still a somewhat disorientating experience when, about midway through her third trimester, the image of Becky shoveling snow from the front of their Victorian terrace stayed imprinted on her mind when she awoke. She opened her eyes, and gradually, their bedroom, gray in the morning light, replaced the gleaming piles of snow outside. The radio clicked on. The reporter read a story about a serial killer who had been burying dead bodies in his allotment; Becky padded to the shower. Laura closed her eyes, drifting in and out of sleep, listening to interviews with the police, the man's wife, his neighbors. She still had a bit more time in bed.

She opened her eyes again to the sound of a crisp white shirt sliding over Becky's arms, and watched her button it up. Laura was glad that she had waited to meet her Miss Right. Ever since she was a child, she had harbored the dream of having a normal family life; marriage and children. That dream had delayed her coming out and caused much angst and self loathing. Even after that, she had been through countless relationships with women who had commitment issues or were reluctant to face the hurdles of IVF or adoption. But Laura had waited, and three years ago, Becky had stepped into her editing suite to watch a cut of a corporate video that Laura had worked on for her company.

Becky bent down and kissed her. The crisp whiteness of the shirt reminded Laura of her dream.

"I dreamt that you were shoveling snow from the front of the house last night."

Becky paused, and looked at her.

"That's strange. So did I, and look—"

Ice crystals silently splattered against the clean, wide window, clinging to the glass before slowly melting and dribbling away, obscuring the light.

By the time she got to Soho, gray at this time in the morning now that the neon lights had been switched off, there was no trace of snow left. It seemed as if there were two streams of traffic: those weary-faced prostitutes, crumbling lipstick clinging to the corners of their mouths, and rent-boys scuttling away in the shadows, and then the fresh-faced media types, texting and talking, café lattes in hand, striding into work. They occupied the same space, but seldom collided, like the moon god Anningan who perpetually chased his sister Malina, the sun goddess, through the skies.

Normally, Laura too would be rushing along with the media types, not paying attention to that other group of people, but today she was more aware of her surroundings. Maybe it was some sort of survival instinct triggered by the pregnancy. Or simply that she was walking slower, due to her balloon-like belly. Harder to dismiss was the fact that she and Becky had had the same dream. It had to be something to do with the pregnancy bringing them closer together. After all, it was Becky's egg that had been fertilized in vitro with sperm from an anonymous donor.

At work, she got started on what was to be her last project before going on maternity leave. It was a job from Piquant, a production company that specialized in those American-style factual programs that were all over the cable channels; Top Ten Serial Killers, Nature's Deadliest Reptiles, that kind of thing. This one was called Abominations of Nature. She turned on her computers, and sat down to log the footage.

She pressed play. A new born calf lay on its side in a dark stable, while a cow lowed dementedly in the background. The calf was trying to get up to go to its mother, who was standing in a corner ignoring it, but its legs kept flailing and giving out. It turned its head towards the camera. It was grotesque; three faces merged together, meeting at one wide bloodshot eye in the middle. She pressed pause. A chill went through her, turning her stone-cold.

When she got home, her head was swarming with disturbing

images. It was exactly the reaction the production company wanted to get from what were, after all, just natural mutations. She ran a bath, and was trying to relax in it when Becky came home.

"You look tired," she said walking into the bathroom.

"Mmmm, a bit. I've just been landed with a horrible project. All about deformed animals."

"Nice," Becky said kneeling by the bath and stroking Laura's belly. She closed her eyes.

"Maybe it's just making me anxious because of the baby."

"The baby is perfectly healthy—you heard the doctor."

"But I'm a geriatric mother!" she said. They had laughed at the phrase upon seeing it on the form at the hospital. She had meant it jokingly, but it had come out with a quiver of hysteria.

"Everything will be fine, darling. Now, what would Madame like for dinner?"

"Hmmm . . . artichoke and truffle soup to start, followed by lobster and saffron risotto, and a crème brûlée for dessert—oh, with fresh berries. I love berries."

Becky bowed extravagantly as she left the bathroom.

"Oh, I forgot to ask about your day," Laura shouted after her.

"The usual. New consultant started today."

After dinner—salmon with celeriac mash—she felt sleepy, even though it was only nine o'clock. Everything exhausted her nowadays and despite the bath, her feet and back still ached.

"I think I'll turn in," she said.

"I'll join you soon. I've got to finish off a couple of things."

Laura went into the bedroom and lay down. After a while, she heard Becky climb the stairs to her office in the loft and close the door.

That night, Laura dreamt that she was standing before a doorway fluttering with red streamers. Through the streamers she caught glimpses of people; a flash of red hair, a trouser leg falling loosely around a worn-out leather shoe, the hem come loose, a pinched nose that looked like Becky's. The streamers brushed her arms as she walked through the doorway, and everything went quiet. The people had vanished. Around her were mannequins with various limbs missing, a chainsaw, crutches, reels of bandages . . . Her skin felt wet, and when she looked down she realized that she was streaked with blood from where the streamers had touched her.

The duvet rustled by Laura's ear, accompanied by a soft moan. She felt drowsy, even though she had slept long and deep. Becky moved over to where she lay on her side. Her breasts pushed against Laura's back, and her breath gently lifted a few strands of hair from the top of her head. Years ago, when she was still learning how to become a editor, someone said that the proximity of sound that you got from a radio mic was the same as the person breathing next to you in bed. She didn't feel like having sex, especially after the dream, but didn't have the energy to resist. It was as if her body and her thoughts were no longer her own, that they belonged to someone else. But who? She felt certain that the strange dream was not hers but it couldn't have belonged to the baby, and Becky? The sensation of Becky's fingers parting her lips and entering her brought her to her senses. The dream had to be hers, springing from genuine anxieties that seemed alien to her when awake. She looked over her shoulder at Becky, who had her eyes closed, lost in her own world of sexual pleasure.

It was a bright, clear day. The sudden freeze had disappeared as quickly as it had arrived, leaving the temperature comfortably cool once more. Laura, however, still felt unsettled. At work, she called Anna. The phone rang and rang, but no one picked up. She hung up and redialed.

Anna was the only one of Laura's friends who had been through the whole pregnancy thing—three times in fact—and might understand what she was going through.

"Wow you are persistent, is everything okay? You're not having the baby are you?"

"No, no nothing like that. Just felt like a chat, that's all."

"Okay, I'm on the school run right now—can I call you back?"

"Why don't we meet for lunch?"

"Love to, but can't today, sweetie, got to make a robot costume for Cas and—"

"Tomorrow?"

"Tomorrow's karate and ballet, and Millie's lost her tutu again . . . What about next week? Wednesday?"

"Okay, see you then."

Laura didn't feel as if she could wait a week before discussing the disquiet that had come over her, but she did not want to bother Becky with such irrational thoughts, especially as they concerned her. She turned back to her screen, where what looked like a huge spider was scurrying along the ground. It was only when you looked at it carefully that you realized that it was a rat, flicking its multiple tails around it as it moved.

She had the dream once more before her meeting with Anna. This time, she was walking along a busy pavement a short distance behind a couple. Neon lights flashed. She recognized the bright coppery red of one of the women's hair, and although she could not see her face, she knew that the other woman was Becky. She followed them to a shop. Along the wall, down its side, a thin hand-painted sign read: NIGHT VISION. Inside, they disappeared through the door with the red streamers. Laura went through after them, and, as before, found herself alone and smeared with blood.

Normally, having spent the whole week in front of a screen, Laura liked to get out at the weekend. But the temperature had risen, making her feel hot and bothered, so she spent the weekend trying to immerse herself in various cooking, DIY and magazine shows. She could not get comfortable on the sofa; her belly, her breasts, her nipples, had expanded out of her control. Until now, she had not experienced any problems with pregnancy, and she even remembered feeling pleasure in the second trimester.

Becky must have sensed Laura's mood, because she offered her cups of tea and cooked for her with a sorry look on her face, like a person who could only chuck buckets of water over a beached whale. Part of her acknowledged that Becky was being a sweet, considerate partner, but the image of her with the redhead stuck in Laura's mind.

The uneventful weekend and Becky's attention must have paid off, because on Sunday night Laura had a different dream. It was of a little girl playing with bandages. She was wrapping them around herself—her arms, her feet, her legs and her head, until only her pale blue eyes showed. They were Becky's eyes. When she woke up, she wondered if she had just had a vision of their future child.

"Oh darling, sounds like a case of pure anxiety. You're worried about childbirth, and the possibility of Becky going off with another woman—especially now, when you need her more than ever," said Anna, stuffing another forkful of couscous into her mouth.

They were in *Vita!* a healthy eatery on Berwick Street. Laura picked at her salad. She got heartburn if she ate too much.

"Yes but ever since that day we had the same dream, I've got the strange notion in my head that . . ." she trailed off, reluctant to put the thought into words.

Anna stopped eating. "What? You can tell me. When I was pregnant, I had the urge to eat mud, and I actually tried it; scooped a couple of handfuls from the garden straight into my mouth!"

"What, you mean you didn't even bother cooking it?"

They laughed. Laura looked at her friend, ". . . the notion that the dreams I'm having are not mine—that I've somehow tuned into Becky's dreams, and can witness her deepest, darkest thoughts. I mean, I never even used to have any dreams, and now—"

"Oh honey, you're just trying to find fault with her. I was particularly irritable towards Miles in my third trimester. I think I was testing him, or even training him, to see if he'd still stick by me, be patient, caring—you know, good father material. But you needn't worry, I'm sure she'll make a wonderful mother."

As she strolled back to work in the sunshine, swelling fingers pressed against her swelling belly, Laura felt as if a weight had been lifted. The dreams, the paranoia and the moodiness were a result of all sorts of hormonal and physical changes. Poor Becky. Poor innocent Becky, she was thinking—when she saw it. Something from the dream world transplanted into reality. As if the moon had been placed next to the sun. A doorway to a shop. Next to it, down the side of the wall, spindly, dark green letters spelled out: NIGHT VISION. She stopped. A man in a suit bumped into her and tutted. She felt herself burning up. Her heart raced. Was she dreaming? Glancing around at the women swishing by in skirts, tourists snapping photos, chit-chatting creatives dashing to and from lunch meetings, she knew that she was not. She stood very still, laboring to breathe, while people weaved around her on the narrow pavement.

"Are you alright?" someone asked. Laura nodded, then, compelled, crossed the road.

It was a couple of degrees warmer inside the shop. A fan lazily turned its head from one corner of the room to another. A man

23

with dirty blond hair and a crooked face sat behind the counter reading a magazine. He looked up at Laura, who stood in the doorway waiting for her eyes to adjust to the dim light, then down at her belly, and back at his magazine. The place had dirty, worn-out red carpets and was filled with rows of pornographic DVDs. It was like any other Soho sex shop, but as the breeze from the fan reached the far corner of the room, Laura perceived the rustle of streamers. She tried to maintain her self-control, and walked along the wall, studying the covers of the DVDs as she went; nubile girls with cotton panties splayed out on beds, big-bosomed blondes in maid's uniforms, a policewoman in pvc . . . At the far end of the room, she looked up. It was exactly as she had seen it in her dream. She reached out to part the streamers—

"You don't wanna go in there."

She paused, and looked at the man at the counter.

"Maybe I do."

"There's nothing in there for you to see," he said. They held each other's gaze for a moment, then Laura dropped her arm and stepped back. As she did so, the breeze from the fan brushed her face and gently parted the streamers for a moment—enough time for Laura to see some discarded mannequins with their limbs missing.

The phone rang and rang, reverberating and mixing with the ringing in her mind. Anna picked up.

"I've just seen it, the shop."

"What shop?"

"The shop in my dreams. *Her* dreams. This proves it; they're Becky's dreams—"

"Calm down. Breathe. Now, tell me, slowly, what happened."

"I was walking back from lunch and I saw the shop. Exactly the same as the one in the dreams, with this sign outside, and that doorway—"

"Sweetie, calm down please. You're worrying me. Think about it; you work in Soho—you must have passed that shop dozens of times."

"Yes but I've never been inside! How could I possibly know about that doorway—" Laura's belly tightened. Something moved inside her. She couldn't breathe.

"Laura? What's going on?"

24

The tightening got worse. "I think I've started having it. Contractions."

As it turned out, Laura was just experiencing Braxton Hicks; practice contractions that eventually passed. Anna talked her through them, and stayed on the phone to calm her down afterwards. Laura left the office soon after their conversation, incapable of getting any more work done that day. As she approached the house, she felt a sense of dread. What was she going to do about Becky? Despite Anna's best efforts, Laura still felt suspicious of Becky. She thought of all their time together and realized that she did not really know her. Only now, through the dreams, had she gained access to Becky's private world. She would have to confront her when she came home, but what would she say? I know you're having an affair with a redhead and have been visiting sex shops because of a dream? It sounded crazy. Maybe Becky would wonder, like Laura was wondering now, who her partner really was. What would be the point in confronting her anyway? As she inserted her key in the lock and turned, she considered just packing her things and leaving.

The smell of frying onions greeted her when she stepped inside. The radio was on in the kitchen, and she heard the sound of water running. She crept down the hall and stood in the doorway of the kitchen, watching Becky chop tomatoes, expertly using the knife, brow knitted in concentration . . . or something else? She wondered what Becky was thinking about. Becky looked up, and they both started.

"Why are you jumping? You crept up on *me!*" she said, laughing.

"Why are you home so early?"

"I could ask you the same question," she said.

"Oh, pregnancy—can't work," said Laura. "And you?"

"I thought I'd make you a nice dinner. Crème brûlée with berries and everything."

Becky smiled, her pale blue eyes betraying nothing. Laura didn't know what to do, what to say. How did one broach the subject of leaving during a perfectly normal conversation? This was her home, and she was carrying Becky's child. If she left now, what would become of her dream of having a normal family life? Maybe Becky just had to fulfill her needs elsewhere while Laura was pregnant—was it really worth giving everything that Laura ever wanted

25

up over an affair and some sex shop? And with the baby almost due . . . No, it was safer to keep up the semblance of normality.

"I'm going for a bath," she said.

That night, she dreamt of the room more vividly than ever before. This time, she ventured further in and noticed, behind a couple of mannequins, another doorway, filled with darkness.

At the weekend, they went shopping. Under the bright lights of the shopping center, with its temperature-controlled air, surrounded by other couples, pensioners enjoying a cup of coffee with a slice of cake, and toddlers ambling in one direction, then stopping and randomly veering off in another, Laura almost felt as if everything was normal again. They purchased a white cot, some organic nappies and baby grows. Laura admired various dungarees and dresses—so fashionable—but they would have to wait until they knew whether it was a boy or a girl.

On the way back to the car park, a woman approached Becky.

"Oh hello! Laura, this is Sian, who's just joined the company," said Becky. She turned to Sian and said something else, but Laura could no longer hear. A ringing sound had started filling her ears, getting louder as she took in the coppery red of Sian's hair, her crutches and her left leg, which ended abruptly just below her short skirt in a smooth, round stump. Then, the contractions began.

She was alone now, cut off from the rest of the ward by a light green curtain. Calming, she supposed, was why they used that particular green in hospitals, except now, that particular green had become associated with hospitals which wasn't so calming anymore. And the smell, that strong smell of disinfectant with a hint of mash potato and urine lingering behind it.

The contractions were, once again, Braxton Hicks. Laura had tried to tell the nurse that something was wrong, but the nurse had insisted that she concentrate on staying calm, for the baby. She had given Laura a pill.

Since then, there had been lots of waiting, and comings and goings, but Laura didn't mind. As long as she was away from Becky. The redhead, the amputated leg, the crutches, the chainsaw, the mannequins with missing limbs, they all fit together, but she couldn't

26

quite figure out how. Not now. Her mind was a bit too hazy.

The curtain was pulled back, its rings screeching along the rail.

"Now Laura, I would advise you to go on maternity leave immediately. It won't do to have you working on a film about deformed animals in your state. As you saw from the scan, the baby is perfectly healthy. Your serotonin levels seem to be a wee bit imbalanced due to the pregnancy, which is probably what's causing the panic attacks, so we're prescribing some pills that will help redress that balance. Okay?" Laura nodded, and left the hospital with Becky, clutching the photo of the scan in one hand, and the pills in the other.

She phoned her boss that night, and explained that she was having problems with the pregnancy. He was very supportive; it would be no problem getting a freelancer in to finish the edit on schedule.

Now that she was on maternity leave, everything was calmer, although she was still drawn repeatedly to that dark room during the night. She wondered what was in there, but every time she tried to find out, she woke up. She took her pills twice a day, and got out of bed late. She liked watching a particular chat show in the mornings, where men and women argued with each other over the paternity of their children. She would watch it with a cup of tea and a slice of toast thinly spread with Seville orange marmalade.

She felt better knowing that some hormonal imbalance was making her anxious, although the alarm bells still rang in her head, just at a lower volume. Like when a pillow is placed over an alarm clock.

Now, instead of worrying about Becky, she worried about the thing growing inside her. The hospital had said that everything was fine, but she found herself staring for long periods at the black and white photo of the scan. Sometimes it looked like a perfectly healthy little baby. Other times, she wondered about the fists—were the fingers just curled up, or did the hand abruptly end there, at the knuckles? Sometimes it hardly looked human; the way that its nose and lips protruded, for example, looked like a snout, as if it were half-human half-pig. It was funny, she thought, how something could exist inside her without her knowing fully what it was.

27

One day, slowly stretching her legs within the confines of the house, she found herself in Becky's study. It was tidy and organized as always, but the sunlight coming in through the window highlighted the dust whizzing around in the air. She opened a filing cabinet at random and looked through the files, all neatly labeled. Tax returns 2010-2011, Receipts 2010-2011, Invoices 2010-2011.

Tired, she sat down and turned on the computer. She went online, and clicked on internet history. Google, HMRC, Guardian Unlimited, BBC News, Recipes Galore, amputee devotees. Laura froze. She didn't want to click, but she did; images of women with stumps where their arms and legs were meant to be laying provocatively on beds or on the floor flashed before her eyes. In a few cases, they were naked. The house shuddered slightly; the front door had just been shut. She turned the computer off and quickly left the study, closing the door quietly behind her. She went down to the bedroom, crawled under the blankets and closed her eyes. She thought of the cat she had had once, who would close her eyes whenever she didn't want to be seen. She heard Becky climb the stairs. The bedroom door opened.

"Laura? Are you okay?"

"Yeah, just tired," said Laura, not moving, trying to keep her voice steady.

"Oh, I was due to meet some clients for a drink tonight. Should I cancel?"

"No—no."

"Are you sure?"

"Yes, I'm just going to stay in bed all evening anyway, so you might as well go out."

An hour later, Becky came in again to tell her that she was off. Laura lay still until she felt the shudder of the front door closing, then went downstairs, and followed her outside. Becky was already at the end of the road, and it was difficult for Laura to keep up. The air was heavy and humid, and Laura was panting by the time she got to the station. She managed to board the adjacent carriage to Becky's and kept an eye on her through the window in the door that separated them. Becky changed trains, then got off at Piccadilly Circus. Laura followed her as she made her way into Soho. It was like watching her worst nightmare unravel. The streets were crowded, and, amidst the flashing lights, screeching black cabs and hoards standing outside pubs and bars blocking the pavements, she lost sight of Becky. It didn't matter; she knew where she was going. She just had to see her there, find out. Know for sure.

She pushed the door of the shop open. As before, it was even hotter inside. The shop was empty. She walked though the doorway with the streamers, their rough papery surfaces brushing her skin. She looked down at her arms, but there was no blood in sight. A few things had changed in this room from the dream; the chainsaw, crutches and bandages had disappeared, but the mannequins were there, and, she discovered as she went further in, so was the doorway to the dark room. As she approached, she heard a woman's voice.

She could see three steps leading downwards from the doorway, the rest was engulfed in darkness. The staircase seemed to lead to a basement. She put her palm against the brick surface of the wall to steady herself and took one step downwards, then another. The heat was suffocating. A tinny, metallic smell that reminded her of blood tingled her nostrils, and then she heard a woman screaming. Her stomach contracted, and she felt something oozing out of her, making her knickers wet. She stumbled back up the stairs and out of the shop.

Of the birth, she did not remember much; the ambulance arriving, the sensation of her bones being slowly crushed inside her, a terrible burning in her vagina. She gave birth to a healthy baby girl, who they named Joanna.

Afterwards, things went back to normal; Laura no longer had any dreams. It was only three years later, when, sitting in Accident and Emergency after Joanna's fingers on her left hand had accidentally got in the way of Becky's chopping knife while she was sitting on the counter watching Becky make dinner, that Laura vaguely recalled the dark room. She was not sure whether it was an actual memory, or the memory of a dream. Had she edited a bizarre story out of fragments of reality at that time, or was she now living the edited version? The doctor came in. She pushed the thoughts from her mind, reluctant to look at what had landed on the cutting room floor.

Forbidden Fruit

Amber Keller

All he could remember was being here in this house and the crows. They were always there, everywhere outside. It was important that the crows did not get into the house. No, if that happened that would be the end of it all.

The man once had a dog. A large mutt of a dog that had fur trailing off its ears.

The dog had left the house one day and never came back. He knew it was because of the birds.

Every day was the same. He would wander the halls, occasionally looking out the windows to confirm his suspicion that they were there, always there.

Each pine tree around his house nestled in the mountainous woods was tall and glorious. Their age could only be guessed. Maybe they were as old as the mountain itself, both existing synchronously, sprouting up from the netherworld as one and separating forms in the dance of life. The crows came with them, spat out from the great Babylonian Tiamat herself as she constructed the ugly necessaries of this world; the things that would keep the balance in nature due to their horrible, murderous ways. Blame couldn't really be forced onto the birds, seeing that this was their way in this life.

Walls and floors of the tiny house were splintered and rotting. Light could be seen through the many cracks. In places, old strips of wallpaper fell in ribbons off the dusty, moldy walls. The kitchen was home to a small, square table standing on unsure legs. One lone chair stood next to it, with two legs broken, and no seat to sit in. A basin and one cupboard also decorated this room, both small and browned with age. The only splash of color in this house was a large, round, red apple standing on the table.

This is what the crows wanted. This is why they never left.

The bright, ripe fruit had always been there, much like the birds. Touching it was unheard of. He had never touched it and the birds stayed outside, only watching. Many times he had come near to faltering, too close on some of those occasions. Fear kept him from caving into his desires.

The brilliance of the shades of red, deepening then fading in spots of a golden-orange hue, the faint, sweet smell, the tiny green leaf affixed to the stem and leaning over the side as if tempting fate to make it plunge, all mesmerized him as he would stare into its beauty. Days were spent gazing at the forbidden fruit, temporarily unaware of the black birds. Not forgetting them, only forcing the information to a far corner in his mind for a small moment.

There would come a time when the man could no longer fight the urge, could no longer hold back his desires. To put it to his lips, taking a deep breath, inhaling the amorous odor, mouth watering with taste buds pulsating in anticipation of the taboo sapor. Dry and cracked lips opened wide to welcome the treat. Heart pounding like the beat of an African drum on a hot summer night. Each finger feeling the smooth, cool, skin, the curve of the shape, the diminutive pits, so hard to see with his eyes.

Unable to wait any longer, he would introduce it into his mouth to experience all of the senses. With the crisp crunch of the bite the juices would explode out of the swollen fruit and fall in trails down his chin. He would rejoice in this moment, savoring each detail with his eyes closed, his pulse throbbing. Nothing existed now except for him and the apple.

The apple was on the floor, resting on its side. One perfectly round bite taken from its formerly immaculate body. Gripped lightly by the man's hand, his body contorted in fantastic angles face down on the kitchen floor.

The crow perched on the edge of the table, beholding the man.

Outside the crows lifted from their places of rest. Swirling above the house, they performed a dance; the last rite of passage. As the sun set slowly on this last day, the mountains rose higher and higher, swallowing the tiny house, and the birds, one by one. Folding in on itself the world became a hardened, porous rock, bubbling in places with the magma and steam. Deep down in the center a black shape came into view. The bird began to flap its wings against the red-orange of the heat.

Bursting forth it flew away.

All Cry

Patricia Russo

"Why do people have to die, Daddy?"

Sam was only six, so Dave tried to be patient with him. Lucia was always on him about that. *He's six, Dave*, she kept saying. *Don't you remember being six?*

Dave didn't, not really. He remembered being eight, but only because that was the year his father had finally broken down and gotten him a dog.

"Daddy?"

"Sammy, put on your seatbelt, okay? Mommy's coming out in a minute."

"*Daddy*, I asked you a question." He bounced up and down in the back seat. He made no move to reach for the seatbelt. Dave sighed and twisted around.

"Sometimes people die because of accidents," he said. "Sometimes because they're sick. Sometimes because they're old."

"But why do people have to die?"

Dave knew where this was coming from. A couple of weeks ago, the mother of one of Sam's first-grade classmates had passed away. His teacher had them all make sympathy cards out of construction paper. Ever since then, Sammy'd been coming out with questions like: *Does it hurt when you die?* and, *If a plane crashes, does everybody die?* and, *How come grandpa died, but grandma didn't?*

Lucia said to listen to Sam's questions. Let him talk, let him ask, let him express himself. Answer him, but don't get too wordy, don't give him more information than he asks for. He's trying to work out how to handle this, don't you see?

She was much better at talking to Sam than Dave was.

"Put your seatbelt on now, okay?"

"Are you going to die?"

"Not for a long time yet."

"Is Mommy going to die?"

"Sammy," Dave said. "Mommy is going to outlive us all. Don't you worry about that." Oh, Lucia would have killed him if she had heard that. Thank God she'd gone back into the house to quadruple-check the alarm system. "Promise me you won't worry about it, okay?"

"Okay."

"And when we get to Grandma's house, don't ask her why Grandpa died. It makes her sad to think about that."

"Okay. I won't."

"Good boy."

"Why do we have to go to Grandma's house?"

Suffering Jesus.

"Because Grandma gets lonely. Don't you remember you talked to her on the phone yesterday?"

"Yeah."

"Remember she said she misses you and how she's really looking forward to seeing you again."

"Yeah."

"Grandma loves you very much."

"I know."

Dave smiled. "She'll have candy for you."

Sam made a face. "I don't like Grandma's candy."

"What are you two talking about?" Lucia leaned in the open passenger-side window. Dave, swiveled sideways in the driver's seat, hadn't seen or heard her approaching. Man, she could make him jump sometimes.

"Sammy doesn't like your mother's candy," he said.

Lucia opened the passenger door and climbed in. "That doesn't surprise me," she said. "Licorice jelly beans. Ick."

"Ick!" Sam agreed.

"Three days with your mother," Dave murmured into Lucia's ear. "The things I'm willing to put up with just because I love you."

"You're a prince among men," she murmured back. She reached up for her seatbelt strap. "Sam, you need help back there?"

"No." He buckled himself in. "Mom?"

"Brace yourself," Dave said. "He's going to ask you where babies come from now."

"I know where babies come from!"

"Of course you do," Lucia said. "Come on, Dave. He's got a

33

picture book and everything." She was smiling, her lips curved only a little, but her eyes full of humor. He loved it when she did that. He loved that expression on her, as if the biggest part of her smile was for him alone. "What were you going to say, Sam?"

"I was going to say, do I have to sleep in that stinky, yellow room again?"

"Hey, kiddo, Mommy and I get to sleep on a fold-out couch. At least you get a real bed."

"Grandma's house isn't very big, Sam," Lucia said. "You know, that was my room when I was little."

"Bet it's the same bed, too."

"Dave," she said, in a warning tone, then suddenly burst out laughing. "Okay, you got me. It is."

"Same sheets, too."

"Now you're pushing it."

Dave shot her a grin.

"Sam," Lucia said, "I'll make you a deal. You behave yourself at Grandma's and next weekend you get to pick what you want to do."

"Anything?"

"Anything."

"At a point such as this," Dave said, "it's prudent to add, 'within reason.'"

"I want to go to the aquarium," Sam said.

"Sure. You got it."

"And I want to go to Pizza Palace."

"I think we can squeeze that in."

"And I want an iguana."

"Told you," Dave said.

"Sam, I think the iguana is going to have to wait until you're older."

"That's what you always say."

"Kiddo, you got a trip to the aquarium and all the greasy pizza you can eat. I reckon you came out ahead in the deal. Okay, then. Everybody ready? Sam, you don't need to pee? Lucia, you don't need to check the motion sensors for the millionth time?"

She slapped him lightly on the arm.

"I peed already," Sam said.

"All systems set for launch, then." Dave switched on the ignition. Lucia slid her hand up his neck, and pulled him gently towards her. The seatbelts made it a challenge, but she still managed to kiss him, hard and deep; there was hunger in that kiss, and a promise. That goddamn fold-out couch, he thought, and when Lucia smiled straight into his eyes, he grinned back.

"You guys are gross," Sam said.

"I love your mommy, kiddo," Dave said. "And there's nothing gross about that."

* * *

"Not Hill Avenue," Lucia said. "Take Consolation Boulevard."

Dave pointed at the GPS.

"Right, don't listen to me. I only grew up here. Computers always know best."

"I'm going to listen to you, dear."

"There are more stoplights on Hill. Consolation is quicker."

"I'm turning. You see me turning?"

"I see you turning. I married a smart man."

"Despite what your mother thinks."

"Quit it. She's crazy about you."

"Your mother's crazy, but not about me."

"I'm crazy about you," Lucia said.

"Now you're talking."

Dave turned when she told him to turn. He took the street she told him to take.

Sam had dozed off in the back seat. They'd stopped once for food, and a million times for bathroom breaks, and they'd still made pretty good time. Forty minutes, maybe less, and they'd be there.

Lucia's cell phone chirruped. "It's Mom," she said.

"Probably checking to see if we're dead in a ditch somewhere."

"Probably wants to know if she can set the table yet."

"Oh God," Dave said. "The meatballs."

"I'll have you know those meatballs are a traditional family recipe."

"But she makes them every time."

Lucia smiled. "She's traditional." She raised the phone to her ear. "Mom? Yeah, we're fine. We'll be there soon. Sure we're hungry. We've been driving all day."

Dave rolled his eyes.

"The traffic's pretty good. Sam's conked out in the back, poor little guy. If he's still asleep when we get there, we'll just carry him into my old room, okay? I love you, Mom. See you soon. Absolutely. I could eat two plates of meatballs and go back for thirds."

Dave groaned. Lucia shot him a look. He raised one hand in surrender.

"No, we didn't take Hill Avenue. We're on Consolation—" Lucia stopped. She was silent so long that Dave glanced over. Her face was ashen.

"What?" she said.

It's the light, he thought. The stupid light in the car. That's what making her look sick.

"What?" she said again.

Her mother burned the meatballs, that's all. Or she wants us to stop at some convenience store and pick up a quart of milk, something like that. Nothing's wrong.

"Dave," Lucia said, "get off the boulevard. Get off the boulevard right now."

"What's going on?"

"Right now!" Into the phone, she said, "Mom, I told him. Didn't you hear me tell him?"

"Get off where?"

"Anywhere! West, west, go west. Mom, it's okay. No, I don't see anything. Everything looks normal. Everything looks fine. Don't worry. We're getting off Consolation. Nothing's going to happen. We're all right."

Dave was trying to get off Consolation, but the only side streets he passed were one-way. "Lucia, would you please tell me what the hell is going on?"

"Daddy?"

"Go back to sleep, Sammy. We're almost there."

"Sam woke up," Lucia said into the phone. "Mom, stop. Stop. It's going to be all right."

Dave gripped the wheel. His heart was pounding, and he didn't know why the fuck it should be. It was barely eight o'clock, and it was July. There was still plenty of light. He didn't see any roadblocks, or construction workers, or detour signs. He didn't see any cops, hear any sirens.

He didn't see any people on the sidewalks.

"You'll do no such thing," Lucia said. "You stay in the house. Lock the windows, all of them. Yes, I can hear it. Go lock the windows, Mom."

Dave could hear something, too. A whining sound, not like an engine noise, not like any sort of mechanical noise. Not like a high wind. Not like any sort of bird cry, or animal call he'd ever heard, though there were probably millions of bird cries and animal calls he'd never heard. Frogs, he thought suddenly. There are some types of frogs that make really weird sounds.

The light ahead of them was red.

"Don't stop!" Lucia shouted. "What are you doing? Dave, for fuck's sake, get off the boulevard!"

"How?" he shouted back. "All the side streets are fucking one-way!"

"Yeah, they're one-way, and half of them are fucking one-way west. Look at the goddamn signs!"

"Mommy," Sam said, in a very small voice.

"I am looking at the goddamn signs, and they're all pointing east!"

Dave ran the red light. He hoped a cop car tucked away in a cul-de-sac would come zipping out after him. Lucia had suddenly, inexplicably, gone nuts, because of something her loopy mother had said, and now he was gunning down an empty street, without a clue what he was running from, or why. A police car would be a relief. Hell, he'd shake the officer's hand and kiss the freaking ticket.

Empty street.

Empty road.

"Lucia," he said. "Lucia, what happened to all the other cars?"

"Daddy?"

"Lucia," Dave said, speeding faster, seventy now, though really he should be looking for those one-way signs pointing west, shouldn't he, the ones Lucia had told him were definitely there, and of which he hadn't spotted a single one, though maybe, it could be, that was because he was too scared to see straight.

Lucia was still on the phone with her mother. "No, you stay in the house," she was saying. "Mom, you stay where you are. We're almost there. We'll be with you in a few minutes." She glanced at Dave, and lowered the phone. He could still hear her mother yammering on the other end. "The other cars got off the boulevard."

"What's going on? You've got to tell me, Lucia. Your mother's freaking out, and you're freaking out, and you're making me freak out."

"You wouldn't believe me."

"Fuck you," Dave snapped. "Fuck you to Hell, Lucia. Tell me, or I'll stop the car right now."

"If you stop the car," she said, in her quiet voice, the one she used when she refused to shout back at him, the one she used to let him know that she was choosing not to shout back at him, "we're going to die."

"Why? How?"

Lucia put the phone to her ear again. "Mom, we're going to have to make a turn at the county line. No, we can't get off Consolation. The side streets are all black."

They were. The streetlights and traffic lights were still lit on Consolation Boulevard, but the side streets he was shooting past were all dark. No, not dark. Black, as Lucia had said. It was too early on a July evening for blackness like that, even if there'd been a power failure that somehow had skipped the boulevard.

"Mom, we're going to make it. I promise. Dave's a really good driver."

"That's why you married me, isn't it? It was the driving skills that impressed you." He'd said fuck you, fuck you to Hell, and he had to say something now, to let her know he was sorry, to take back those words.

"No, it was the way you hung your toilet paper roll that captured my heart."

Half the tightness in his chest disappeared, just like that. "I love you. What I said before—"

"Mom, I have to talk to Dave now. I'm still here, but I need to talk to Dave for a minute. Hold on, okay?" This time, she didn't just lower the phone. She put it on her lap. "When we hit the county line, we have to turn west. Even if the road is dark. It's essential that you do that."

"Fine. Whatever you say. But please, I'm serious, I'm begging you, tell me what's going on."

"Do you hear the crying?"

The whining sound, the sound he'd never heard before, that couldn't be frogs or hyenas or anything natural. "Yes."

"It's the dead. They cry. They cry for bodies."

38

"What are you talking about?"

"They want to come back, Dave. They hate being dead."

"Are you nuts? Have you completely fucking lost—you don't even go to church!"

"This has nothing to do with church." Her voice dropped. "They all cry, Dave, all of them. They can't break through everywhere, but they try. And a little rip in the fabric between our worlds is all it takes for a swarm of them to come through. There are people who know how to patch up the cracks, but the dead are so many, and so . . . relentless. They are all around us, you know. I saw one swallow up a perfume-spritzer in the mall once. When we're dead, we'll do the same."

"Lucia, you can't really think—"

"Why do you think there's nobody on the street? Everybody with a speck of sense has taken cover."

"What do you want me to do?"

"Keep driving. We'll be safe once we get to my mother's house."

"Because your mother's a secret government zombie slayer?"

"Because it's an old house. It's strong, it's been patched up over and over. My mother's lived there all her life, and not one of the bastards has broken in there yet. She's very good at patching. And they're not zombies. They are the dead."

"Mommy?"

"Sam," she said. "Close your eyes. Go back to sleep. Everything's going to be all right."

The dead cry? They break into the world to swallow up the bodies of the living? Her mother was a patcher of cracks between the worlds of the living and the dead? He could turn those sentences over a million times, and not find any sense in them.

What he did understand was Lucia's fear. That fear made him stop arguing, stop protesting. He would do anything for her, always had, always would.

"Keep driving," she said. "Don't stop, not for anything."

He listened to her. He did exactly what she said. At the county line he turned west. Lucia was talking to her mother again, but he couldn't hear her. The crying was in his ears, blocking out everything else. The noise was real, that much he had to accept. He couldn't hear the car engine anymore. He couldn't hear his own breathing.

A wave of blackness swept toward them as soon as he turned off the boulevard. Dave set his teeth and drove straight through it. It's like a tunnel, it's just like a tunnel, he told himself. A tunnel without any lights. The car's headlights didn't help. It was as if the darkness had coated them, and coated the windshield as well. He couldn't see a thing outside. He drove on for an eternity. He felt Lucia's hand grip his knee. The eternity went on and on.

And then they were through the blackness and into gray, a deeper, thicker gray than was normal for an early evening in July, but it was gray and he could see. He turned his head to give Lucia a quick grin, and then something hit the car.

And something hit the car again.

"Don't stop!" Lucia screamed.

He heard that. He heard that, through the crying. But the car juddered and slowed, though his leg ached, his fucking thigh hurt from pushing the gas pedal so hard. There was a shape in the gray-ness, a shape of a darker gray, not quite black. The shape moved. The shape had substance. It struck the car again.

"What do we do?" He could see the shape, almost like a per-son, blurred and featureless but for a gaping mouth. It was crying. It was crying so loud he could not think. "Tell me what to do."

The car slowed and slowed. They were creeping now, ten miles an hour. But they were out of the blackness and into gray, and that had to be good, that had to be better than being in the blackness, didn't it?

"We're going to have to run for it," Lucia said. "You take Sam. We'll split up. It won't be able to go after both of us."

She was so cool, so calm. Terrified, still, but keeping it to-gether. She'd stopped talking to her mother. She'd put the cell phone away, Dave didn't know when. He hadn't been paying attention. Now she undid her seatbelt. "Sam," she said, "Daddy's going to pick you up, and then he's going to run. You hold on tight. Promise me, Sam. You hold Daddy tight."

If Sammy answered, Dave didn't hear it. He could hear only Lucia, Lucia and the crying, Lucia and the shape thumping the car. He glanced at the speedometer. Christ, they weren't even going five miles an hour now.

Lucia unlocked the passenger door. "Dave, get ready."

"No! We can't split up."

40

"It's our only chance. I'll go first, draw it off. You get Sam out of the back seat, and run as fast as you can."

"Lucia, no," he said. "No. Together. We go together."

She wasn't listening. He'd asked her to tell him what to do, and now she expected him to do it.

He would do anything for her, but how could he do that?

She gripped the handle of the passenger-side door. "You have to be quick. As soon as I'm out, you grab Sam. Sam, are you ready? Good boy. That's right, take your seatbelt off. When you see me open my door, you open yours, but wait for Daddy."

"Lucia, no."

"We'll meet up at my mother's house," she said. She didn't look at him. She doesn't want me to see her eyes, Dave thought.

The car was barely moving. The shape blocked the road. It stretched, and as it stretched, its grayness altered to a lighter hue. Its mouth gaped wider.

This wasn't a ghost. It was a being of some kind, but how could it ever have been human?

Except, wasn't it the most human thing of all to be selfish, to take what you wanted, snatch what you needed, and the hell with the other guy; a starving man would grab food out of a child's hands. People killed each other for parking spots.

The car stopped.

The shape advanced.

Lucia flung her door open, and leaped out. Dave scrambled after her, not even thinking of the driver's side door, thinking only of Lucia. He was clumsy, couldn't get his legs to move right. He plunged out head first, and barely got his hands under him in time. He couldn't see her. He pulled himself out of the car, and screamed her name.

There. There she was, running like a high school track star, long strides, arms pumping, not looking back. The shape flowed after her. The shape cried.

"Daddy?"

Sam was standing next to him. He'd gotten out of the car on his own. He gazed up at Dave, fearful but obedient.

Dave held out his arms. "Come on, Sammy. Up you go."

Fearful but obedient, Sam let Dave pick him up. "Put your arms around my neck," Dave said. "But not too tight, okay? Don't squeeze, or else Daddy won't be able to breathe."

41

"Okay," Sam said.

It had been a long time since high school. Lucia was already flagging. The shape flowed after her, at a steady pace.

Dave ran. Sam was heavy, and his feet bumped against Dave's legs, but Dave ran. He ran directly at the shape. "Hey," he screamed. "Hey! Not her!" Even with Sammy in his arms, he could run faster than Lucia. He had to run faster than Lucia. "Not her!" he screamed.

The shape hesitated. It wavered, blurred, stretched itself a little more. Then it turned toward him.

Dave kept running. Sam's grip was loose. Dave put his hands under Sam's armpits. It was easy to break the boy's grip. He was only six.

It took Lucia several seconds to realize that the shape was no longer following her. By the time she whirled around, Dave had already hurled Sammy at the gray, wavering form. It let out a tremendous cry. Sammy screamed. Lucia screamed. Dave stood, panting; the gray shape enveloped his son. Sam disappeared from sight in an instant. The gray shape folded, contracted, turned darker and darker, smaller and smaller. As it diminished, Sam's form began to reemerge. He was lying on his back in the middle of the road. The shape became a black clot no bigger than a fist, sitting on Sam's chest. And then it was gone.

The light of an evening in early July came back.

Sounds, the sounds of wind, and birds, and traffic, came back. A dog barked in the distance.

"Lucia," Dave whispered. "Are you all right?"

Sam sat up, slowly. He touched his face, his arms, his legs. He breathed. He didn't look at either of them. He stood up, with care, and with care took a step, and then another. He walked away, past where the car had come to a stop, stumbling at first, but after a moment moving with more ease. Dave watched Lucia watch him go. He never took his eyes off her face. When Sam vanished from Lucia's sight, she fell to her knees.

Dave hurried toward her.

"How could you?" she said. "How could you do that?"

"It's all right, it's all right. Lucia—"

She was shaking her head. He wanted to grab her, hold her tight, but when he took another step closer she raised her head, and he saw utter blankness in her eyes.

"Who are you," she said.

She was in shock. Naturally. It would be impossible not to be in shock. He was in shock, too. "Lucia," he said. "It's me. Come here. Give me your hands."

"Get away from me," she said. "Get in the car. Go home. If I ever see you again, I'll kill you."

It was shock, simply shock.

"I love you," he said.

She stood up. Her eyes were dry.

She walked away from him.

Dave ran back to the car. He followed her, at a snail's pace, all the way to her mother's house. He watched her go inside.

Her purse was still in the car. Her cell phone was still in the car. Her suitcase was still in the trunk.

She'll understand once she's had time to think about it, he told himself. He'd done the only thing he could.

Dave sat in the car all night, believing that.

Part of him continued to believe it for the rest of his life, an existence that endured for another thirty-seven years.

"I won't cry," he said. The hospice nurse was fussing around with his drip. "I'll never cry."

"You can cry if you want to. It's all right. It's natural."

She didn't understand. He wasn't talking to her, anyway.

"Do you want me to sit with you for a few minutes?"

"No."

The hospice nurse patted his arm absently and left the room. "I won't cry," Dave murmured. In his hand, he held a photograph of Lucia. "I promise." She couldn't hear him, of course. She wasn't there. He was speaking only to darkness.

Darkly Dreaming in Black Waters

Jason Andrew

"The ocean is more ancient than the mountains, and freighted with the memories and the dreams of Time."
- H.P. Lovecraft

Seagulls squawked as they glided past the bow of the *Susan B. Anthony* punctuating the white noise of the rhythmic hum of the diesel engine. Chief Joshua Heller sipped his bitter cup of coffee and buttoned his peacoat. He paced along the portside of the ship, adjusting the binoculars strapped around his neck, trying to keep from directly facing the arctic wind. The horizon shone brightly with colors of red and orange brightening the dark cloud on the horizon.

Heller enjoyed Morning Watch. It provided a few hours of serene quiet before the bustle of running the ship and herding bored passengers. He sniffed the air. The familiar briny scent of the sea soured as if eggs had exploded in the galley.

His ears twitched. Numbness overtook his arms, but he could still feel the veins in his arms and chest pulsing with blood. Why did he feel such dread? The recons reported that the fleet was still a week away from the predicted Nazi engagement zone.

Heller wiped the sweat from the back of his neck after a third rotation around the ship. Bleary-eyed crewmen filtered onto the decks muttering. Why was everyone waking so early?

He tilted his head, licked his thumb, and tested the air. The brisk winds dropped then died as though the ship sailed into the eye of a hurricane. Where were the seagulls? Those sea rats followed the ship across two oceans and three continents. The last time they had disappeared was just before the Nazi Wolf Pack engagement off Algeria last year.

He scanned the horizon once more with his binoculars. Sparkling glint of metal reflected brightly against the choppy waters of the Atlantic. The object was just at the outer range of his vision.

It could be a mine, flotsam from previous wreckages, or a waiting U-Boat. Heller signaled the bridge. "Metal object sighted fifteen-degrees off the port bow."

The shrill general quarters whistle pierced the air. Crewmen frantically rushed to their battle stations. Heller returned to his gunner's nest and prepared for battle. He imagined the bridge crew warning the rest of the convoy and the cargo ships turning to give the object a wide berth. Recon seaplanes buzzed overhead and circled the area. The crew waited silently. Heller wiped the sweat and grime from his hands on his pants.

He checked the horizon once more searching for any incoming targets. The Nazi Wolf Packs sank nearly a thousand ships in just under two years. Had they expanded their hunting zone?

The ship's whistle blew three times. The gunnery crew sighed with relief. Heller tilted his head unable to believe what he heard. Was it possible the fleet wasn't in danger? It had felt so horrible.

"Chief Heller. Chief Heller!"

He signaled the runner. "Here, Seaman."

The fresh faced boy that looked barely out of school saluted. "Bridge wants to see you."

Heller closed his eyes and rubbed his temple. "Please don't let it be garbage."

He followed the seaman silently up the winding set of stairs to the upper deck and then finally to the bridge. It was a hive of busy officers and technicians scrambling from station to station. Maybe he hadn't wasted the time of the fleet after all. Captain Hartley puffed on his pipe listening to a hurried ensign whisper into his ear. "I think I understand, Ensign." He turned to Heller. "Chief, how the devil did you spot it?"

"Spot what, sir?"

"The damned U-Boat, Chief." The Captain scratched his graying beard. "How did you spot it dead in the water?"

"The seagulls disappeared, sir."

"The seagulls?"

Heller gestured out the porthole to the empty sky. "They only disappear during a fight, sir."

The Captain laughed. "There won't be a battle this day, Chief, but our nets have brought aboard an unexpected haul."

"Captain?"

"The U-Boat is dead in the water. Barely floating by the look of it. You speak German, don't you, Chief?"

"Aye, sir."

The Captain nodded, very satisfied. "You'll be joining Lieutenant Nicholson's boarding party as his second." He gestured to the young officer, barely out the academy, with big ears. "Your orders are search and salvage, then report back. The fleet can't stay here indefinitely."

"Aye, sir."

"It wouldn't hurt any of our service records if you brought back prisoners, but it's not worth dying over."

Nicolson swallowed and nodded to Heller. "Assemble a team to ride over on the skiff. We'll need a welder and any technicians you have with submarine experience."

Heller flashed a salute already running through candidates in his mind. "Aye, sir."

* * *

The skiff circled the long way from the *Susan B. Anthony* to the craft. The top hatch of the U-Boat floated haphazardly just above the water line like a cork that might be pulled under at any moment.

A ring of dead sailors floated near the hatch, bumping against the metal from the tide. Heller felt a strange twitch in his gut. Why would the sailors have drowned in such calm waters? He nodded to Medina and McGrath and they leveled their rifles at the bodies. Heller cut the motor and allowed the skiff to quietly float through the corpses clanging against the metal of the ship.

They reached over the side of the skiff and pulled one of the corpses aboard. The dead sailor wore a cracked drager mask and a brown survival vest. Heller plucked off the mask to reveal the pale bloated face of a young man frozen in a hideous scream. Red-shot eyes stared up at them unblinking.

Lieutenant Nicholson was the first to speak. "Cover that poor bastard's face."

"Aye, sir." Heller slipped the mask back on the corpse. "Looks like he's been dead a couple of days."

The short technician shook his head. "Can't be, Chief."

"How's that, Carver?"

"I've worked many a summer on the fishing boats." Carver

looked out at the flotsam of dead flesh and shivered. "A body can't just float around without something taking a nibble on him, Chief."

Medina laughed. "Maybe the Nazis don't taste too good."

"The Captain said we needed to be quick." Lieutenant Nicholson gripped the sides of the skiff. "Let's get this over with."

Medina and McGrath heaved the large red and green acetylene tanks onto the U-Boat and then steadied their rifles. Heller knew he could trust them to keep their heads in a firefight and shoulder their share of the load. Not much more you ask for in a situation like this.

Carver climbed onboard and then started examining the hatch. He had transferred to the *Susan B. Anthony* at the last port from the USS *Constellation*. "Chief, this is the Alptryume. Type nine U-boat. Long range. Deep divers. This thing'll get you where you want to go, but don't take too many turns."

"See if you can blow the hatch."

Carver shrugged his shoulders. "The hatch isn't locked."

Lieutenant Nicholson scowled. "I don't like the feel of this, Chief."

"Why wouldn't the crew have scrambled onboard the U-Boat?" Medina asked. He turned to the rest of the crew. "A good portion of it must not be flooded."

"Must have been a gas leak." McGrath cackled at the fate of the Germans. "The Nazis use Mustard gas and God knows what else. Maybe the bastards got a taste of their own medicine."

"Could've been a problem with the O2 scrubbers." Carver shook his head disdainfully. "Might have given them all the bends and drove them all batty if they went too deep. I've seen it before."

Heller locked eyes with the Lieutenant. It was always a bit difficult working with a fresh face officer looking to make their bones. He waited for the eventual nod of approval before continuing. "Stow the speculation until we've hit port. We've got a job to do." He pulled his revolver from his holster. "I'll go first. Medina, I need you topside keeping watch. There's only room for one of us down there."

The large Cuban laughed and cocked his rifle. "Thanks, Chief."

Carver turned the tiny metal wheel and then pulled open the hatch. Heller dropped a flashlight into the darkness and then quickly aimed his revolver. It clanked against the metal ladder and then the bulkhead before finally landing upon the deck with a loud crack. Emergency lights flickered. He squeezed through the hatch descending into the darkness overwhelmed by a garlic-tinged, metallic aroma and the funk of sweat and decay. Once he reached the bottom, he fumbled for his flashlight and quickly scanned the chamber.

Another young face with a hideous scream twisted almost into a laugh. What caused his eyes to bulge like that? This poor bastard had his throat cut. There were dozens of bodies strung about the floor as though they had been trampled over to get up the hatch. "Clear! But be careful where you step. You won't like it."

Carver, McGrath, and Lieutenant Nicholson descended the ladder one by one. Carver quickly found the circuit breaker and reset the power illuminating the gunmetal grey bulkheads and dead sailors. They had fought each other with knives, with their bare hands, and in one extreme case with his teeth. "Did all of them get the bends at the same time?"

"I don't think that's statically possible, chief."

Lieutenant Nicholson gestured to the hatch leading to the rest of the U-Boat. "Let's see what can be salvaged."

Surprisingly, most of the length of the U-Boat seemed safe with almost breathable air. They found the bridge, crew's quarters, and most importantly the engine, clear over any overt breaches or leaks. The hatch to the bow of the U-Boat had been sealed and reinforced with welding.

Heller peered through the porthole. The chambers beyond had been flooded. Flickering emergency lights illuminated the hovering bodies of the dead in a strange green hue. An amorphous collection of bubbling oily tar drifted in front of the glass. "Looks like an O2 line's been cut here."

The bubbles popped with rainbow sheen and then reformed. He wiped the sweat from the back of his neck. What must it have been like to die like that? Surrounded by the freezing dark. Choking on the ancient filth from the bottom of the sea. He stopped himself from gagging reflectively. Heller coughed forcing himself to return to business. "Looks like some sort of oil leak."

"What's that way, Carver?"

"Torpedoes, cargo, and the galley, Chief."

McGrath wrinkled his nose. "I've had German food. Count ourselves lucky."

Lieutenant Nicholson paced the length of the bridge. "Why

is the U-Boat submerged, Carver?"

"From the looks of it, the crew went mad sir." Carver studied the instruments. "It wouldn't take much to repair her. But I'd want to take her to dry-dock to fix that forward section."

"Full sweep then," the Lieutenant ordered. He gestured to the blood soaked papers and maps. "Look for anything important. I'll report back to the Captain."

Carver glanced around at the exposed wires and broken equipment. "This is going to be a nightmare to properly repair, Chief."

"That seems appropriate." Heller winked at the seamen. "After all, Alptryume does mean nightmare in German."

* * *

Lieutenant Nicholson returned to the Alptryume two hours later with supplies, tools, and twenty extra men. During that time, Medina and McGrath stockpiled dead sailors in the aft section. Once he pried open the Captain's office and Medina removed the grinning corpse sprawled over the desk, Heller discovered a treasure trove of files, maps, sketches, and cargo manifests.

Medina shivered. "This one looks like he blew his brains out during a conniption fit."

"That's how I want to go. Laughing my keister off."

Carver managed to restart the oxygen scrubbers, but it still smelled like a fishing cannery during low tide. Gunny Lucius assembled the new crew of the Alptryume in the bridge near the table with maps and charts.

The Lieutenant addressed the men. "Captain received word from Norfork. The Pentagon has just made it priority one that we take this boat to US soil. The fleet has to make it to English soil or the war effort could be severely damaged. Norfork dispatched the USS *Decatur* to rendezvous with us. If weather holds, we should rendezvous in two weeks. Questions?"

Carver raised his hand. "Sir, we won't be able to fire torpedoes until we've been to dry-dock."

"Norfork is well aware of the situation and has ordered evasive action in any conflicts. If the boys in the lab coats get hold of this tin can we could end the war."

Medina looked around the bridge comically. "Sir, I didn't notice showers onboard."

"The Germans don't build for comfort, Seaman," Lieutenant Nicholson said wryly. He nodded at Heller. "The Chief will have your assignments. Do your best and I'll personally see to it that there will be a full week of liberty when we reach American soil."

The supplies were loaded and the men began to remove the dead. The Alptryume had barely enough room for the men on board so they buried all the dead at sea. Lieutenant Nicholson recited the Lord's Prayer and then McGrath blew the Boatswains whistle.

Once the covey disappeared into the horizon, Lieutenant Nicholson issued the order to dive. Heller wasn't even aware that he was holding his breath until they had been under the waves for at least a full minute.

After a full twenty-four hours on the Alptryume, Heller understood why Carver had transferred off ship. He had to walk in a perpetual hunch or risk braining his skull against one of the overheard compartments. Life on a submarine was an exercise in silence and living in the filth of others. The lack of showers quickly brought a new level of funk in the cabins. Breathing became more labored. The scrubbers were working, but in the end it was still recycled air. Lieutenant Nicholson managed the general operations of the Alptryume and assigned Heller the dull task of compiling the papers of the crew and to determine a previous course.

The Germans were a very organized people. The former Captain of the Alptryume had taken very detailed notes. Heller read cargo manifests and inventories. The Alptryume had resupplied in Brazil three times in the last six months. Why would they visit South America?

Several of the nautical charts and maps pointed to an obvious answer. The Alptryume had been exploring the rim of Antarctica. The manifests in the cargo hold suggested an expedition of some sort. Black and white photographs of a smoldering mountain labeled Erebus in fine print. That named sounded familiar. Heller scanned the tiny bookshelf above the desk and then finally found what he was looking for. *The Zoology of the Voyage of HMS Erebus & HMS Terror* published in 1846.

The Captain's journal was of little help determining their true objective. It had been found partially in ashes in a waste bucket. It must have occurred just before the Captain elected to blast his brains out with a service revolver.

His temples ached. The nonsense thoughts hurt his brain. Why would the Nazis waste such resources during the war? They must have thought there would be some weapon or resource they could exploit. He decided to resolve the madness of the Nazis in the morning.

Heller skipped dinner and tried to get comfortable in his new bunk. It smelled of smoke and sweat, but he didn't have any other choice. It was a quiet lull of desperation. The air was humid. What wouldn't he give for fifteen minutes topside right now?

Sleep did not bring peace to his mind. *He dreamed of the towering Erebus volcano high upon the ice shelf of Antarctica in a land undisturbed by man. Beyond the ice wall there was a vast abandoned city of ancient black stone with structures shaped like rigid cubes and alien spiral cones. And from there came the terror of the colossal amorphous bubbling protoplasm waiting to be awoken.*

He awoke with a start as though his very heart had been incased in ice. Silently, he slid to his feet and began to pace the length of the boat. The hum of the diesel engine brought a much-needed sense of familiarity. He almost felt better until he reached the bridge. The haggard faces of the crew told him that none of them slept well.

He walked past the sealed hatch three times before forcing himself to look through the porthole once more. Clearly, he had imagined the bubbling rainbow oil eyes. The oil had settled. He no longer saw the dreaded amorphous ink cloud. Then why was he still afraid?

By morning, the rest of the crew also felt the unexplainable dread. Why would they feel such terror now? This crew had been through years of war and blood. Dead sailors left behind no ghosts. Heller pushed it out of his mind and returned to the studies again skipping breakfast.

Some of the words on the cargo manifest weren't German. What was a *Shoggoth*? Was it some sort of code? He started scanning the stolen codebook for any clues when the shrill whistle of the boatswain's mate cut him off. Danger?

Heller rushed to the source surprised to find the grinning corpse of Boatswain's Mate James McGrath. A bloody wrench rested on top of his chest. Heller knelt down to check his breathing. Someone had bashed in the side of his head.

Medina stood shaking in the corner. He cried and laughed

at the same time. With disbelief, Heller realized that the seaman's hands were filthy with blood.

The Alptryume was a large U-Boat, but a cramped location. Members of the crew quickly joined them. "Damn it, we're running silent." Lieutenant Nicholson and two marines parted the crowd. Blood pooled around the body.

"What the hell happened here?"

"He came at me, sir. I couldn't fight him off." The Lieutenant glanced down at the beaten body of McGrath and then compared him to hulking frame of Seaman Medina. "I had to stop him from waking it up."

Lieutenant Nicholson nodded to Gunny Lucius and they bound him in chains and locked him in the supply closet. Heller desperately tried to gain permission to speak with the prisoner but the Lieutenant was resolute. At dawn, Alptryume surfaced for an hour to recharge the batteries. Seaman Mario Medina was hanged by the neck from the mast in front of the entire crew. "This is a war and discipline must be maintained. Dismissed."

Morale did not improve quickly. The next three days, the crew performed their duties as though in a fog. Heller found it difficult to continue to read the reports. He paced the length of the boat always stopping at the sealed hatch, looking through the porthole into the flooded cargo hold seeking any sign of the black oil.

At the end of the first week, Heller had found several other non-German words of strange origin and noted them in his log. One worn journal had a single unintelligible phrase scribbled frantically over and over. *Tekeli-li.*

It had been the first morning he had awaked without pain or dread. A loud *bang* blew through the submarine. Heller rushed frantically to the bridge. Carver desperately tried to weld a metal plate onto the bulkhead. A dead sailor lay limp in the center of the cabin. Gunny Lucius tended to Lieutenant Nicholson's wound. "This whole crew is going mad!"

"Just like before," Heller muttered under his breath. "What happened?"

"Turner shot me," Lieutenant shrieked exacerbated. "Said I was taking him to Hell. Can you imagine that?"

Heller nodded at the two marines. "Looks like you boys took care of that for the Lieutenant. Can you take him back to his cabin and get him patched up?"

The wound on his leg clearly hurt. Sweat dripped from the Lieutenant's face. "Chief, we have to meet our rendezvous!"

"Aye, sir." Heller made a formal show of saluting for the crew. "We'll pull through as always."

* * *

Heller concentrated on the motions of his arm while trying to remember the stories his uncle told him about the Battle of Langres. *Do the job. Ignore everything but what you need to do.* He steadied himself with one hand and applied his weight to the saw. The blade shined from the overhead light.

Lieutenant Nicholson's agonizing scream reverberated throughout the submarine. Carver and Lucius forced him back onto the map table using all of their weight to keep him there.

"Give him another shot!" Heller ordered.

Carver grunted, trying to keep the squirming Lieutenant still. "That could kill him."

Heller steadied the leg with one hand and concentrated on keeping his continued motion to saw flesh, grinding on bone. "I think we're already doing a good job of that."

After the morphine flooded his system, the Lieutenant had a moment of lucidity. "Please don't take my leg, Heller!" Heller ignored the Lieutenant and pressed on. "Carver, I order you to stop him."

"Your leg has the gangrene." Heller resisted the urge to look at the leg. Rotten flesh, the color of pyrite, sprinkled around the burnt patch-worked skin of the Lieutenant's calf muscles. "We have to take it or you'll die, sir."

Heller ignored the screams. He had been in charge for almost seven days. They had been due to rendezvous with the USS *Decatur* in less than twenty-four hours. Carver decoded the message over the radio:

Delayed a week, proceed to Norfork.

Heller had been counting on the antibiotics on the *Decatur* to kill the gangrene and save the leg. But now, another day or two and the inflection would spread to the Lieutenant's heart.

His arm ached; surprised at the endurance of the limb, Heller dropped the saw. Carver applied the tourniquet. Gunny Lucius handed Heller the next tool required in the operation. He donned the dark goggles and lit the blowtorch.

Now for the hard part.

* * *

Heller took to avoiding sleep altogether. The nightmare returned more vividly each time he closed his eyes. Why did the Nazis
seek this horrid city? What eldritch secrets lost to the ages had they
discovered?

The Captain of the Alptryume clearly had drifted to madness the last few days of his life. Heller managed to piece together
fragments of the journal describing the Antarctica Expedition and
the resulting retreat to Europe. Why did the Captain order that hatch
sealed?

He tried to keep the crew calm. Just a few days and they
would reach Norfork. They would be safe. He wasn't certain he
could ever use that word aloud again after this trip. He paced the
length of the boat, always stopping at the sealed hatch. Once again,
he checked the porthole. The flooded chamber was empty as it had
been for the last week.

Empty?

Weren't there corpses in there?

"Carver!"

The technician rushed from the radio station. "Yes, Chief?"

"Where are the bodies?"

Carver checked the porthole. "Maybe they floated to where
we can't see them."

"All twelve of them! That thing I saw when we checked out
the boat. It's in there. That's what the Nazi bastards were looking for
in Antarctica. A Shoggoth! Show yourself!"

"There's nothing there, Chief."

Heller smashed his fist against the glass. "Show yourself! I
know you're in there! Tekeli-li! Tekeli-li! They thought they could
control you, didn't they? Use you like a guard dog."

The putrescent tar crept along the glass of the porthole;
bubbling rainbow eyes formed, melted, and then reformed. Heller
stared into the blackness. Did he imagine that hateful face laughing
at them? How had he missed the malevolence of the monster? It
cried forth in their minds. *Tekeli-li! Tekeli-li!*

"What is it, Chief?"

"A monster. A working stiff just like us. Sleeping thousands of years and ready."

"Ready for us?" Carver stepped back from the creature. "Ready for what?"

"To get back to monster's work. We can't take this back. Once it gets out, it can't be stopped."

"It seems trapped in there."

"The Nazis tricked it into submission. They didn't count on it being brilliant. Carver, I need you to take us to the surface."

Carver followed orders and Heller sounded general quarters. The crew prepared to abandon the Alptryume. "What are you doing man?" Lieutenant Nicholson asked, still delirious.

"There is a creature in the cargo hold. We can't take it back."

"Nonsense boy, that's what they're hoping for. It'll end the war."

"Some things can't be undone. You can't fight evil by hiding under the skirts of greater evil."

The Alptryume popped out of the water. The marines prepared the emergency craft and the remains of the crew prepared to abandon the U-Boat. "We can't just leave it there. Someone else will find it."

"We're not abandoning the Alptryume to the elements, Carver." Heller nodded to the survivors. "You're in charge. Get them to the shore."

"What'll you do?"

"I'm taking the Alptryume for one last dive. We're going to find a nice place at the bottom of the ocean."

"It'll get out eventually, won't it?"

"I'm buying us time. Time to fix the Nazis and figure out if we deserve a place on this world."

He waved uneasily to the crew and sealed the hatch. The Alptryume delved into the dark waters of the Atlantic. Heller set the controls to an irreversible course fearful of the creature taking control of his mind. *Tekeli-li! Tekeli-li!*

The pressure of the dive weighed upon him. Heller didn't have the luxury to endure a gradual dive. The force of the creature's mind could dominate him given enough time. Metallic pitched whines ripped throughout the U-Boat as the bolts in the bulkheads began to shake. If it escaped the Alptryume, Heller desperately hoped that the weight of the ocean would crush it.

He started to fade from consciousness. White light shimmered on the edges of his vision. A loud crack signaled the shattering of the porthole. It came upon him quickly wrapping its soft tentacles around his neck and shoulders pulling him into it. The bubbling protoplasm tingled then numbed his body. Beat by beat his heart slowed. Vile images of the lonely eternal waiting for the stars to change drowned his mind. He understood the Shoggoth's plan at last!

As the Alptryume descended through the dark waters of the Atlantic, Heller dreamt of the ancient city that awaited them at the bottom.

Untouchable

Amanda C. Davis

The floor was lava.

Emily crouched on the arm of the sofa and surveyed her options. The rocking chair. Dangerous, but tempting. The armchair was perfect, but it was all the way across the room; she'd need an intermediary. There was the bookshelf (too high) and the little wicker chair that held a decorative doll (absolutely, positively forbidden to touch—she'd learned that the hard way). But the lamp stand . . .

She stretched an arm just to see how far it really was. Her fingers brushed the edge. She got up on her toes on the very tip of the sofa's arm. She could make it. It would be an incredible act of derring-do, but she could make it. She steeled herself for the leap. Like they said in the cartoons: one small step for man . . .

The front door banged open. Emily fell backward onto the cushions. She heard her father's shouts before she saw him, so she sat up fast—had he seen her jumping on the furniture? But he was shouting at her mother, not her, and he moved so quickly through the living room that she doubted he even saw her.

"Nothing. Don't take anything. Shoes, get shoes. Where's Emily?" He spotted her and swept her up. In a dizzying few seconds they were in the front room. "Put your shoes on. We have to go."

"Go where?" said Emily.

Emily's mother tried to help with the shouting: "Paul, you're acting crazy! Just stop for one minute." But Emily's father was much better at it—and by then he had Emily on his knee and he was grinding the sneakers over her footie pajamas without even undoing the velcro. It hurt, but Emily knew with deep certainty not to mention it. She didn't say anything. Not when her father stood her back up; not when he faced her mother and shouted right over her:

"Trust me, Lisa. We have to move. *Now.*"

Emily's mother's face went strange and hard; it got lines and looked old, all at once. She grabbed Emily into her arms. Then off they went, out the door to the garage, into the car—not even into

57

the car seat!—and the car went screaming out of the garage into the street.

Emily sat on her mother's lap and tried her very hardest not to cry.

"Paul, please. I need to know what—"

"It was an accident. At the plant. I don't know what happened. I only saw, and I knew. I knew we were working on something bad. What's wrong with me? Why didn't I stop them before this?"

"Is it—"

"I didn't stop to think. I just left. We'll just leave. Once we're gone, we'll think of something, we'll be okay."

"Where are you taking us?"

"I don't know, Lisa, I don't know. I don't care as long as we just—"

He stopped shouting then, but it didn't get quiet because another sound happened: a terrible screech. Emily's mother screamed and that made it worse. Her arms went around Emily even harder, so hard it hurt. Emily buried her face in her mother's chest with her eyes closed tight . . . so she didn't see. She didn't see anything. But everything went crazy, up and down, side to side, and then everything hurt, and then—

Then she was sleepy as if it was morning. Then she was cold. She opened her eyes.

It was dark. She was in her mother's arms. It felt wrong. "Mommy," she said and reached for her mother's face, but couldn't find it. Her mother didn't move.

"Emily."

Her father was wrong. Folded over. The car was wrong. She saw the seats hanging above her. But her father was there on the floor of the car that used to be the ceiling, looking at her. Talking to her.

"Emily. You have to be really brave. You have to leave us here and go away."

She said, "No no no no," like she used to, not long ago, before she learned her words—in the days when no matter whether she was angry or sad or confused or tired, she could only say *no*.

"Yes. Listen to Daddy."

Something soft thudded against the window. She looked across her wrong-way Daddy to see a man scrape past, very slowly.

His hand clung to the glass like a bad squeegee. It fell away when it hit the door handle.

More thuds. Another man. A woman. A whole lot of men and women . . . she peeked back and front and out of her own window, and saw them everywhere. Slow. Strange. Wrong.

"Listen to Daddy, Em." She looked back. "You have to be a big girl. Get out of the car. Go through the woods. Find someone to help you. Someone who looks . . . ." He made a weird sound. Blood came from the side of his mouth. "Someone nice. Like a policeman or fireman or teacher. Someone. But Emily, listen . . . ."

"Daddy, no, no. . . ."

"Don't touch the people. The people are . . . poisonous. They're bad. Don't touch."

"The people are lava," said Emily.

"Yes," said Daddy, and he made the weird noise again, only she thought he kind of smiled. "The people are lava. Don't touch the people, Emily, but go as fast as you can, and we love you, and you'll be safe, and go . . . go . . . ."

"Daddy, no!"

But he had stopped talking. He didn't even make the weird noise.

One of the back windows was gone, just a ring of sharp teeth in the door. Emily crawled over the ceiling floor and squeezed out. It wasn't hard to fit. She fell with a thump and stood up. All around the road there were people walking and swaying and standing still. They were all wrong. Far off she saw the edge of the forest, where Daddy had told her to go.

"The people are lava," said Emily.

Then she wasn't small or scared. In an instant, she was brave and confident, an explorer, an adventurer, and she laughed in the face of lava. She was an expert at this game. She could make it. Like they said in the cartoons: one giant leap for mankind.

Emily began to walk.

The Wager

Matthew Fryer

Poppy bolted upright as a key rattled in the front door.

"Shit!"

Stabbing her half-smoked Camel into the ashtray, she leapt from the sofa and switched off the television. The professor wasn't supposed to be back home for several hours.

She shoved the bottle of port she'd been drinking under a cushion as the outside door opened and footsteps entered the hallway; two people by the sound of it.

Time to disappear.

Poppy turned to the wardrobe. The antique behemoth was over two meters tall and almost spanned the entire back wall of the parlor. It had several ornate drawers, twin sets of doors and a central, full-length mirror topped with a curvaceous arch.

Poppy clambered onto the chair nestled in the corner. She grasped the side rim of the wardrobe, jumped and scrambled up on top. Wincing at the noise, she slithered forward onto the blanket stashed up there and flattened her back against the wall. Fortunately, the wardrobe had a deep, carved rim, lining the edges like some kind of decorative castle battlement. Poppy nestled down into the blanket, trying to shrink into the shadows as Philip Frost's deep, gentle voice drifted down the hallway.

"Would you like a cup of tea?"

"Never mind tea, you got anything stronger?"

Poppy wilted. That voice belonged to Thomas Blake, one of the professor's colleagues from the university. Although Poppy had never actually seen him, he had bludgeoning footsteps, drank like a sailor on shore leave and possessed a sarcastic temper. God alone knew why the quietly dignified professor kept such company.

"Help yourself to a glass of vintage port," Philip said patiently. "There's a bottle beside the stove."

No there isn't, Poppy thought. *Shit.*

"It's not here," Blake said.

There was a pause. "So it isn't."

"Sure you didn't drink it all?"

"Unlike yourself, I enjoy life's luxuries in moderation."

"Maybe you just forgot? Or put it somewhere else. Only to be expected at your age."

"I assure you, my faculties are very much in order. As you will discover when I win our wager."

"Never gonna happen."

"We digress. I distinctly recall placing the bottle there last night. Somebody has been in here and moved it."

"What about that fat bitch who does your cleaning?" Blake asked. "Bet she likes a drink."

"Mrs. Pegg only works Monday afternoons."

"Maybe we should take a look around."

Poppy cursed silently. Mrs. Pegg was usually the only person who ever poked around the parlor, and it was obvious from her wheezy, undignified grunting that she was obese. There was no danger of her clambering on the furniture and accidentally discovering this little sanctuary, but now it seemed a hunt was underway.

Poppy had been homeless for three years, not that the threadbare council terrace she previously occupied could have ever been considered a home. Since her mother had died of breast cancer when she was twelve, she'd shared it with George, her worthless cliché of an abusive step dad, who didn't give a fuck about Poppy, and only regarded her as someone to tidy up his mess, bring him booze and slap around if she ever spoke out of line. Tired of the joyless existence and the stinging back-handers, Poppy left for school one rain-drenched morning and never returned.

After a couple of years of sleeping under damp cardboard and resisting the whispered solace of heroin, a feature in a discarded magazine had caught Poppy's eye. It was about a Japanese girl who'd lived in a Tokyo banker's apartment for several years without detection, ensconced in an unused storage cupboard. With nothing to lose, Poppy decided to try it for herself and discovered that if she selected a property carefully, it wasn't as outrageous as it sounded.

Whenever the risk got too high, she fled. Professor Philip Frost's large estate was her third pseudo-squat since she turned eighteen last year. He lived in a large, gabled house built from dusty stone that used to be part of an old priory. It had plenty of rooms, and of course, an enormous antique wardrobe. As the professor worked long and regular hours, Poppy had plenty of chance to climb down from her sanctuary and relax. The fridge was well stocked and although living in a room the owner actually used—albeit very occasionally—was a risk, it was simple complacency that had let Poppy down.

She peered over the rim of the wardrobe to be sure that in her haste, she'd properly hidden the port beneath the cushions. Her heart sank. While the bottle was out of sight, her docked cigarette still smoldered in the ashtray, a trail of smoke wriggling up towards the ceiling.

As footsteps moved across the hall from the kitchen and into the lounge, Poppy considered making a dash for it. Unfortunately, the window of the parlor was small, and since the sill was lined with faded picture-frames and candlesticks, she'd never be able to clamber out without knocking things over and bringing the cavalry. She knew the back door was locked, and it seemed unlikely she'd get past the lounge unseen. Poppy slumped back down, opting that her best move was to just keep quiet.

She dragged the blanket from underneath her body and covered herself up, cringing as the wardrobe issued a coffin-creak. Hopefully it would look as though the blanket had been tossed up here by the lazy cleaner.

Muffled voices drifted in from the lounge.

"Anything missing?" Blake asked.

"I don't believe so."

"How'd you afford all this stuff anyway?"

"I work for a living. You should try it some time."

Blake ignored the jibe, left the living room and stomped down the hall. He stopped by the open parlor door and Poppy held her breath.

"Gotcha," he said, stepping inside, and Poppy's stomach clenched. "You better check this out!"

Philip's soft footfalls entered the room.

"Look," Blake said. "Looks like we interrupted someone's smoke break."

Philip walked across to the sofa. "Ah. And the mystery of the missing port is solved."

"They've probably scarpered by now."

"We should make sure. Would you please check the rest of

the house? I'll lock the front door and make sure all's well with the wager."

"I'm on it."

"And please don't drink all the port. I have plenty of sherry and wine, but that is a vintage to be savored."

As Philip left the parlor, Poppy took her flick-knife from her pocket. Blake thumped across to the sofa and the stopper squeaked from the port bottle, followed by a series of hearty gulps.

"Ah, that's the stuff," he breathed and belched loudly. At least he clearly thought the intruder was long gone. He wandered around the room casually and stopped before the wardrobe.

"Anybody in here?" The doors beneath Poppy squeaked open one at a time. "Jesus, you really hoard some crap." Blake slammed them shut.

Poppy tensed as the chair beside the wardrobe groaned under Blake's weight. She rested her thumb against the flick-knife's trigger. She was gonna have to stripe the fucker and then run for it while surprise was still on her side.

Wood splintered and Blake crashed to the floor.

"Shit!"

Several seconds later, Philip hurried back into the room. "What on earth is going on?"

"The fucking chair collapsed on me! Why don't you throw some of this junk out?"

"That *junk* happened to be a mahogany and canework Georgian original."

"You can bill me!"

"I might just do that. Are you quite finished rolling about on the floor?"

"I've twisted my ankle. And got a splinter."

"Do you need an ambulance?"

"Very funny. I'm good."

"That's a matter of opinion."

"Is the wager okay?"

"I keep the cellar door securely locked. The wager is safe."

Poppy had no idea what 'the wager' entailed. Living on the streets had fostered a fear of being cornered and she never set foot in unexplored territory—especially not a cellar—unless confident there would be somewhere to hide or an alternative escape route.

"Did you see on top of the wardrobe?" Philip asked.

"Yeah, just. Before that piece of fucking firewood dumped me on the floor."

"And?"

Poppy clenched the flick-knife tight, sweat greasing her palm. The professor wasn't leaving any stones unturned.

"There's just an old blanket. What were you expecting? Somebody lying there with a glass of port, wanking over a picture of your sister?"

"Well then if your injuries permit it, would you mind checking upstairs?"

Poppy exhaled silently as footsteps left the parlor, at last allowing her wired muscles to unwind. Christ, it didn't get much closer than that.

As Blake stamped angrily up the stairs, Poppy decided to wait until he went home and Philip was in bed for the night. In fact, if she hung on until Philip went to work tomorrow, she could bag some valuables to pawn.

"You can come out now," Philip said.

Poppy froze, heart punching against her ribs. Philip spoke again, his voice strangely calm for one confronting a mystery intruder.

"I know you're up there. Please show yourself and don't attempt anything foolish."

Still holding the knife, Poppy pushed back the blanket and sat forward, seeing Philip up close for the first time. Dressed casually in blue jeans, tan suede boots and a matching jacket, he was slightly built with shoulder-length, yellow hair. His eyes were deep set in a craggy face that nevertheless still possessed some of the attraction he no doubt had in abundance as a young man. Poppy saw the source of his relaxed demeanor. He held a gun.

"Come down and let's be done with all this silly business."

Poppy's mouth went dry. While she had experienced the wrong end of a gun before, it was always a bucket of ice to the soul. Fortunately, Philip didn't seem angry, rather his posture suggested relief at discovering that she was just an ordinary young woman and not some drooling, battle-scarred crack-head.

Poppy was more worried about what Blake would do when he eventually joined the party.

Philip smiled warmly. "I won't let Mr. Blake harm you, if that's what you're worried about."

Poppy decided to play it safe for now. She surreptitiously pocketed the flick-knife, carefully clambered over the edge of the wardrobe and dropped to the floor.

"My name is Philip and this is my house. Who might you be?"

"Poppy."

Philip gestured to the sofa with his empty hand. "You commit a very leisurely break and enter. Were you not concerned about being caught?"

"I just wanted to get warm, something to eat," Poppy said. An ageing bachelor like this would hopefully be putty in her hands, although he'd detect a deliberate manipulation.

"And something to drink it seems," Philip chided gently, but his eyes sparkled with humor.

"Who the fuck are you talking to?" Blake yelled down the staircase.

Philip frowned. "Myself! It's more engaging than talking to you!"

"Well excuse me for interrupting! You just sit about chatting to yourself in a fucking mirror while I risk my arse poking about *your* smeggy old house for burglars!"

"Charming fellow," Philip chuckled then winked at Poppy. Despite the gun, she suddenly had the feeling everything was going to be okay.

"You're homeless I assume?"

Poppy nodded.

"My poor dear."

"Sorry," she said. "I just wanted to get off the streets for a while."

"And off the streets you shall be. I have a spare bed."

"What?"

"I'm willing to play host. A temporary arrangement, naturally."

"But . . ." Poppy began, caught off guard.

"Think nothing of it," Philip said, dismissing her hesitation with a smile.

Poppy tried not to radiate the suspicion that jangled in her brain. She might have expected a cup of tea and a sandwich before being sent on her way from this oddly generous man, but being offered the spare room mere seconds after they'd met? Nobody was

65

that naïve, surely. Did he think homeless people were a bunch of cheeky scamps out of a west-end musical? Was anybody really that out of touch? It had to be a ruse. Maybe he was going to try and fuck her.

Philip nodded towards the door. "I'll show you to your accommodation."

The warning bell in Poppy's head shrieked like a Klaxon. "Actually, I need to go. Sorry for all the trouble and thanks, but I'm staying with a friend tonight and he'll be wondering where I am."

"We both know that's not true. You're just being polite, bless you. This way please." Philip waggled the gun at the parlor door. His smile, while the same as before, didn't seem benevolent any more. Something dark gleamed behind it. Dread spidered up Poppy's nape and across her scalp.

"Are you okay, my dear?"

"I really need to go. I'm grateful, I really am, but . . ."

"You don't have any choice," Philip interrupted.

Poppy's street sense kicked in with a bang. She considered trying to sneak out the flick-knife, but if Philip saw he'd confiscate her only weapon. Maybe she should play ball for now then take him on the stairs before Blake got involved?

"Whatever you're thinking, I wouldn't advise it. Even if you somehow avoid getting shot, Mr. Blake will be down the steps in two bounds. As I'm sure you've noticed, he's an uncouth hooligan. Unless you behave, I won't protect you from him. This way."

Bide your time.

Poppy walked stiffly from the parlor and turned towards the stairs. At the end of the wood-paneled hallway, the cellar door yawned, a rectangle of pure darkness that spilled shadows onto the floor. Poppy had never seen it left open before.

She grasped the balustrade and was about to begin upstairs when Philip spoke quietly.

"We aren't going up there."

Poppy froze.

Philip stepped up to the cellar door and although the gun never wavered, he momentarily took his eyes off Poppy to locate the light-switch. She seized the opportunity, slipped the flick-knife from her pocket and managed to palm it deftly in one slick, practiced movement, holding it against her thigh. Philip flicked a switch and lamps glared, bathing the brick walls and descending steps in cold, white light.

"Down you go," he said, standing to one side.

Poppy approached the door, eyeing the gun. She'd have to pick her moment carefully. Philip followed in silence as she began down the concrete steps.

The cellar slowly came into view and Poppy squinted against the glare of fluorescent lamps that burned along the low ceiling. As her eyes adjusted, the image cleared and her street sense shriveled to a useless bulb of terror in her guts.

Philip's gun nuzzled her spine and she stumbled down the last few steps.

The cellar had been converted into an operating room. The walls were covered in white plasterboard, shelves stacked with drug ampoules and trays of surgical instruments. A custom-made operating table formed the centrepiece, its steel struts and macabre clamps gleaming cold. Medical equipment cluttered the corners: anaesthetic tubing, cylinders of oxygen and nitrous oxide, an examination lamp. To the left was a deep sink beneath a metal cupboard sporting biohazard symbols.

Of all the furnishings, Poppy's gaze was drawn to the back of the cellar where a shallow cot had been constructed. It took several seconds for her to realize that what lay upon it was real.

"Oh God, no," she breathed, her whisper distant beneath the staccato terror in her veins. Philip nudged her and she lurched towards the cot in a trance.

All that remained of the naked victim was a ruined torso and a head; Poppy couldn't even tell the victim's gender. The arms and legs had been removed, as had any trace of external genitalia, leaving scabby ridges of skin, yellow with bruising and webbed with broken capillaries. The fleshless trunk was striped with surgical scars, dipping and rising across sharp rib-bones and down into the sagging pit of the abdomen. Some of the wounds were healed but the bigger incisions, such as the one that stretched from sternum to pubis, were pink and inflamed as though they'd been stitched then re-opened several times.

And its *head*?

It was scalped, the exposed skull glistening a creamy pink. The victim had no external features, just knots of scarification where the nose and ears should have been; its eye sockets were empty and black. The lips and cheeks had been snipped away, right back to the jaw, leaving a ghastly grin.

Various drips, tubes and electrodes were attached to the body, but the monitoring equipment at the cotside was switched off.

"This is Alfie," Philip said. "The subject of our wager."

Poppy's subconscious screamed to act now and attack Philip before it was too late, but she was in shock, barely able to cling to the flick-knife in her palm, let alone use it.

"Why?" she managed to croak.

"Mr. Blake and myself have contacts with a terrorist organization who want specific research into long-term, physical trauma. I don't know their ultimate plans, but they require answers that traditional medicine cannot provide, and they pay extremely well to get them. It's sadly indicative of the brutal world in which we live that the most difficult, illegal and unethical research is the most handsomely funded."

Poppy couldn't take her eyes off the thing in the cot. She felt her gorge rise and hunched, spattering her shoes. Philip waited until her heaving stopped before continuing.

"I concluded my research a couple of months ago. I was about to terminate young Alfie's life support and cremate the body, but Mr. Blake expressed a curiosity as to how much the human body could take. Rather than waste the perfect opportunity, we decided to have a little bet. I have removed all Alfie's external appendages and organs. Internally, I excised one of his lungs, a kidney, his spleen, stomach, gall bladder and most of the small bowel and colon. I took his larynx, tongue and thyroid. I was going to remove the teeth also, but I rather liked his radiant smile. It's sweet, don't you think?"

Poppy thought that Alfie's skullish leer was the single most demonic thing she'd ever seen in her life.

"Although a patient can lose several of these structures and survive, we wondered if it would be possible to cope with losing them *all*. I wagered fifty thousand pounds that it was. Mr. Blake disagreed, and he was correct. There was still a pancreatectomy to go, a tricky procedure, but I was confident of success."

"He only just died?" Poppy said in a hoarse whisper. Maybe she was stalling, but didn't really know. Her brain spun, struggling to process the horror.

"Yes. I discovered the body earlier while Mr. Blake was in the parlor, breaking up my furniture while looking for you."

"Please. Just let me go and I won't say a word."

"You would go straight to the police, and rightly so." Philip sighed. "Much as it pains me to concede defeat against such a man, I'd better call Mr. Blake and weather the inevitable gloating."

Poppy wiped port and bile from her lips and sucked in breath, hoping it would somehow clear her scrambled thoughts. If Blake came down here, she wouldn't stand a chance of getting out alive.

Think, damn it. Say something, anything, just stall him . . .

"No, don't call Blake." Keeping the flick-knife out of sight, she turned to face the professor. "I've got an idea. Why don't you send him home, and then take Alfie's pancreas out tonight? Then when Blake comes back, put the heart monitor on demonstration so he thinks Alfie is still alive."

Philip raised his eyebrows, impressed.

Poppy continued, trying to keep him distracted. "Someone did it on telly once. It's got to be worth a shot, you might still get your fifty grand."

Philip had definitely loosened up but maintained the space between them, gun poised. "Interesting idea. And the operation would be easy as there's no actual risk to the patient any more." He shook his head. "But no. Unfortunately, Mr. Blake would notice the deception. And anyway, this is an honorable wager made in good faith."

Poppy would have laughed at the psychotic old bastard's refusal to cheat on a handshake if her blood hadn't turned to sludge. Footsteps thundered along the hallway above then began down the steps to the cellar.

"Too late anyway," Philip said as Blake lumbered down the stairs, ducking low to avoid banging his head. He was a hulk of a man with jet black hair and hands like shovels, crammed into a suit that looked as though it would rip any moment. The perfect henchman.

"I knew you were talking to someone!" He marched across, glowering down at Poppy with febrile anger. "Who the fuck is this?"

"This is Poppy. She was on top of the wardrobe, where you claimed to have checked."

Blake frowned, his thick black eyebrows knitting together, and glanced at the eviscerated torso. "Hang on a minute. Is Alfie dead?"

"I'm afraid so."

Blake's anger vanished in a blink and he beamed like a

schoolboy. "I've won the wager?"

"You have."

"Yes!" Blake punched the air. "I knew you couldn't do it, you fucking mental, old quack. That's fifty grand you owe me."

"Indeed."

"Only the pancreas to go. So close, but no cigar!"

"I think I know what went wrong. If I'd left the kidney until last, it might have delayed the acidosis."

Although the gun still nosed in Poppy's direction, both Philip and Blake's concentration had wandered with their discussion. Adrenaline flooded her system.

Springing the blade, she leapt. The professor jumped as the steel blade flashed towards his throat and the gun fired, the deafening bang sending Poppy's heart into overdrive. The shot missed, plaster clouding down from the ceiling. The knife skimmed Philip's throat and Poppy glimpsed a victorious flash of red before huge hands grabbed her, one around her neck, and flung her hard against the wall. She shrieked, the flick-knife falling from her grasp. A fist cannoned into her side and she dropped like a sack.

Poppy wheezed as fireworks of pain seared up through her back and squeezed the breath from her lungs. Philip leaned against the wall, still holding the gun but clutching a handkerchief to his throat. Hopefully she'd got him good.

"You okay?" Blake asked, retrieving Poppy's flick-knife from the floor.

"Yes. Fortunately, just a nick."

Poppy choked on a sob.

"Ever thought of actually disarming someone? She could've had your fucking throat out!"

"Thank you, Mr. Blake. As you've probably guessed, spontaneous violence is not really my area of expertise."

"No shit."

"He was gonna cheat!" Poppy blurted, finding breath.

Blake stared at her. "What?"

"I swear. He was going to send you away and take out the pancreas and put the monitor on demonstration mode so you'd think the body was still alive! He told me, just before you came down!"

Blake narrowed his eyes at Philip and for a hopeful moment, Poppy thought her plan might actually succeed. The barbarian would get riled, start a fight with the professor and she'd be able to bolt.

"Nonsense, of course," Philip said calmly. "Such skulduggery would be doomed to exposure. She's lying, a transparent attempt to set us upon one another."

Blake weighed it up then nodded. Tears filled Poppy's eyes.

"But regarding the wager, Mr. Blake, I'd like another chance."

Blake stared at the professor for a moment. In perfect synchronization, their gazes turned to Poppy.

"Double or quits?" Philip said.

"One hundred grand?" A grin spread across Blake's face, so wide that it almost resembled the butchered corpse in the cot. "You're on."

At Winter's End

Brad C. Hodson

The ache in his bowels returned. It thumped like a heartbeat and ripped him from his dream. He tried to open his eyes but they were crusted shut. He had to dig his knuckles in hard enough to create stars for the flakes to loosen. He blinked three times. Struggled to hold his lids apart. Everything was dark and blurred. It reminded him of summers spent at the lake, when his view of the submerged world was little more than silt and algae.

A green light cut through the murk. He turned toward it, reaching out, willing his eyes to focus. They ached from the strain. His fingers stretched farther and his liver-spotted hand came into view. His vision cleared.

He had been reaching for the flashing mountain peaks that skipped their way across his heart monitor. He jerked his hand back, confused.

The dream had been so vivid. He had been convinced that he really was thirteen, that the past fifty-nine years had been the dream. He struggled to sit upright and the pain hit him again. His insides screamed at him, panicked at the discovery that three feet of his colon was missing. He ground his teeth together and took several deep breaths before pressing his weight into the pillows stacked behind him.

The room was still dark, but now that his eyes were working he could at least make-out shapes. The rectangular shadow against the wall. The cube hanging from the ceiling's corner, reflecting a tiny bit of green light back from its screen. The black mass of curtain separating him from his roommate, whoever that might be.

His mouth was dry and he wondered what time it was. He fumbled for the call button and waited. He had just about given up and settled on sleeping again when the door cracked open. Light from the hallway crawled across the white tiled floor and up the wall. A nurse tiptoed in, stopping to peek at the bed on the other side of the curtain, before walking over and checking his machines.

"How are you tonight, Mister Samuels?"

She turned and smiled and, even with all his pain and discomfort, he couldn't help but smile back. Her short blond hair and blue eyes reminded him of his late wife, though her face was quite a bit rounder. She probably weighed thirty pounds more than Carol at that age, but he found her thick waist and thicker breasts much more attractive than when his wife had finally been that size.

He felt a pang of guilt for thinking of Carol that way.

"I'm thirsty," he said.

She smiled again and touched his shoulder. "I'll get you some water."

She left and was back with a large plastic cup in minutes. His hand shook as he lifted it to his lips.

"Need a hand?"

He shook his head. "No. I've got it." When he was finished he wiped his chin dry. "What time is it?"

She glanced at her watch. "Two-thirty three."

"Is there some kind of pill to get rid of this pain? Maybe help me sleep?"

She grabbed a clipboard from the foot of his bed and scanned it. "I'm sorry, Mister Samuels. You're not supposed to have any more medication until the morning."

"It is morning."

"You know what I mean. How bad is the pain?"

He shrugged. "Manageable, I suppose."

She laughed. "Thank you."

"For what?"

"Your honesty. Most patients whine and play it up, whether it's for drugs or just sympathy."

He groaned and settled back into his bed. The wind picked up outside and shook the window.

"Is there anything else I can get you?"

He shook his head. She stood and nodded. As she was leaving she stopped and stared at the empty dresser and the empty shelves. She sighed. "Let me know if you need anything else."

He closed his eyes. He kept them closed until the door shut, then threw the blanket off and sat up. Throwing his legs over the side of the bed sent a bayonet stabbing into his guts. He grimaced and leaned forward, his hand feeling along the length of the wall until his fingers found the drawstring for the curtain. Careful not to wake his neighbor, he gave the chord several short, slow tugs until the curtains were wide open.

Something rustled behind him. He turned and saw the curtain fluttering between him and the other bed. He eyed it for a moment, hoping he hadn't woken whoever it was. He didn't want to struggle through another awkward conversation.

The curtain settled and he was satisfied he wouldn't be disturbed. He turned back to the window.

A thin sheet of icy rain dulled the city's lights until they were just a thousand orange pinpricks. He stared through the gray-white and tried to find that unique intersection of lights out there, that strange three-four-three-five square that framed the area down West Olson Avenue where he and Carol had raised their children.

There. He had climbed the rafters on the office buildings out this way when they were little more than steel skeletons awaiting concrete flesh. Though he had never had occasion to look for it from the hospital, he had spent his dinner breaks staring down at where his wife and children were from very similar angles. He had nearly broken his back during those years on the rafters, working from sunrise to well past sunset day in and day out, coming home in time to eat a few of Carol's brownies or cookies, read his children a bedtime story, and then slide into bed with his wife.

Those had been good years, that time after Korea and before Vietnam, when the country prospered and hard work was still appreciated. Every weekend he had taken his kids to a movie or a ballgame and his wife out for dinner and the theater. He'd taken an entire week off in the summers, packing the family up in the station wagon and hauling them off to his father's lake house, where he taught the boys to swim and fish while Sarah played with the O'Connell girls next door.

Family meant something once. But Carol's death had severed whatever glue had bonded them and the individual pieces of the Samuels family had scattered across the country.

Would they have even cared that he was in the hospital now? He didn't know. He had kept his surgery a secret from everyone outside of the Sunday night meetings of *Los Conquistadores*. Every member of that august body of septuagenarian poker players had already been through several major surgeries and none of them even batted an eye at his pronouncement. He didn't know how he felt about that. What was it the nurse had said about why patients lied?

For drugs and sympathy? Seems he had a need for both.

One of the lights on West Oslon blinked a few times, threatening to go out. His breath caught in his throat. He wasn't sure why, but the idea of those lights dying scared him almost as much as when Carol had first been diagnosed. It struggled to stay lit, but eventually vanished, leaving a tiny black space in the strange Morse code of lamps.

He was suddenly very aware of the hole in his bowels, the newly formed emptiness inside of him. It was absurd, the idea that this fluke of the Department of Water and Power should have some effect on him. He had no answers as to why.

A family lived there now, a young black family he had seen when overtaken by a whim last summer to drive by and take a glimpse. They had planted rose bushes in the front yard, built a garage where his shed had stood, and replaced the white exterior he had painted every other summer with aluminum siding. He wondered if they noticed the light and if it shook them as it did him.

The bed creaked behind him as his neighbor's weight shifted.

His bladder tickled. The last thing he wanted to do was urinate right now. What would *that* pain be like? He was afraid to find out.

He thought of the dream he had been having. It was of the day he almost drowned. Deep under the lake, sunlight dancing across the surface, his foot pinned between rocks from playing a game of quarters with the beautiful girl he'd just met. It was the fifth that she had thrown and he hoped to impress her by catching each one. The silt on the floor had shifted and rocks clamped on his ankle. His lungs burned from holding his breath. His vision leaked away.

Carol dove down and pulled the rocks away. As she struggled and he faded away, he saw something.

A dark shape scrambled across the bottom of the lake, head cocked to one side, hands outstretched. It reached for him.

The rocks had given way right then and Carol pulled him to the surface. He sucked in a cool breath and blinked the black from his eyes.

"I've got you," she'd said. "Nothing will ever happen to you while I'm around."

A low moan from behind him. A cough. Another creak. Silence.

75

The tickling grew stronger. He'd have to take care of it soon. He was tempted to use the bedpan, but didn't like the idea of pissing in the same room as a stranger. It was going to hurt walking across the room to the bathroom, but he wanted the privacy.

The curtain rustled again. He could hold it long enough for the restless sleeper to calm.

The machines hummed and flashed next to him. Would an alarm go off if he disconnected himself?

He looked back out the window. This time the intersection proved more elusive. His eyes moved back and forth, up and down around where he thought it had been. He was worried that he wouldn't find it with only four lights, and that worry sunk down into his bladder. The tickling grew worse, threatened to burst inside of him. His eyes lingered on a trio of lights clumped close together, certain they were the key to finding his intersection.

The tickling settled into a stabbing pain. When his eyes flickered around and rested on the trio for the eleventh time, the realization that those three lights were his intersection enveloped him. He sucked in a sharp breath and his bladder let go. Hot piss erupted against the inside of his hospital gown, spraying back against his shins and flooding onto the floor.

Why had another light gone out?

He was nauseous. Unsteady. His weight shifted one way, lurched the other. He pressed a hand against the freezing window to right himself and stay on his feet. The world rocked back and forth around him like he was on a ship fighting through a storm, pitching him shoulder first into the window. His feet pressed into the warm puddle and lost friction. He landed hard on his ass.

He sat there, ass and shoulder aching, covered in urine, until his head stopped spinning. The pain inside doubled its attack. He doubled over and ground his teeth together.

When everything had returned to a dull ache, he looked up over his bed. There was a gap in the curtain now. Behind it was thick ink, too deep and dark to see whoever peeked out at him. He waited for them to ask if he was okay, but whoever it was never said a word. Why were they watching him at his most vulnerable, observing him like some goddamned zoo animal?

"What the hell are you looking at?"

The curtain fluttered.

He gripped the window seal with one hand. Grunted. Pulled

himself to his feet. Is this what he had to look forward to? A few years of pissing himself and falling until his own lights went out?

He shuffled back over to his bed and sat. What was happening to him? Was it the surgery? The drugs that he thought had worn off? Or simply the hunger of age eating away at him? He tried to shake it off. He needed rest. Sleep. Then tomorrow, he assured himself, in the daylight, everything would be better.

He pulled his legs up onto the bed and maneuvered back onto his pillows. One of the chords had slithered around his calf and he had to twist and kick to untangle himself. He took a deep breath. Closed his eyes. Tried to let sleep wash over him.

Instead, he thought of Carol. Not the small, sagging, shriveled, wheezing Carol that she had been at the end, but the strong, vibrant Carol she had been when he met her. She was so beautiful and his heart had instantly been hers. The vision came to him unhampered by time. He thought this was thanks to the dream.

Her hair had been the color of the sun setting through autumn leaves. Her smile was whiter than winter's first snow and her eyes the blue of a bright spring day. Seeing her there that summer, he thought she had been emblematic of all seasons, of life itself. Years later they had gone to Scotland on their honeymoon and he had watched the sun set through an ornate stained glass window from the fourteenth century. Those bright colors were the only thing that ever compared to that first viewing of his Carol. The window depicted the Virgin Mary's ascent to Heaven and he had said to his new bride that he hoped when his time came it would be just as beautiful.

He heard a wet slapping sound next to him, a foot hitting the floor. He opened his eyes and looked to his left. The curtain was wide open. The space behind it was still too black to see, but he thought he could make out the shape of the pillow. The bed was otherwise empty. He scanned the room.

It was also empty.

"Hello?"

The only sound was wind rattling glass.

He sat up again. Looked to the window.

Where his intersection had been there was nothing but a dark circle, a black hole that had appeared in the middle of the old neighborhood.

Cold sweat ran down the back of his neck. He shook his head

hard enough to rattle his teeth. Tears slithered down his face.

The surgery, it seemed to him, was not the success that those doctors thought.

He heard the wet slap behind him again.

And again.

The floor felt colder against his feet as he stood. He walked through his urine, hot only moments ago, but now ice splattered over the tile. He pressed his hand against the freezing glass, covering the black spot.

He stared at his dim reflection in the window. It was faint and gauzy, like a ghost in an old film. Is that what he'd become?

Behind him was the weak outline of the room. The dresser. The television. His bed.

A dark shape shuffled across the floor. Every movement was in time to another slap. He searched the reflection for a face, for any discernible feature at all, but there was only darkness. Darkness like the area outside his window that he now covered. Darkness like his life had been since Carol left and his children stopped caring.

He fought the urge to turn and look. He didn't know if he could see it if he did, didn't know if he wanted to. A part of his brain, still clinging to rationality, sifted through its catalog of information, trying to determine what would cause such a hallucination. But he knew what it was.

Slap.

He had summoned it, here at the end.

Slap.

It was his, had been his since that day at the bottom of the lake. Carol had saved him from it, but she was no longer around. It had waited all these years, lurking at the bottom of the lake, afraid of the light. But all the lights in his life were gone.

Slap.

He closed his eyes and thought of that stained glass window. He thought of Carol and all her seasons. He thought of a life once lived under his palm.

Slap.

A cold hand wrapped around his neck and he thought no more.

Revivified

Maria Alexander

A hand in a white latex glove moved over the tray, rubber fingertips delicately probing each blade lying on the gauze covering its surface. The glove was banded at the wrist to the sleeve of a white surgical gown. At last the hand chose a reedy silver knife that caught buttery globs of light on its polished surface.

On a table beyond, the back foot of an albino rabbit rapped against the surface. Its body was neatly fastened with leather buckles and straps to the surface of a metallic tray with deep grooves along the edges. The rabbit's pink eyes widened as the knife tip touched its back leg.

Then, methodically and remorselessly, the knife sliced open the leg joint. The scarlet rivulets gurgled and splattered from the wound before they merged in one of the carved grooves. The animal screamed in fiery agony, its body convulsing against the inescapable metallic plate, blood staining the white fur, splattering the white cloth that covered the table with bright red spots . . .

I awoke in mid-convulsion, chest thrust to the air, stomach sour with terror. My neck and back separated reluctantly from the damp sheets and pillow. I hastily stripped off my long cotton nightgown and rolled to the other side of the bed where it was cool and dry. Breathing heavily, heart flailing against my ribcage under the haze of exhaustion, I eyed the clock radio. 4:32 a.m.

I closed my eyes and took long, tempered breaths to slow my racing heart. I tried to fall back asleep, but instead I just laid there, replaying the nightmare in my mind. That white room, the tray covered with gauze and menacing surgical knives . . .

When I went to work later that morning, the programmers were already in the bull runs: two rows of cubical desks provided computers and workspace for six programmers, one QA engineer, a UI specialist and the technical writer—me. I dropped my backpack on the floor beneath my workstation and headed off to the kitchen where Ricardo, our portly Italian CEO, had installed a real espresso machine. The aroma of freshly ground espresso delighted my nose. Tevan the QA guy was putting the finishing touches on his latte when I entered. "Hey there, Tevan."

"Hi, Anita," he replied. "How are you?" The words rattled in his mouth like chipped marbles.

"Oh, God—tired! I keep waking up at four-thirty in the morning. It's really strange." I grabbed the freshly rinsed utensils and started measuring my ground coffee.

"Really? I never slept better in my life." He adjusted the brown plastic rims of his glasses. His grayish-blue eyes glimmered like ground glass in the soft fluorescent lights.

Our technical lead, Noel, leaned into the kitchen doorway. "Hey guys? Team meeting in five minutes, okay?"

"See you." Tevan shuffled back towards the conference room while I finished the noisy business of brewing. As I sipped the foam, Judy, the HR manager, called to me from her office adjacent to the kitchen.

"Anita? Can you come here a sec?"

"Hey! What's up?"

Judy's desk stood next to a massive white linen couch with colorful velvet pillows that begged for the pressure of people's backs. I was half mesmerized by the overstuffed cushions as we spoke.

"You know," Judy said, "I'm having the same problem! I keep waking up at, like, four-fifteen!" She slumped forward, propping her chin on her palm as she looked off in the distance, hand groping for her enormous Starbucks cup. Her bottom lids bulged with fatigue. "I heard that four a.m. is the hour of the liver, that we wake up then when our livers need detoxing. Do you think that's it?"

Considering how much Judy loved to schedule our happy hours, she probably needed a detox or two. I smiled. "Maybe. Or maybe it's the heat." I raised my cup to her. "Sorry. The Ginger Man wants us. We'll chat later?"

As I entered the conference room, I stopped cold when I saw the white board. In dark blue dry erase pen, someone had scrawled:

Test as if your life depended on it

I pointed at the whiteboard. "Who wrote this?"

"Ricardo," Noel said. "He's just being funny."

"He should leave funny to the professionals."

"I think he's worried we won't make this deadline for J&J." Johnson & Johnson, that is.

"Ya think?" I replied.

One of the programmers closed the conference room door.

"Okay, everybody, listen up." Noel rolled his chair back into place at the head of the conference table. We called him The Ginger Man because of his wiry bright red hair and face dusted with freckles. "We've recruited three more people to do testing this week. Judy, Beth and Mark will be running Tevan's test scripts. Do you guys have any questions? How's your testing going?"

For the last six months, they'd made every mistake the last startup had made: modifying the code with features to quaff the whims of a single *potential* client (J&J wasn't signed yet); burning out the development team with repeated crunch times; distributing unreadable marketing collateral because they couldn't afford to hire a real marketing writer; changing the business plan every week; hiring and firing Sales Directors at lightning speed.

I only took this job because the last layoff was so abrupt, I didn't want to lose the cash flow. I had a terrible habit of just taking what came my way. I was a somnambulist in my life. It had to stop—*stat*—but I didn't know how to rouse myself.

Our work made little sense.

The code we were developing was part of some bigger, secret pharmaceutical project for J&J and possibly the government. They wanted the ability to connect disparate biotech and pharma databases so that they could create a single massive molecular database. Government lab databases had to be able to connect, too. The challenge was that many of these databases had incompatible formats for recording chemical compounds. Our software was to solve the incompatibility issues.

My job was to document how our software worked. I sometimes had to call J&J developers about integration issues. They more than once hinted that we were "not alone" in the problems we faced. Were other companies like ours performing the same work? They wouldn't say. Why would the government sponsor work that joined corporate and political interests on such a wide scale?

The repeated crunches were killing our database guy. He'd left two weeks ago. Why they wanted this in such a hurry was beyond me. Market pressures were one thing, but this?

Just as the meeting was about to break, the caffeine slipped into my bloodstream and the insulin jolt broke the fog of exhaustion. "How's our funding, Noel? Any word?"

Noel rolled his lower lip up under his tongue and made some notes on his legal pad. "I have no idea. We have to ask Ricardo about that."

"Where *is* Ricardo? We never see him anymore." Our affable CEO no longer haunted our bull runs to engage the programmers in small talk. These days he occasionally disappeared into the conference room with men in dark suits for long discussions, presumably about money.

"He's around. All I know," Noel said, "is that we've slipped three deadlines and tomorrow's a hard one." He lowered his voice. "We can't do that again."

* * *

Instead of going out for lunch, I took a nap in the car, which was parked in my assigned space behind the German deli. I ran the air conditioner. As I dozed, the broad-shouldered, Aryan owner talked worriedly on her cell phone as she paced beside her husband's black Bronco.

She sipped from a tall paper coffee cup, dark shadows under her eyes.

* * *

That night, the wobbly elevator doors slid open and I ambled down the scuffed hallway towards the door of my overheated Hollywood apartment. The halogen light sconces created the seedy haze of the partially exposed hallway. The apartment door across from mine stood open maybe a foot. A thin whistling slipped through over the music of Marilyn Manson.

As I fumbled with my keys, I peeked inside.

A cigarette smoldered in a crimped aluminum tray squatting on the cheap coffee table. Wearing chewed-up, black Docs and a sagging Led Zeppelin tee, my neighbor sat on the couch, mousy hair cascading over his shoulders. He loaded a shotgun, methodically pressing and sliding each red cylindrical shell into the barrel. When he finished, he pumped the gun and the metal clapped sharply.

I shoved the key into my door lock, twisted it, and ducked inside.

* * *

I fell asleep easily and dreamed. This time the rabbit's blood surged from a bright red line carved across its abdomen. Its eyes fluttered as it swooned from the loss of blood. A growth of some sort blossomed on the rabbit's neck under the fur. Two hands covered in latex gloves clipped a long metal tag to one of the rabbit's ears, its thin pink lips snarling and trembling in anguish.

I was unable to move or see what kept me from moving.

And then I awoke.

4:27 a.m.

* * *

When I opened my apartment door the next morning, the brown emergency fire door was shut, closing off the hallway from the elevators. My neighbors Aaron and Waka were just leaving their apartment to walk their retriever, Bastion. Aaron had East Coast charm and eloquence, which he applied to a successful sales job. He and I shared the same birthday—not just the day but the year, too. His personable, chatty wife was in school getting her Ph.D. in criminal psychology. They both waved, and Bastion pulled on his leash, eyeing me eagerly.

"Hey! How are you guys?"

"We're good." Aaron yawned. "Tired, but good."

"How are *you*?" Waka asked. Aaron handed her the leash as he strong-armed the fire door. He propped it open so we could get to the elevators. Aaron's face was haggard, pasty, bloated. Waka, on the other hand, looked fresh and happy.

"I'm exhausted," I said. "I keep waking up at four-thirty a.m. It's really wearing me down."

Waka jerked a thumb toward Aaron. "Him, too. And then he kicks me! And I was sleeping like the dead!"

"Must be sprinklers or something coming on at the same time each morning," Aaron said.

"I don't know," I said. "I wear earplugs because of the ghetto birds." The police helicopters that buzzed our neighborhood often descended in the dead of night, lowering their beams into our courtyard just below my window.

Bastion jumped up on me, golden paws clawing at my jeans. I scrubbed love into his ears with both hands and he licked my nose.

As I got into my car, Aaron and Waka descended to the sidewalk with Bastion. Aaron yawned and rubbed his right eye with the back of his hand.

* * *

That afternoon, Noel and the other programmers holed up in the conference room for a final bug scrub. I hadn't high hopes that the software was clean. It was layoff weather. For weeks I'd felt the quiet. I didn't have enough to do, which is always one of the big signs, and what I'd been doing lately—testing—wasn't my job at all. The problem was that we just didn't have enough time to incorporate these last-minute feature demands. They were easy enough to document, as we were told exactly what they had to do in J&J's specs, but making the code obey the requirements was another story.

Meanwhile, I blearily searched online—*again*—for the possible cause of my sleep problems. I had tried everything: going to bed late, going to bed regularly, giving up caffeine (except my morning coffee), giving up alcohol, melatonin, chamomile tea, warm milk, reading, drinking myself blind, staying up later than usual. I worried that I might be suffering depression, but couldn't figure out what was depressing me. I mentioned the problem to friends, but none offered any insights. All of them were sleeping peacefully.

I checked one of my favorite online news portals. An article jumped out at me. *Is the Sandman Slacking?*

They described my malady perfectly: dreams of victimization followed by sudden awakening around 4:30 a.m. According to the article and hundreds of comments, my problem was widespread. Reports of sleeplessness had increased 25 percent in the last three months according to polls. Experts quoted in the article attributed it to an epidemic of reactive hypoglycemia, a result of all the low-carb dieting. Sufferers often awakened in the middle of the night with cold sweats after nightmares. I read the article twice.

My phone rang.

"Good afternoon. This is Anita at Genware. Can I help you?"

The line crackled. Several men and women were talking excitedly; someone wailed in the distance.

"Hello? Who is this?" I checked the caller ID panel on my office phone. I instantly opened a "white pages" website and ran a reverse lookup on the phone number.

Then, a young man's voice, swollen with grief: "We're not going to be able to stop it."

"Stop what?" I entered the company name in Google and found their website. It was a small company just like ours but in Massachusetts.

His voice wavered. "Does the rabbit bleed in your dreams, too?"

Shocked, I hung up.

Everyone filtered out of the conference room. Most of the programmers were joking with each other about their video game skills or drinking prowess. Noel was poker-faced. He dropped into his ergonomic chair, leaned back and read his email.

I was too afraid to ask how it went.

* * *

That night, I muddled home in a cloud of obsession.

As I stood at my apartment door, I hefted my backpack, picking through the keys on my key ring, when I heard the *shussss* of my neighbor's door opening behind me. I slid the key into the lock and swung my head around to look.

My neighbor stood in his doorway, watching me with a milky stare. His eyes were circled with black eyeliner, a tear drop painted at the corner. He might have been in his mid 20s. He held out his hand. "I'm Evo."

I shook it. "I'm Anita. Nice to meet you."

He pinched his nose idly and gazed at the industrial carpeting. "Hey, uh . . . can I ask you a question?"

I turned to face him, crossing my arms. "Sure."

"Are you sleeping okay?"

He must have heard my conversation with Aaron and Waka this morning. "Why do you ask?"

Shifting nervously in his dirty Docs, he crossed his arms, too, then uncrossed them, scratching the back of his head. "Well...

I've heard people talking about it . . . and . . . I just wanted to say that I'm having trouble, too. But I'm not having . . . this is weird, I know . . . but . . . it's like I'm sleeping *too* good."

I eyed him for more than his poor grammar. "Too good?"

"Yeah. And I sleep too long, too. I just can't wake up sometimes." Sadness smoldered in the creases of his eyes and his bottom lip trembled like the rabbit's in my dreams. "My girlfriend left me because she thinks I'm drinking again, but I swear I haven't had a drink in almost a year!" He fished in his faded black jeans' pocket and withdrew what looked like a shiny new poker chip with the letters "10 Months" and "AA" printed on one side. "It's my chip. My sponsor gave it to me last Thursday night."

A faint memory surfaced of my Uncle Chris, who had gotten sober eight years ago. He slept like the dead for the first year or so while living with my parents. "But isn't it normal for recovering alcoholics to sleep a lot?"

"Maybe. I just thought I'd let you know that it's not just you. I hear everyone talking. At work, too. Even these guys." He indicated the door around the hallway corner on the same wall as mine, where a Russian couple lived with their teen daughter. "Everybody. They're mostly like me, but sometimes like you."

I dropped my backpack on the floor and leaned back against the wall. Evo knew more about my neighbors than I did. "What do you think is happening?"

"Something's coming." He placed his hand on his neck and grimaced, his gaze trailing down the hallway to the stairway and then up to the ceiling. His gaze seemed to penetrate the upper floors. He wouldn't explain.

* * *

The next morning, my alarm went off. My sleep had been dreamless, slick as a black satin bed sheet.

As soon as I stepped into the office and set my backpack on the floor by my workstation, Judy emerged from the conference room, holding a file folder. "Anita? We need to talk. Can you come inside?"

The UI designer was sobbing quietly at her workstation. Most of the programmers hadn't arrived yet.

Tevan was gone. His thick glasses and grayish-blue eyes no

longer reflected the QA scripts running on the computer screen. He was a single dad with a small child.

This was it.

I walked to the conference room with Judy and took a seat by Noel at the table. Ricardo the CEO was there as well, but he sat deflated like a week-old birthday balloon, his pillowed cheeks sagging.

Judy explained that Noel and I were being laid off. Noel looked stricken. I then realized it was killing him as much to see us let go as it was for him to lose his own job. I wanted to put my hand on his arm as Judy gave the layoff speech I knew so well, but I let him shoulder his own uncertainty.

As soon as Judy gave us our severance and paperwork, I broke my silence. "Judy, have you been having nightmares?"

She looked taken aback, but said nothing. Ricardo's eyes quivered like a junkie.

I continued: "Does the rabbit bleed in your dreams, too?"

"You need to leave. Now." Ricardo's mouth sneered like a drunken carnie waving a battered cane.

I asked Judy if I could clear some files off of my computer.

She nodded, nervously glancing at Ricardo. "Is a half hour long enough?"

We filed out to our desks. A flat moving box now sat collapsed on the floor by each workstation. I slapped the box open and piled my belongings inside, zipped up my files and emailed them to myself at home. As I worked, Ricardo slipped back into his office and closed the door. He sat at his desk behind the translucent, pockmarked glass wall of his office, his profile a blur to everyone in the bull pen. When I finished, Noel pointed at the box. "Can I help you with that?"

"Yeah. That'd be great."

As we walked out to the parking lot behind the deli, Noel asked, "What the hell was that rabbit stuff about?"

"I'll tell you, but first . . . " I asked Noel if he ever knew why we were operating the way we did. He'd been through a few startups himself. He had to have seen what was coming.

He set down the box on my car trunk. "I just thought like everyone else did, that, if we could pull it off, we'd be rich. There's always that chance, eh? And, honestly, we were close. I don't know why they let us go like this. Sure, we might slip a day, but it looked like we might make it. Is this related to the rabbit—"

A loud *crack* broke distantly from inside the office. And then a woman screamed. And screamed. And screamed . . .

I ran towards the office, sleety dread sluicing my stomach. Before I reached the back door, Noel pitched himself at me and tackled me to the ground. I struggled but capitulated to his superior strength and sense. We stayed like that, sobbing in each other's arms as the police sirens seeped into the parking lot.

* * *

Ricardo had taken a pistol from his desk and shot himself. As I huddled alone at home, I imagined him sitting at his desk behind the translucent, pock-marked glass wall of his office, his profile a blur as always. In my imagination, a split second after the *crack*, a spume of blood hits the glass with a smattering of brain tissue and skull splinters. The blur slumps forward onto the desk as a bright red clot of tissue slides down the pane and drops to the floor . . .

I pictured this. Over and over.

Does the rabbit bleed in your dreams, too?

Somehow I knew it wasn't just because his business had failed. Those men in dark suits never brought briefcases like real investors. More like government men.

I thought about my life, which was as colorless as that operating room. I had been as dumb as that rabbit until these events slid their blade into my overindulged skin. We had all been like the rabbit in my dream: passive, voiceless, waiting for the next pain. We never asked bigger questions, never fought bigger fights.

The longer I thought about it, the angrier I became. *Something's coming.* Fuck that. If I'd been asleep at life's wheel, this had slapped me awake.

At nightfall, I turned off the lights in my apartment and turned on the floor fan. The breeze licked at my calves as I climbed into bed. I laid there for nearly an hour before breaking out the bright orange earplugs, rolling them between my fingers and wedging them into my ears.

And I slept.

One of the knives moved towards my naked flesh as I struggled violently against the leather straps binding my forehead, ankles and wrists. My bare legs were pulled apart, pubic hairs straying into the hinges between my crotch and thighs. The hand angled the knife towards my body. I brayed in agony as the knife gouged that tender articulation point, leg to groin, a heavy spray of blood drenching the latex glove.

My eyes opened, the oppressive premonition squatting on my chest. My heart erupted with each beat like fireworks in my chest. I plucked out the earplugs, grabbed the maglight by my bedside, and scrambled out of bed to the family room window. The courtyard lights between my apartment and the next were dead. People were talking nervously in Russian through an open patio door. The occasional scream interjected in the restless darkness. Someone ran down the street beyond our gated courtyard, shouting.

I ran to the front door and opened it. The smell of last night's cigarette smoke singed the air. In the heated shadows of the hallway, the air pulsed. The maglight revealed that the brown emergency door was closed again, blocking the elevators. I heard Bastion's staccato barking over Aaron's faint yet distinct voice. "Wake up, Waka! Oh, dear God! *Wake—up!*"

I crossed the hallway and pounded on Evo's door. "Evo! Evo, can you hear me?"

No answer.

As Aaron wailed in despair, I laid my hand on Evo's door knob lever and pushed down. The tumblers clacked with welcome. I leaned on the door and it gently swung open. *Shusssss.*

"Evo? *Evo!*"

I swept the massive circular beam through the bare living room. Evo lay on the couch, arms curled around his shotgun. Boxes of ammunition sat half open on the table. He slept peacefully, like a baby rather than a tormented alcoholic.

Training the maglight on his face, I carefully untangled his fingers from the slick barrel. The gun came to me as if he were giving it to me. I tucked a box of ammunition under my arm and ran back out into the hallway to Aaron and Waka's apartment door.

"Aaron! Get out here!"

A sniffling pause. "I can't leave her."

"We can't do anything for her. We've got to protect ourselves."

Silence.

"Be a fucking rabbit, then!"

The door opened slightly and Bastion bounded out. Aaron's tear-stained face met mine briefly—eyes hollow with hopelessness—before he slammed the door shut. Bastion circled me protectively between raucous barks, then bolted past the laundry room and up the metallic stairs, stopping periodically to check if I was following.

Something's coming.

We wound up the outer side of the building and climbed all four stories to the roof, my bare feet slapping the warm steel steps. I followed the trail that Evo's eyes had traced nights before. Up.

I crested the top stair and broke into the full warmth of the Los Angeles night. The air conditioning boxes with their rusty gratings silently flanked the long walkway to the pool area. From my rooftop, I could normally see all the lights of Los Angeles—downtown, the flats and up into the Hollywood Hills. But now the entire city was steeped in pitch except for the roar of helicopters sweeping the city and the flicker of headlights as people fled in their autos. Car horns blared and drivers threatened each other as traffic knotted at the base of the Highland onramp to the 101.

They would never escape.

Bastion and I skirted the pool to reach the broad recreation area, which was littered with armless chaise lounges. I lowered everything gently onto one of the chairs that was pointed at downtown Los Angeles. I sat cross-legged on the chair with the box of ammo open before me, awkwardly grappling the loaded gun I only knew how to use from movies. Bastion sat beside me, panting. Sentinel and soldier. I pressed the cool barrel against my cheek as I watched the horizon. As my eyes grew accustomed to the dark, I noticed others did likewise on apartment rooftops, huddled in blankets. Some wept. But many were armed, angry like I was.

And then it started.

A bluish murk boiled over the edge of the horizon. Muted explosions of tangerine light rumbled under the belly of the murk as they came.

And, oh, how they came. From somewhere closer than stars, yet beyond our bones. Vivisectionists and virologists, with distended onyx eyes and mouthfuls of deadly machinery. Crowded on the inverted bases of mammoth pyramids, needles of electricity writhing across scraggy walls.

Whatever it was that we—and perhaps hundreds of companies like ours working together, unwittingly—were making for J&J, for the government, for whoever it really was, it was intended to stop this.

We had failed.

Of course, I didn't know this for certain. All I knew was that those who were awake would not go down without a fight.

And those who slept would never awaken again.

One For The Road

Jason V Brock

Three a.m.

Elizabeth was tired: bones heavy, neck stiff, eyes burning. The rhythm of the white dashed line reflecting off the interstate made her feel so

very . . .

drowsy . . .

"Gotta stay awake!" She reached over to the dashboard and cranked up the radio. For a moment—as she belted out a few lyrics of choice metal—she was more alert. Even with that shot of adrenaline, though, Elizabeth could barely fend off the highway hypnosis. Her energy ebbed quickly. In the mirror, her eyelids were droopy, whites bloodshot in the dim luminance of the speedometer. She cracked the window for some fresh, cold air.

"Jesus, that's *too* cold!" She rolled the window back up, shivering. Mid-January in the Pacific Northwest was no time to be cruising around with the window down, especially on a night like this.

"What I *really* need is to get to Seattle . . . " She had known better than to start the trip from Eugene so late, but the argument with Derrick had taken her off-guard. She had no idea that he was so jealous about her taking the new management position. She now regretted snubbing his offer to accompany her.

He should be happy for me! For us! More money, better benefits . . . There's no reason for him to be so insecure after all this time.

Just thinking about it made her anger flare.

I should have stopped over in Portland . . . but they said the orientation meeting was supposed to start at eight-thirty sharp . . . if I can just get to Seattle, maybe I can snag a couple hours' sleep . . .

Before . . .

Before sun . . . rise . . .

92

Elizabeth jerked the tiny car back onto the interstate, roused by the roar of the tires on the wake-up strip next to the shoulder. She was scared wide-awake now, heart in her throat, mouth like cotton. The blasting radio seemed distant. Around her—hurtling through darkened space—there was nothing; it was as if she was the only human alive on the planet.

Three-thirty. Meeting at eight-thirty . . . Seattle's still at least another hour and a half out . . .

Elizabeth settled into the seat with renewed resolve, taking a swig of diet soda from the can between her legs.

"I read somewhere even a twenty minute catnap can help when you're tired. Maybe I'll just do that. Set the cell phone for thirty minutes, then keep on grinding . . . Stay over in Seattle tonight before I go back; Derrick'll understand . . ." Checking the fuel gauge, she saw that she had more than enough gasoline to get to the Emerald City. In the yellow glow of the headlights, a sign came into view:

Rest Area: 2 Miles
Next Rest Area: 63 Miles
Safety Break: Free Coffee
Wi-Fi Hotspot

She smiled to herself. "Perfect."

* * *

The pale sodium-arc lamps cast an eerie pink illumination on the empty asphalt of the parking lot.

Creepy.

She parked under one of the light posts, double-checking that all of the doors were locked. She cut the radio off, sitting for a minute with the engine idling, taking in the surroundings. It was drizzling now, mixed with a few flurries of large, wet snowflakes.

Directly in front and to the left of her was the entrance to the ladies room, and opposite that was the men's lavatory. In addition to housing the restrooms, there was a tiny, dark Plexiglas-encased building where elderly volunteers normally offered free coffee, tea, cookies. A halo of moths threw themselves at the sputtering fluorescent lights of the small complex.

93

Many times Elizabeth had seen different older couples at this very rest station, which was a lot more inviting in the daytime, chatting jovially with travelers who would stop to stretch their legs or make use of the facilities.

"Nobody home tonight though." She cut the engine. *I'll just use the bathroom, get back in the car, lock up, and nap for a few minutes . . . then head on up to Seattle.*

A sudden gust made the trees rustle. The place was strangely forbidding, draining her normal moxie; she swallowed, throat parched.

Better make it quick . . .

* * *

It felt good to empty her bladder. Elizabeth had not realized that she had been holding it for so long. As she cleaned up, she heard the door creak open. Her blood pressure spiked. *Just another woman needing to pee . . .*

The person was walking quite slowly, the reverberation of their steps on the tile very measured, as though they had difficulty moving.

I won't flush; I'll just excuse mys—

Dark shoes shuffled into view under the door of Elizabeth's stall as she buttoned her pants. The person on the other side said something in a hoarse voice, then loudly rattled the handle.

"Coming out—I'm done!" Elizabeth yelped, mentally reflecting on how rude it was that this person would not use one of the other unoccupied commodes. She threw the door open.

Time ballooned: for how long, it was impossible to discern. The old woman in front of Elizabeth was staring with huge, runny eyes, blood pumping from a ragged gash under her jaw.

The injured woman reached out with a gory hand. "H-h-hel m-me pl-please," she rasped.

Elizabeth stifled a shriek, dodging the old woman's outstretched arm, never taking her eyes from the blood-soaked vision. The woman, shirt saturated with red, tracked her—watching as Elizabeth backed toward the door.

"H-h-help! No!" Blood foamed in the raw wound as she collapsed, her strangled pleas bouncing off the tile floor.

Suddenly Elizabeth was outside, sweat pouring down her

back, stomach roiling as the noxious scents of urine and oily wet pavement collected in her nose. The wind stung her face, but she was too shocked to react. Looking down, she noticed a trail of bloody footprints.

"Oh God, oh God, oh *GOD!*" she screamed, now fully comprehending the reality of what she had seen.

"God," a husky male voice said, "ain't got nothin' to do with it, lady . . ." The voice was emanating from a silhouette sitting on the hood of her car. The glowing, orange tip of a cigarette was the only visible detail of the hulking figure.

Glancing around the parking lot, Elizabeth could see that it was still deserted—not a car in sight. She froze, watching the cigarette burn brighter, then dimmer as the man took a drag in the darkness.

"Shame about Grandma, huh? She's been stumblin' around for ten minutes . . ." The man stood, flicked the cigarette to the ground, then began walking toward Elizabeth.

Another scream blossomed in her throat. She looked around, her knees starting to buckle. The car was only thirty feet away at most—but between it and her was *him.* It may as well have been the distance between the Sun and Pluto. She could always retreat to the bathroom, but then she would have to deal with the old woman, and there was no way to lock the only entrance . . . or exit.

Immediately to her left was the door to the little room where the volunteers resided when dispensing coffee and snacks. She noted that the door had a keyed lock.

As the man closed the gap between them with his colossal strides, Elizabeth leapt to the door.

"Oh, God!" She turned the knob and pushed, seeing stars as hyperventilation brought her close to passing out.

Miraculously, the door opened. She fell into the comforting blackness of the small room, whimpering involuntarily. She kicked the door closed just as the stranger was upon it, pushing the button lock in, then—

Nothing.

Elizabeth huddled on the floor, regarding the hard lines of the utilitarian furnishings: a wooden, stiff-backed chair; a miniscule sink; the built-in countertop, which served as a desk. The unhealthy cast of the greenish fluorescents outside was the sole illumination. The terrifying man was nowhere to be seen; her ragged breathing was loud in the cramped space as her heartbeat began to slow. She felt better as her muscles relaxed. It was a very 'dead' room acoustically, compared to the resonant bathroom. Every noise seemed clipped off the instant it was completed, as though the gloomy air itself was consuming the sound waves.

She was shaking as she grabbed the edge of the counter and peered through the scratched lucite windows. The only thing she saw were some snowflakes swirling among the naked trees just past the parking lot.

Who was that poor old lady? And that guy—did he do that to her? Christ! She closed her eyes, imagining the woman dying in the toilet.

The little room was still: she heard the muffled whistle of wind, the patter of falling rain and snow. If she held her breath, she thought that she could just make out the sound of icy grass and leaves crunching as the man stalked outside. Her ears tightened on her scalp.

He's out there!

"You come on out," he proclaimed, out of sight. "No sense prolonging this."

Just then, the doorknob shook violently, punctuating his demands; Elizabeth's chest ached from the pounding of her heart. She scuttled farther from the doorway, scanning the tiny chamber for another place of entry. There was none. It was a claustrophobic room, with high, bare ceilings—like a tomb or mausoleum. She hated tight spaces normally, but, under the circumstances, she was grateful that it was no larger than it was: she could at least view the entire room at once.

"We ain't got all night for these games, bitch!"

Abruptly, the rattling and banging ceased. She strained to look from the dirty windows, trying to be as inconspicuous as possible—nothing, just her snow-dusted old sedan in the gradually whitening lot.

My car! If I could just get to it . . . I'm sure I could make it if I ran. She felt for the keys in her pocket: still there. She moved quietly over to the door of the little room, watching for any movement outside.

Wait—Derrick! I'll call Derrick; he might be able to meet me, even if I have to wait 'til morning in here . . . No—911 first, then Derrick. Elizabeth patted her pockets for her cell phone.

Damn! I left it charging in the car.

A shape materialized in the corner of her eye. It scared her to realize that only a couple of inches of wooden door separated her from this man. She crouched down, but her eyes were riveted on him. He walked over to her car once more, smoking another cigarette. The rain and snow had subsided for the moment. He was large, and seemed in decent shape, but otherwise she could make out no real details.

If I can just hold on 'til daylight, maybe he'll leave . . . But I'm so tired . . . and the meeting . . . damn it!

He was sitting on the hood again, vapor trailing from his silhouette. After a few moments, he stood up, trolling around her vehicle like a shark.

If he leaves I'll break for it . . . but what if he's waiting for me on the other side of the door, or behind the room? Her hand moved instinctively to her throat as gruesome images of the old woman crowded her mind.

Who knows how many times he's done this before. I guess I'd better just wait it out.

As she watched, he strolled up to the shack; she tried to make herself small again.

"Who are you kidding? We both know you're in there," he said, backlit by the streetlights. "I can see you! Think you're gonna wait me out, huh? Well, that little lock ain't enough to stop *me* . . ."

With that, he stormed out of sight. Elizabeth thought her heart must have stopped as she waited on him to pound the door in. She sat there in a ball, breath shallow in the darkness.

Nothing. She strained to hear over her own pulse. She was miserable: legs tingling from lack of circulation, fingers stiff from the cold as it permeated her shelter. Her coat was in the car along with her purse and phone. Her intention had been to use the toilet and get back into the car as quickly as possible.

The best laid plans . . .

A shadow crossed her vision and she recoiled. It was a car.

* * *

As Elizabeth watched, the powerful beam of a searchlight washed over her vehicle. *The police!*

"Thank God!"

A finger of illumination probed the area around her car, then slowly moved away, bathing the surroundings with bright light, like an artificial sun in miniature.

Elizabeth jumped up in the dark room. She was reacting, her numb body moving automatically, as if gripped by some out of body experience. She began clawing at the window, her gaze never leaving the police car. She went to the door; it was sticky, but after a few hard yanks it gave way, just as the cop doused the lamp and started to pull off.

"*NO!* Don't leave me here!" She screamed, barreling out of the tiny room with all of her might.

All she could think of now . . .

absur d int er val of time passing

Was narrowing the gap . . .

DistanceGrowingTheCloserSheGets

Between herself and the patrol car. . . Finally: the cold wet metal and glass of the doorframe.

The officer flipped on the blue emergency lights, swinging the searchlight in Elizabeth's direction.

"Thank God! Thank God!" Elizabeth could see the white's of the cop's eyes through the moisture-beaded driver's side window. A woman in her mid-forties, hair pulled back in a tight bun.

"Help me! Please—he killed the old woman! *Oh God*, help me!"

"Hold on! *Who*, lady? What's the problem?" the officer demanded. Exiting the car as the police scanner blared, the entire place was now splashed with sapphire from the twirling lights on the roof of the vehicle.

"I don't know! I-I've been trapped in the visitor's reception room for a while—he's out here! Please, let's go! *Please!*"

"Wait—you're fine—I'm here; I'm not gonna to let anything happen to you, okay? Catch your breath."

Elizabeth was shaking uncontrollably in the cold. The officer unholstered her weapon as she placed a hand on the girl's shoulder; gradually Elizabeth calmed down, her hysterical yells dissolving into sobs of relief.

"Wait here—I've already called for backup. Where did you see this dead woman?" the cop asked, looking into Elizabeth's eyes. Elizabeth studied her, slightly dazed as her body began to unwind, to relax; she pointed a shaky finger at the building near her car. It began snowing again, harder.

"In there," she whispered. "In the women's restroom."

"Okay—stay here. If you see or hear anything unusual, scream, run; don't worry about me. I've got this." The officer brandished her gun, then stroked Elizabeth's hair. "It's going be all right, honey."

She watched the woman move cautiously toward the restroom. The officer carefully opened the rusty door and disappeared inside. Once she was out of sight, Elizabeth's anxiety slowly resurfaced. She sat down on the edge of the driver's seat, mesmerized, waiting on the woman to reappear, to tell her that she had imagined it all.

The radio suddenly broke the hypnotic silence, startling her; Elizabeth realized that her hands were numb and stiff from the wind blowing through the desolate parking lot, driving an icy mix of sleet and flurries into eddies under the revolving blue lights. The hackles on her neck rose.

"Think that bitch is gonna help you?" His hoarse, guttural voice was the last thing Elizabeth heard—a scream stillborn in her chest—before whiteness exploded behind her eyes. Fighting the slide into unconsciousness, she crumpled to the unyielding pavement. The world receded—cold, wet snowflakes pelting her face, swirling away as she stared into a dark, mournful sky . . .

* * *

Far away, she heard voices in the gloom.
"Took you long enough to get here—"
"There was an accident on I-5 . . ."
"We've got a problem—"
"I know, I saw . . ."
"Yeah, things got a little out of hand—thankfully you got here when you did."
Elizabeth opened her eyes: she was in a squad car, lying in the backseat. She sat up quickly with a sharp intake of breath.
"Look who decided to show up—sleeping beauty!"
In the rearview, she saw the dark eyes of the female officer looking back at her.
"Wh-Where are we going?" Elizabeth asked, bewildered and aching from where she had been struck.

99

"To Olympia," the officer in the passenger seat replied. He peeked back through the partition, then lit a cigarette. "But we got a quick stop to make first."

"You . . . " Elizabeth whispered. He resembled the horrible man from the parking lot, but it was hard to be certain. It sounded like him, though. She screamed, frantically kicking at the door.

"Hey! Relax, lady!" the male officer shouted, exhaling smoke. "You were being watched the whole time; that rest area has been under surveillance for a few weeks. The old lady was one of the perps we were after—"

Elizabeth stared at him in disbelief, shocked into silence. "Wh- what are you talking about?"

The female cop spoke first: "She was part of a ring that's been shaking people down. Their M.O. was to abduct people and rob them—pretend there was some sort of 'medical emergency'—"

"Wh- where is she? Is she alive?"

"Oh yeah; my partner's got her in custody back at the rest stop," the man replied, stubbing out his cigarette. "Along with her partner, the guy that knocked you out. Good thing I showed up when I did—"

"Yes," the other officer seconded. "You were very lucky."

Elizabeth was confused.

"Where are we going, then? You said we had another stop to make—oh, God! My orientation!—can I go back?"

"As soon as we take a statement; we're headed to the hospital first, then the police station."

Elizabeth sank back into the seat of the patrol car.

So much for my new job . . .

The male officer lit up again, taking a long draw; the smoke made the air in the car dry and sharp. The woman glanced over at her partner. They exchanged a brief, knowing smile, then both of them started to laugh. The woman cut off the blue lights, which Elizabeth realized had been going without the siren. The rainy highway—vast and bleak—yawned before them in the dark.

The hairs stood on Elizabeth's arms: she suddenly realized that she was cuffed. Her face felt flushed, hot, and her stomach plummeted. *Something isn't right!* Her throat began to hurt. Her scalp was taut on her skull, as if someone was pulling her hair out by the root . . .

100

* * *

The last thing Elizabeth heard, his ragged breath hot on her ear:
"Told you that bitch wouldn't save you . . ."

The last things Elizabeth felt:
The rain, snow and wind chilling her damp face; a tangy congestion in her sinuses; a searing pain in her throat; the sensation of weightlessness in her extremities . . .

The last thing Elizabeth glimpsed as her eyes closed a final time:
The body of the dead female officer, soundlessly caressed by the spinning blue lights of her cruiser—face crushed. Next to her, propped against the blood-sprayed patrol car, was another carcass— this one decapitated.

Before the light faded forever, the last thing Elizabeth thought:
What is . . .

is he going to . . .
do with my . . . *head?*

A Cat Named Mittens

Bob Macumber

Samantha gazed lazily through the window of the French doors, her tiny hands resting between her knees. She slouched forward in her chair, defeated and vulnerable. Unpleasant thoughts began to crawl around in her head: *What if Mittens never comes back?*

The storm was ravenous and unrelenting. It was said to be the worst storm to hit the Shallow Creek area in over half a century. Record amounts of rainfall pummeled the earth below. Entire farm crops were submerged under water, storm drains over flowed and flooded the streets. The damage was estimated to be in the millions and expected to rise.

Grant shared his daughter's misery. Whenever Samantha hurt, he couldn't help the feelings of guilt and desperation. He always wanted to be the one with all the answers, to be the one who knew what to do in any situation, to be the one person to triumph over the most incredible odds. Only that wasn't the case. The reality of the situation was far more hopeless.

That fucking cat sure picked one hell of a time to disappear, Grant said to himself angrily.

He leaned over the kitchen sink, peering out the window. The storm wasn't letting up. If anything, it was getting worse.

Grant walked up beside Samantha and began to gently rub her back.

"Why did Mittens runaway?" Samantha asked.

"I doubt he ran away, honey. He's probably just taking shelter from the storm."

"He always comes home, daddy . . . always." Samantha sighed, propping her chin up with her little hands.

Grant knew she was right, but he couldn't tell her that.

"Mitten's a tough cat. He can take care of himself," Grant assured her.

Samantha looked up and flashed a limp smile.

"How about this," Grant said. "I'll put on my rain coat and

check the yard. Maybe he's hiding in one of the sheds or the old chicken coop. Sound good?"

For the first time all day, Samantha had a genuine smile.

* * *

A deafening crack of thunder greeted Grant the moment he walked out the front door. *What did I get myself into?* He surveyed the soggy landscape that waited to embrace him. The rain was so heavy that it was almost impossible to see the old sheds along the tree line. Grant took a deep breath, flipped up the hood of his rain coat and stepped off the porch.

What a fucking nightmare, he told himself. *This is ridiculous.*

The old chicken coop was a rundown eye sore. The roof was sunk in where a large tree branch pierced through the summer before. The walls were so badly worn by the weather that they resembled pieces of drift wood. *I should have tore this thing down last year,* he thought.

The door to the chicken coop swung open with a high pitched creak of rusted hinges. Instantly, the smell of rot and decay attacked Grants' senses. *What a mess.* A heap of rusted junk was piled up to the sunken rafters. Old appliances, ductwork and worn-out tires created a small labyrinth; a perfect place for a cat to hide.

Grant briefly examined the chicken coop. There wasn't enough light to see much of anything and the only sound to be heard was rain beating on cedar shingles.

"Mittens . . . here, kitty, kitty," Grant called out while snapping his fingers.

He stepped further inside.

"Come on, Mittens. Let's go, buddy."

Nothing.

After giving the place one more look over, he stepped outside.

Grant checked every shed, but came up empty handed. He wanted so desperately to find Mittens alive and well. Being able to deliver that cat into his daughter's arms would have been a truly uplifting experience. But all he could do was go back inside and face his daughter's heartache.

As Grant made his way back to the house, he was startled by

a high-pitched bark. He turned in time to see a Beagle in a little, yellow rain coat trotting towards him. It approached with subtle caution before brushing up against Grant's leg, demanding a petting. *Who the hell dresses their dog in a rain coat?* Grant laughed to himself.

"Coco, get over here, now!" a voice yelled out.

Grant looked up and saw his neighbor, Mrs. Fisher, standing along the tree line. She was bundled up tightly in a bright orange rain coat.

To be fair, Mrs. Fisher wasn't a sweet, old lady. She fell short in the looks department. She was short, homely and dumpy.

"What are you doing out in this mess?" Grant queried.

"I could ask you the same thing," Mrs. Fisher said bluntly. "Coco loves the rain. He hates taking a bath, but he loves the rain."

Grant did his best to fake a smile. He knew all about Mrs. Fisher and her eccentric behavior from the minute he moved to Shallow Creek. She always seemed to be part of the rumor mill. The stories about her were endless, each one more outrageous than the last.

Sometime in the late eighties, Mrs. Fisher's husband went missing. It was a well known fact that Mr. Fisher had a serious problem with women and gambling. It was a problem that landed him in hot water on a regular basis. Most people believe that he got mixed in with the wrong crowd and ended up owing a serious debt to the mafia. Others think he simply ran away from his domineering wife. But a select few seem to think Mrs. Fisher got fed up with all his gambling and womanizing, so she killed him and buried him in her flower garden.

Small towns, Grant thought.

"You haven't seen Mittens around have you?" Grant asked.

Mrs. Fisher slapped her hands to her hips. "You mean that mangy cat that shits in my garden?"

Grant almost burst out laughing, but he bit his lip instead.

"Have you seen him?"

"Nope," she said without compassion. "I haven't seen the little beast."

"Well, if he shows up on your doorstep can you give me a call?"

Mrs. Fisher melodramatically rolled her eyes. "If he shows up, you'll be the first to know. That's if he hasn't drowned in all this rain."

Grant grinded his teeth. He thought about telling the ornery old cow to piss off, but he took the high road instead.

"That's one thing we don't need . . . more rain," Grant said.

"Well, the worst is yet to come," Mrs. Fisher snapped. "It's going to get worse before it gets better."

Grant stared at her blankly. *How can someone be so callous?*

Without giving a second glance, Mrs. Fisher called her dog and walked back into the woods.

Grant watched her waddle down a narrow trail that connected both their properties. She continued to yell commands to her hyperactive Beagle and it continued to ignore her. *That settles it,* Grant decided. *I'm putting up a fence.*

* * *

Samantha poked at her spaghetti. Her attention was focused outside the French doors. She knew when Mittens made his return, it would be at those doors.

"Come on, honey," Grant said. "Can you try to eat some more?"

"I'm not hungry," Samantha murmured.

"You *need* to eat," Grant protested. "You haven't eaten anything all day."

Samantha sighed deeply, snatching a piece of garlic toast off her plate.

A familiar sight caused Samantha to leap from her chair. Two little paws scratching at the window, followed by two wide eyes peering through the glass.

Mittens came home.

Grant chased Samantha to the door. "Wait for me." But the door was already open and the cat was inside.

Mittens looked like a drowned rat. His fur seemed more like oil sludge, ready to fall off his body at any moment. His eyes shifted around the room suspiciously. He cowered close to the floor, shaking uncontrollably.

Grant grabbed a tea towel off the counter. He gently cradled the cat in the towel, trying his best not to frighten it.

"What happened to him, daddy?" Samantha asked.

Mitten's was in rough shape. He had multiple lacerations around his neck and shoulders. The end of his snout had a cut that extended from his nose to his bottom lip. The left side of his face received the most punishment. One set of whiskers was severed off, along with the tip of an ear.

"Looks like he got into a fight with another animal," Grant assumed.

"Is he going to be alright?"

One word kept swirling around in Grants head: Rabies.

"He's a tough little cat. I think he'll be fine."

Samantha's eyes began to well up with water. Her face went hot and red. "He doesn't look fine."

"Mitten's is tough as nails!" Grant beamed. "We'll take him to the vet first thing in the morning and get him all fixed up."

Samantha smiled while wiping tears from her eyes.

Rabies . . . the animal that attacked him could have had rabies. Grant knelt in front of his daughter. He delicately grabbed her arms, looking deep into her sad eyes.

"Honey, it's possible that Mittens could be sick, so for tonight were going to keep him in the basement, alright?"

Samantha struggled with her father's words.

"Mitten's has all his shots," Grant assured her. "This is only for tonight. He's safe now."

* * *

The howling storm wasn't enough to drown out the noise. He heard it alright. No doubt about it.

Grant sat up and listened for the sound that had woken him from his sleep on the couch. The sound that chilled him to the bone.

He only heard the storm, until . . .

A cry.

Not a human cry. This was much deeper. A throaty rasp that resonated throughout the house, resting its sickening call deep into Grant's consciousness.

It's coming from the basement, he thought with absolute certainty.

When Grant flicked on the living room light, nothing happened. *Light must be burnt out.*

He carefully felt his way to the kitchen. The usual green glow from the stove clock was gone. *Storm must have knocked out the power*, he told himself.

106

Grant tried the kitchen light switch, but it only proved what he already knew. *Shit!*

* * *

Grant probed the darkness. The flashlight beam investigated every step before resting on the bottom. Mittens was nowhere in sight.

The unfamiliar cry echoed throughout the cavernous basement.

"Here kitty, kitty," Grant called out, while carefully searching every corner.

From across the room, Grant spotted Mittens. He was perched on the window's ledge, staring outside at the falling rain.

Mittens was frightened. He growled and hissed, striking the window furiously with his claws. Each attack was more savage than the last.

"Mittens!" Grant yelled. He shone the light directly on the cat. Its eyes glowed eerily.

Mittens scowled at Grant, as if he were studying him. Studying his rhythm to time an attack. Searching for that one weakness.

Within seconds the cat was on him.

He cried out in pain as Mittens ripped into his arm. His front claws gripped tightly, slowly tearing from side to side. His back claws worked freely, rapidly slicing Grants forearm.

Grant managed to snag the scruff of Mittens' neck. Crushing it angrily. This only infuriated the cat more.

He shook his arm aggressively while trying to pry Mittens off with his free hand. But the more he attempted to free himself, the more the cat dug in.

With one merciless blow, Grant spiked Mittens against the cement floor. The thud was sickening, yet musical.

Grant half expected another attack, but . . .

Silence.

All he heard was his own rapid heartbeat.

He scooped up the flashlight, spreading its beam around the darkness. *Where the hell did you go?* Grant thought, keeping his guard up in case Mittens advanced out of nowhere.

Every cut on his arm throbbed. He stared at the bloody mess in disbelief. Most of his wounds were superficial, but the soft belly of his forearm had several deep gouges. *Something is seriously wrong with that cat.*

Grant froze and listened intently. His heart was jammed in his throat. He felt disembodied, numb and nauseous all at once. He heard Samantha scream.

* * *

Samantha stood on her bed, holding a pillow in front of her like a shield. Her eyes were wild, filled with fear and confusion. Hot tears streamed down her cheeks.

"Daddy! Mittens is scaring me!" Samantha cried out.

Grant plucked her from the bed. He held her close, frantically searching for any sign of Mittens.

"Shhhhh it's okay. I'm here now," Grant said.

"I don't want him no more! He scares me!"

"You're safe now. I won't let anything happen to you."

Sounds of glass smashing against the kitchen floor startled Samantha and Grant simultaneously. Grant sprinted towards his bedroom, Samantha bobbing in his arms. He slammed the door behind him.

"Are you hurt," he asked, sitting Samantha on his bed. "Did you get scratched?"

Samantha managed to answer 'no' between heavy sobs.

"You have nothing to be scared of now."

He handed the flashlight to his daughter, asking her to keep it on the closet. He reached deep into the closet and pulled out a canvas shotgun case. Inside was a 10 gauge, pump-action shotgun. *Better to have it and not need it, then to need it and not have it,* Grant told himself. He didn't like guns, but when you live in the country, it's almost a requirement.

Seeing the weapon made him dread his inexperience. He inherited the shotgun when his father died, but other than some target practice last summer, it hadn't left its case.

"How come you have a gun?" Samantha said.

"Grandpa gave it to me."

He pulled a box of shells out of his sock drawer, dumping the shells onto the dresser. Four shells left. Three in the magazine, one in the chamber. He slammed a shell in the chamber, aggressively closing the slide. He then slipped each additional shell in the magazine tube.

Samantha cringed when her dad loaded the shotgun. This was a side of him she hadn't seen before. He was bold, threatening. "You're going to kill him aren't you, daddy?"

Her words hit him hard. As he gazed into her crying eyes, his heart broke. "No, honey. I promise you."

"Yes you will! You're going to shoot him!"

Grant squeezed Samantha tightly. "Shhhhh, it's alright."

"You told me he was sick, daddy. He's just sick. He didn't mean to."

"The gun's to make sure your safe. That's all," Grant said.

"I'm alright. See?" Samantha held up her hands, twisting them around so he could see every inch.

"You're right. You look like a million bucks," he said with a smile.

Grant grimaced in deep thought. He needed to get Samantha out, so he could deal with this problem on his own. *She's safer that way*, he thought.

"I'm going to take you over to Mrs. Fisher's, okay? And you can play with Coco until I get a hold of a vet."

Samantha nodded.

Grant grabbed the shotgun and then carefully opened his bedroom door. He motioned for Samantha to pass him the flashlight. "Stay close," he whispered.

The hallway felt more like a labyrinth. Grant moved apprehensively around every corner, keeping his daughter in tow.

A brilliant flash of lightning illuminated the entire kitchen. Shattered glass was everywhere. Among the ruin of broken glass was Mittens. His lifeless body cradled by a cold floor.

Grant sheltered Samantha's eyes. "Don't look at him." They stepped past Mittens, but something caught Grant's eye.

Mittens' body began to quiver. It contorted violently followed by a chorus of snapping bones. His abdomen began to swell, stretching skin beyond physical limits. Something ripped through the skin, sending a splatter of blood across the room. A claw similar to a scorpion's claw protruded from the cat's bloated belly. The creature writhed and slashed ferociously, until it spilled out all over the floor.

It was an abomination. The nightmare creature loosely resembled a centipede. Two muscular claws stuck out from its otherwise tube like body. It appeared to be an arthropod, but its trunk wasn't in segments. Each leg had no set pattern. They stuck out in a macabre fashion, like jointed needles ready to tear flesh from bone.

Samantha's shrill screams broke Grant from his hypnotic state. He quickly ushered her out the front door. "Wait for me right here! Don't move!"

"Don't leave me, daddy!" Samantha begged.

"I'll be right back." He gripped the shotgun tightly. "Don't move."

When Grant slipped back inside, the creature was gone. Only tiny blood tracks along the kitchen floor remained. He tracked each bloody print, unaware of the immediate danger he was in.

The creature clung against the ceiling directly above Grant's head. Its long antennae twitched rapidly as it searched for its prey. Still clinging to the ceiling with its hind legs, it quietly reached down and dropped onto Grant's shoulder.

The attack was swift. Grant instinctively pulled the trigger, sending a shotgun blast into the kitchen cabinets. He tripped backwards and smashed heavily into the pantry doors, knocking the creature loose.

Terrified, Grant went still. He silently watched the creature crawl onto the counter top. It turned in his direction, flexing its inch long mandibles. He noticed it was barely three feet long, but its grip strength was unmatched by anything he had ever felt.

Sweat stung Grant's eyes. He was more afraid now, than he had ever been in his entire life. He felt vulnerable, alone. His shotgun mocked him. He had dropped it during the struggle. It may have only been a few feet away, but it rested directly under the creature's perch. *It's twice as fast as me*, Grant bemoaned. *I'd never make it.*

A familiar sound stunned Grant, sinking his heart deep into the depths of his stomach. It sounded like a door opening. His eyes darted to his left and standing over the thresh hold was Samantha.

Instantly, the creature scurried down the counter towards her. Grant pounced on the shotgun. Grabbing it by the barrel, he clubbed the creature repeatedly. Its exoskeleton was hard as rock. Unfazed, the creature wrapped itself around the stock and crawled its way onto Grant.

He screamed as the creature tore a chunk of flesh from his chest. It was ravenous. Using its mandibles like scissors, it burrowed its head deep into Grant. He clutched the creature, and with every

110

ounce of strength, began to pull it from his wound. It wrapped its entire body around his forearm. Grant smashed the creature against the kitchen counter. It tightened its grip, using its claws to anchor itself.

Samantha was panic-stricken. She cried uncontrollably.

Grant snatched one of the creature's clawed arms. Twisting it backwards, he forcefully ripped the arm downwards. Thick, white mucus oozed from its socket. The creature let out a garbled screech and retreated.

"Is that all you got!" Grant snickered, falling heavily to one knee.

Samantha picked up the flashlight, carefully approaching her father. "Daddy? Are you okay?" Her words were mumbled beneath heavy sobbing.

"Daddy's hurt. We need to go to Mrs. Fisher's right now."

Grant was slow to his feet, using the shotgun like a crutch. He gazed back into the darkness and knew that somewhere in this house, it waited for him.

* * *

Blood dripped steadily onto Mrs. Fisher's welcome mat. Grant faltered slightly, propping a hand against the door frame to keep from falling.

Samantha stood next to her father. She buried her head deeper into her coat, trying hard to keep away from the pouring rain.

Mrs. Fisher finally came to the door.

She wore a fuzzy, pink nightgown that accentuated her plus-sized figure. Oversized hair curlers lined her scalp, creating the look of a disgusting wig.

The door opened as far as the chain would allow. She hid behind a candle. The small flame danced on her nervous face. "Who is it?"

"It's Grant. We need your help," his voice trembled.

"What happened?"

"Just help us . . . please!" Grant shouted weakly.

The door slammed shut. A few moments later, they were inside.

Grant staggered into the kitchen and crashed onto a chair. He shivered wildly. His clothes were drenched in rain and blood.

Coco barked from the living room, but he wasn't brave enough to investigate any further.

Suddenly, Mrs. Fisher took charge of the situation. She became a different person. Strong and level headed. Genuine compassion flowed through her veins.

She stripped Grant down to his under wear and wrapped him up with a large, hand stitched quilt. Blood soaked into the quilt's fabric. "What happened to you?"

"Our cat," Grant said, his heading drooping to his chest.

Mrs. Fisher ignored his comment. She helped him to the living room, sitting him in front of a wood-burning fireplace.

"What happened to your father, Samantha?" Mrs. Fisher asked, while helping the girl from her coat.

"A . . . a monster got him," tears welled up in her eyes. Every adult told her monsters weren't real. But they lied. Monsters were real and they were worse than any nightmare.

Samantha sat next to Coco. He licked her hand, snuggling his head onto her lap. His tail thumped the couch cushions in excitement.

Mrs. Fisher stoked the fire and then began tending to Grant's wounds. Scrapes, scratches, cuts (some deep, some not) and bruises made a road map across his body.

"So, a monster did this to you?" Mrs. Fisher said.

He nodded, keeping his eyes closed. "Something like that."

Grant winced when she began cleaning each wound with peroxide.

"You know how stupid this all sounds, right?"

He smiled, but it was weak and fake. He didn't want to sit there and contest truths. He had lived through a vicious encounter by an unknown creature. A crime against nature. Believable or not, it was true.

"My husband was about your size. I still have some of his clothes." She disappeared into a bedroom.

Grant surveyed the candle-lit living room. Samantha had fallen asleep with Coco on her lap. She whimpered quietly. *She'll have nightmares for years*, he thought. *I know I will.*

Mrs. Fisher returned with dress pants and a flannel shirt. She turned her back while Grant got dressed. He noticed the walls were plastered with pictures. From weddings to birthday parties, every photo featured a smiling Mr. and Mrs. Fisher. Her smile was infec-

112

tious. She glowed with a certain radiance not much people have. But something happened in her life to change all of that. She took on another persona. For whatever reason, she became the person he knew today.

Mrs. Fisher noticed Grant's wandering eyes. "That's Paul. My husband."

"I'm sorry for being snoopy."

"Don't be. That's why I put them there." Her eyes hardened. The tears dried up for good, but the hurt was still there.

"You both look happy," Grant said.

"We were . . . at one time. I'm sure you heard the rumors around town by now?"

"No," he lied.

"It's okay. I've heard them all. The truth is . . . he left me." She sighed deeply, fixing a crooked picture frame. "He came home one night and said he'd had enough. That was twenty years ago."

Grant said nothing.

"I knew there was another woman. He denied it, but I knew."

"My wife left me and Samantha," Grant blurted out. He didn't know why he said it, it just felt right. "Leaving me was one thing, but abandoning your only daughter . . . "

They continued their conversation, oblivious to what Coco heard slipping through his doggy door.

The Beagle was far from a physically imposing animal. Its bark was much worse than its bite. Any other day it would have ran off with its tail firmly between its legs. Any day, except today.

It happened fast. Coco pounced on the creature as it climbed the wall. He bit deep into its hind end and shook as hard as he could. The creature jerked free. It lunged at Coco, but he was quicker. He side stepped and ended up mounted on the creature's back. From there, he bit into its exposed head.

Mrs. Fisher couldn't believe her eyes. Her little dog was fighting with a monster. Fighting with an intensity she didn't know he possessed. But his triumph was short lived.

The creature wrapped its body around Coco, squeezing out a sharp yelp. Its jaws began tearing out chunks of flesh and fur.

Grant swiped the shotgun from off the kitchen table and took aim. He was forced to make a decision: Kill the creature while it's vulnerable, possibly killing the dog or attempt to save the dog, risking everybody's life. The decision was easy. He squeezed the trig-

113

ger.

Mrs. Fisher shoved Grant, sending the spray of pellets away from their intended target. She was livid. A sense of blind rage swept over her. She swung at the creature with an old corn broom. Strike after strike, she pummeled her dog's attacker. Blood stained the brooms bristles red.

Grant yelled at her to move, but it fell on deaf ears. All her intentions were set on saving Coco from certain death.

When the creature released its grip, a blood bathed ensued.

It scurried under Mrs. Fisher's night gown. She cried out in pain as blood began to stain the crotch area of her gown. She punched and pulled at the creature as it climbed her meaty frame. Inch by inch, it ripped its way to her soft throat.

Before Grant could help, the creature bit into her throat. The bite severed her windpipe with ease, sending an arterial spray cresting through the air.

Mrs. Fisher collapsed to the floor, her hands still fighting the creature. She gasped frantically for air, but only a wet gurgle escaped her mouth. After several agonizing seconds, she was dead.

The creature stood on its hind end. Swaying back and forth like it was dancing to some macabre harmony. Its mandibles chattered rabidly as it reveled in the blood of its freshly killed prey.

Grant seized his golden opportunity. The first shotgun blast tore the creature in half, sending a splatter of white mucus and entrails across the kitchen.

The second shotgun blast slammed into the creature's freshly disjointed upper half. Mucus sputtered out of each pellet hole, leaving the creature in a mangled heap.

Grant found Samantha huddled behind the sofa, her hands clasped tightly around her ears. *With all the hell that unfolded tonight, it will be a miracle if she escapes without severe psychological problems.*

"Samantha?" Grant said. He leaned in closer. "It's all over, honey."

Samantha looked up. Her eyes were swollen and red, but just as beautiful as ever. "Is it dead?"

Grant nodded. "It can't hurt us anymore."

Something began to stir in the kitchen. They could hear the distinct sound of sharp nails clicking against kitchen tile.

Grant loaded his last shotgun shell, ready for whatever came his way. Limping through the doorway was Coco.

The dog was in bad shape. Ugly lacerations and deep gouges covered his torso. The battle scars of a little warrior.

* * *

The rain had slowed to a drizzle and the sun began to peek over the horizon. Samantha carefully followed Coco as he hopped slowly across the yard. Grant smiled at them, but his thoughts took him elsewhere.

He had collected the creature's remains and put them in a Tupperware container. Even in death, the creature was something to fear. Its lifeless eyes were fierce, full of hate.

There were so many questions and not enough answers. What was it? Where did it come from? Was it an undiscovered parasite or an experiment gone horribly wrong? Maybe it's extraterrestrial?

Grant frowned at his own thoughts. Then he thought of Mrs. Fisher lying on the kitchen floor, cold and alone. For a brief second he wondered if there was an afterlife and if she had gone to a better place. *She deserved better,* Grant thought. *Nobody deserves to die that way.* He thought about how to explain the incident to the police. They would have to believe his story; he was holding the proof in his hands.

But Grant wasn't aware of the changes taking place within the container. These changes were taking place at a cellular level. Dead cells began to activate, regenerating tissue and organs. Only these cells were re-arranging the pre-existing structure. They were slowly developing a new creature, a better creature.

Nature's perfect predator.

Old Nick's Game Town

Dominic E. Lacasse

Name: Old Nick's Game Town
Location: About fifteen miles south of Paxico, Kansas
Rating: One star

Travelers are urged to avoid this uninspired send-up of the classic American tourist trap. Located fifteen miles or so from Paxico, Kansas (a town of less than 300 people hunkered firmly down in the tornado belt), Old Nick's is nothing if not an unpleasant reminder that these roadside attractions need to offer seediness as *part* of their appeal, not as their sole attraction.

What struck this reviewer most forcibly upon arriving at Old Nick's Game Town was the clear and simple lack of effort that went into its construction and operation. It is a small cluster of wooden buildings blasted by the wind, all in dire need of paint and structural repairs. There is a mostly-intact wooden fence that runs around the property, terminating in a large plywood image of the familiar horned and goateed head of our friend, Old Nick himself. One drives one's car through the devil's mouth to access the parking lot. This wooden façade and the accompanying sign show some of the best workmanship the site has to offer; through clever manipulation of perspective, the proprietor has actually managed to make this most stereotypical image seem genuinely creepy.

However, beyond this image (and the simple fact that this man somehow operates a Satan-themed roadside attraction in rural Kansas without nightly pitchfork-riots) there is little to praise at Old Nick's Game Town. The games, mostly of the pinball and whack-a-mole variety, are old and malfunctioning, most in need of repair and a good number out of order entirely. There are a few small and routine carnival rides—a little devil-headed roller-coaster, a teacup ride cleverly disguised as bubbling cauldrons, etc. The main attraction is a small, artificial pond, upon which the guest is invited to take a ride in small canoes that are available for hourly rent. The pond is small

116

enough to paddle across in less than two minutes or so, but here the proprietor has done something this reviewer had never seen before; under the water are stone devils and anguished souls, reaching up at the little boats with gnarled fingers and open jaws. The effect, it must be said, gives one a distinct feeling that one actually is hovering over the gates of Hell.

The teenager had been to the old tourist trap near Paxico earlier that day, and now he was asleep and he was dreaming.

Dreaming that his mother and father had been in a car accident and they were both in critical condition. By that strange logic of dreams, he had chosen not to go to their bedside to be with them, but instead he had decided to return to Old Nick's.

It was the dead of night, and the moon was high and full. It cast a ghostly blue pallor over the flat, featureless desert. The sand beneath his feet was gritty and harsh even through his shoes; it was not pleasant to walk here. He hadn't noticed that in the daytime.

The booths and outbuildings were closed, of course, their plywood doors shut, locked tight with big padlocks. But there was nothing preventing access to the pond at the end of the walkway, nor, he soon found, were the small canoes nearby locked to anything. For no reason he could discern, he took one of the canoes and dragged it to the shore of the little pond. Taking a paddle in his hand he pushed out into the still water. He was utterly alone and there was not a breath of wind. He heard the soft sound of the waves from his boat lapping over the shore of the pond's edges.

He peered down into the water. The light of the moon refracting through the wake of his canoe cast strange tiger patterns of light and shadow across the snarled features of stone Satans, dissolved their individual characters and reduced them to a forest of limbs and faces. Human hands, reaching to the light to be delivered from their torment. Human faces, their lips peeled back from their teeth in silent sunken shouts of anguish and terror. And here, and there, things not human; hands with fingers that were themselves simply jagged claws, faces with insect-like bugging eyes and mad grins filled with stone teeth. There was such detail that it was almost difficult to look at, the light passing in gentle waves across the pond's bottom, it seemed paved with suffering and gleeful torture.

Pulling his eyes from the scene below him, he was startled to see that he was not alone in the boat. There was a woman in the bow. She was naked and she had her back to him, her face in her hands, and she seemed to be weeping. He wanted to say something but he was terrified to disturb the silence, as though speaking would awake some horrible beast that lay sleeping. As he watched, she leaned to the side of the boat. Her hand gripped the opposite gunwale and her bicep trembled, as though she were exerting great force to stay in the boat; but her body was being pulled, slowly and gently, over the edge, and when her grip suddenly relaxed she fell, without saying a word or making a sound, and her body made only the slightest splash as it slipped under the waves. He looked for her where she had fallen but she was not there.

And then he saw that there was someone else present, standing on the shore of the pond. It was the owner of the park, standing silently with his arms folded and his eyes closed, and the boy was going to bring the canoe to shore and apologize and ask if he had seen the woman falling into the pond, but before he could do so a thundering voice was blasting his mind and he gripped the paddle with white knuckles and sat paralyzed, stunned to immobility by the power of the sound in his mind.

YOU HAVE COME SEEKING THE SILVER JUDGE, HE COMES HERE TO MEET YOU, HE THAT CANNOT BE NAMED, THE WORDS UPON HIS FEET ARE NOT KNOWN TO MEN AND HIS DECREE CANNOT BE CHANGED, YOU HAVE COME OF YOUR OWN WILL SEEKING THE SILVER JUDGE AND HE COMES HERE TO MEET YOU.

And then, from the side of his eye, the boy SAW HIM. He could not turn to him, saw only a form of silver leprosy-sickening color that stunned him and made him feel like dying, made him feel like nothing, that everything he knew could be blown away like a grain of sand by the thing that had come to meet him. He was told what he was to do, and he did it. He chose to do it.

He was in the hospital and there was screaming all around him. Two prone figures lay at his feet, black bruises around their necks, his parents. Dead. The screaming was other patients in the ICU, restrained in their sickness and injury, unable to stop him and unable to run they could only watch him and howl their fear and their confusion. He looked at his hands and knew in his heart that he had chosen this for himself.

When he woke with a start he knew that it had been just a

118

dream, but it provided him no consolation. His parents were asleep in the next room, living and breathing, he had done nothing wrong, but he felt a blackness in his heart because he knew that even if it had only been a fantasy, he had done what he had done because he had made his own mind up to do it, the silver judge had not forced him, had only . . . had only what? Explained.

Old Nick's Game Town offers tourists a glimpse of the stereotype of the tourist trap, shoddier by far than even the most ill-conceived attraction that seeks to do the job honestly. It is a parody of its own genre, and aside from the masterful and legitimately scary carvings beneath the artificial pond, there is nothing here for the serious traveler. Add to this the fact that it takes nearly two hours out of one's way between the two nearest Kansas cities of any size and it is indeed surprising that the place has stayed open long enough to fall into the state of disrepair that it is in.

Parking (of course) is ample and basic provisions can be purchased (flashlights and batteries, playing cards, hot dogs and soda, and the like) but there is no gas station nearby, so if you're determined to stop into Old Nick's I would suggest that you gas up before you arrive, lest you be doomed forever to the ministrations of his plywood imps and goblins.

Dear Grammie,

Our trip is going good. Mommy says we're almost out of Kansas and we're making good time. Daddy said I should write you a letter about something that I saw yesterday. There were deer in the road ahead of us and they were really pretty. We also went to a roadside stop to have lunch. The gate had a big devil's head and it scared me, but Mommy said it was just wood, and when we got through to the other side and I looked at the back of it I could see that she was right.

It wasn't a very fun place but Daddy and me played pinball and we all had hot dogs. There was a pond with canoes, I wanted to go out in one but Daddy said that it was too expensive and that we needed to get back on the road. I really wanted to go though so I think that's why I had this funny dream as we were driving away.

I was on the pond in a canoe and I was all by myself. It was nighttime and I was cold. I saw shapes under the water and they were moving, I didn't want to look at them because they scared me. So I looked toward the shore instead and there was a man or something standing there. I don't know what he was but he made me feel sick to my stomach or even the kind of sick where you have to go to the hospital for a long time and people don't know if you're going to be OK ever. He was silvery and tall and I think he had long arms but I don't know, and where his feet were was kind of fuzzy, like he sort of mixed into the ground with his feet or something.

And I heard this voice in my head that says: 'I know that you're looking at me.' And I feel really bad but he says: 'It's good, keep looking at me, keep looking, keep looking, keep looking.' So I do, and my boat is moving toward him but I can't stop it and I don't even want to stop it. And then my canoe is on the shore and he's close now and I'm scared but I'm also like I want him to be there. It's hard to look at him, like my eyes go other places when I try to look at him, or he moves around, goes fuzzy or something so I can't see him.

And he holds something out to me and it's a pretty glass flower, red and green and yellow and it's the prettiest thing I ever saw. And he says in my brain: 'Do you want this?' and I say 'yes' and I reach for it but he pulls it away and I feel like he thinks it's funny but I want it so bad. And he says again, 'Do you want this?' and I say that 'I do' and he holds it out but when I take it I feel something go out of me, like air going out of a balloon or mustard coming out of the bottle and all that's left is this empty bottle that you throw in the trash. I don't know what went out of me but I know it's gone and it still feels gone while I'm writing you this. But I don't care and I take the flower and I'm running to the car to show Mommy and Daddy and I trip and the flower falls and smashes in a million pieces on the ground.

I woke up with Mommy and Daddy shaking me because I was crying in my sleep and when I woke up I kept on crying and I couldn't tell them why it was so bad, and it's still bad. Do you know what happened?

I will write you again in a few days but our trip is going really good. Daddy says to tell you that he will call you from the hotel tonight.

Love,
Ashley

In conclusion, unless you have a particular fascination with aquatic statuary, or you're really dying for a hot dog and you happen to be driving through the absolute dullest part of Kansas, Old Nick's Game Town is not worth the time. A lesson learned; a novel idea is not enough when it's done poorly and without heart. There's nothing out of the ordinary here, so drive on, weary travelers, and get your kicks somewhere where the devil doesn't roam.

Origin Story

Christopher Hawkins

"If you had a super power, what would it be?"

"You mean, what would my power be if I could pick for myself? Or what would my power be if I was a character in a comic book and I ended up with a power that fit me as a person?"

A moment's pause, and then, "I hadn't really thought about it that way, but let's do the second."

Phil shrugged. "Well, knowing my luck, it would be something completely useless. We're nowhere near an ocean, so it'd probably be something to do with fish. Talk to them, summon them, make them do stuff. It may not seem like much, but if someone ever committed a crime in a pet store or an aquarium, I'd be your guy."

Darryl didn't look up from the issue spread out on the counter in front of him. "I guess that would make you The Crayfish."

Phil. Phillip Cray. The Crayfish. He stared past the panels in his own book and realized that he'd probably just earned a nickname that would last him the rest of his life.

"What about you?" he asked.

Darryl answered immediately, as if it was something he kept on the tip of his tongue at all times, ready at an instant's notice. "I'd have the ability to compress matter, to make it so small that it could pass through quantum holes in space-time and travel instantaneously from one point in space to another."

"Oh, is that all?"

"It's enough."

"And is this the power that you'd pick or the power that fits your character?"

Darryl didn't answer. If it was because he was too lost in the world of his comic book or because he'd just lost interest, Phil couldn't tell. Darryl was like that, so Phil had learned. He'd latch on to whatever hotbutton geek-issue crossed his mind, pursue it, debate it and argue it into a corner until it no longer suited him. Then he'd pretend he'd never brought it up in the first place, especially if he found himself on the losing end. Phil didn't complain, though, since Darryl was the one who signed the checks that kept him behind the counter of Fantasy Flight Comix and well away from the certain horror of The Respectable Job. Besides, Darryl was mostly an okay guy. Mostly.

It went on like that for most of the day, Phil on his side of the counter, Darryl on his. They made almost perfect counterpoints to each other, Darryl with his girth, his close-cropped hair and glasses, Phil with his stringbean physique and grunge rock scruffiness.

It was a Thursday, which made it a slow day. All the serious collectors had come the day before, when the new issues came in. Thursday customers, what few there were, were tourists, and greeted with indifference bordering on scorn. As they browsed the racks there was an almost funereal, library-patron way about them, as if they knew that they had entered someplace holy, that they were treading somewhere they could never truly belong. Darryl and Phil took their money all the same, rarely making eye contact, silently reveling in their self-ascribed superiority.

It was late in the afternoon, after the single-issue sales and the countless others who left empty-handed, before Darryl spoke again. He shifted his weight back on his stool and turned to Phil, his brow furrowed in thought.

"This fish power of yours. How did you get it?"

"You mean the cosmic event that forever transformed mild-mannered Phillip Cray into The Crayfish, unstoppable force for justice?" Better to own the nickname now. Maybe Darryl would see it didn't get to him, and he'd just lose interest.

"The very same."

"Hypothetically?"

"Hypothetically."

Phil thought it over, suddenly taking pleasure in the game. He hit upon the answer and grinned. "Mobsters."

"Mobsters?"

"I saw too much, and they had to get rid of me. So they tie me up, throw me in the trunk of a car and drive me to the pier. They hook weights to me, they throw me in, and I drown. Then a shark comes by. Maybe he's looking for food. Maybe he's sent by the sea gods to help me out. Anyway, his fin grazes one of my ropes and cuts it. So, I float free and as the tide comes in, I get caught in a school of fish that pushes me up on shore. That's when, suddenly, I start to breathe again. And I can talk to fish. *Voila!* The Crayfish is born!"

"That's already been done a hundred times."

"But not with fish."

"Sure it has. I could name at least three."

"Well, now you can name four."

Darryl shrugged and went back to his book. "I thought you said you didn't live near water."

"All right, smart guy. You think you can do better?"

"Hmm?"

"All that matter shrinking whosamawhatsit."

"Compressing."

"Compressing. Whatever. How do you come by that little gem?"

Darryl closed his book and raised his head, a gesture of seriousness and respect-for-topic that Phil had seen only once before. "I don't know. Maybe it was one of those things where I always had it and it just took this long to develop. Maybe it's a cosmic event and it lets loose powers in other people, too. Maybe it's something that just happens. One day you're normal and the next day . . . boom."

As he spoke, there was a faraway look in his eyes, an earnestness that seemed to belie the disdain and apathy that was as much a part of who he was as his sweat-ringed t-shirts.

"Those have all been done, too."

"Yeah, but not like this." He looked up at the clock and allowed himself a little grin. "It's a quarter 'till. Let's lock up early. I've got something to show you."

Five minutes later, they were out in the crisp, fall air and well into the six-block hike from the store to Darryl's place. The big man moved with quick, determined steps. His head was down and forward, as if he meant to stay ahead of his own bulk, as if gravity itself was propelling him along. Phil followed at a stutter-step, almost having to trot to keep up.

That phrase, 'I've got something to show you,' always preceded something wondrous. If not wondrous, then at least noteworthy, even if it was noteworthy only to Darryl. Phil wondered with a vague sense of anticipation what it would be this time. Perhaps some vintage action figure he found online. Maybe a bootleg episode of some long forgotten television fantasy. Doubtless, it was some artifact of significance, the latest addition to a vast collection, over which Darryl would beam like a proud parent. Whatever it was, he was in a hurry to get back to it.

Their path took them down a street where, up ahead, three lean, straggle-haired kids stood at the corner. One straddled a bike while the other two shoved at each other playfully, getting rid of pent-up energy. They were not quite teenagers, but carried themselves as if they were in a hurry to get there. Darryl lowered his head even more as he approached them, and Phil could see that this wasn't the first time he had crossed their path.

One of the shovers noticed him first. He stopped shoving and made a show of trying to be casual as he elbowed the kid on the bike. The kid on the bike smiled and began to stare at Darryl as he lurched toward them. Before long, all three of them were staring, wicked little grins on each of their faces.

Those grins said it all, every insult that came to their minds, every name they could have called him, had called him, and would have called him if he had been alone. Phil and Darryl passed them, and as they did, Phil could hear the whispers, the muffled snickers that followed after them. He caught himself searching the ground, looking for a rock to throw, but banished the thought as soon as it came. There were better things ahead: all the wonders of Darryl's collection, new and old. Best of all, that look on Darryl's face, the awe and pride that cared nothing for the unspoken insults of little children.

"There has to be a point to it." Darryl sorted through his keys, the metal frame of the screen door propped against his arm.

"A point to what?" Phil asked.

"The fish. Your power. There has to be a reason for it or it doesn't make sense."

"Why does there have to be a reason?"

The door popped open with a squeak and let out a breath of air, cloth and human, like old laundry. "Because without a reason, it's just a gift. A gift doesn't mean anything. It's just something you get."

"What's wrong with that?"

"Everything."

Darryl's living room was something that should have belonged to a man three times his age: a battered couch with yellowed doilies on the armrests, an old pull-chain lamp with a broken shade, a dusty carpet marked by matted clumps of cat hair. Amid it all were the boxes, tidy, age-worn bins, full of magazines and papers, stacks of comic books well known and long forgotten. They'd been piled high and deep, with little trenches of bare floor left behind in case anyone should ever want to peruse them.

The place was so familiar to Phil that he rarely gave it a second glance. But something was different today, and though he couldn't quite figure what it was, it caused his eyes to linger. The answer was there, almost close enough to grasp, but then Darryl spoke again.

"With a gift, you don't have to give anything back. But if there's a *reason* for the gift, then it becomes a mission. Suddenly you have a purpose in life. It's the power that gives you that purpose. Or, maybe you had the purpose all along but didn't know it until you received the power. Either way, there's a point to all of it."

Phil could see the excitement in the big man's face, the single-minded insistence of his stance, of the way he held his mouth. His thoughts immediately shifted to the front door, to the number of steps, the number of seconds it would take for him to reach it and open it. The feeling came and went, replaced by a wave of shame.

"So," said Darryl, "what's the point of your power?"

"What's the point of yours?"

"That's the real question, isn't it?" His face registered the hint of a grin, a wistful, far away look. It was gone in a moment, replaced by his usual grim stoicism. "Come on," he said. "What I want to show you is right downstairs."

Again, that feeling of hesitation. Phil felt it send tingles from the base of his neck up into his scalp. His feet felt heavy, getting ready to run. He might have done it, gone sprinting for the door and out into the street, had Darryl not reached for the door to the stairs and started down them, ahead of him.

If he had seen the doubt on Phil's face, he gave no sign. He just trundled down the wooden steps, boards creaking with age and strain as he made his way. If he had waited, insisted somehow that Phil go first, then there might have been cause to go running out the door. But Darryl had gone first, and that made him harmless. Still, Phil did not want the big man behind him.

Darryl stopped a few stairs down and turned back to face him. There was a look there that Phil had not seen before. It was more than the usual distant acceptance. This was something closer to friendship.

"I trust you," he said. "You know that, right?"

At once, Phil realized that he might just be the only friend that Darryl had. He was a poor friend at that, one who barely tolerated his existence on most days, only taking an interest in his life when there was some new treasure to be seen. The shame came over him again, this time to stay. Darryl started down the stairs again, and this time, Phil followed.

"The thing about having a power is that it lets you do stuff that you always wanted to do, but that you knew you couldn't because you weren't strong enough. But it's stuff you have to do, stuff you were born to do. All that you've been lacking your whole life was the means."

They were almost to the bottom now. Phil could see the first few rows of Darryl's action figure collection, tiered displays like in a museum. He knew that there were more just like it around the corner, but suddenly, he didn't want to see around that corner. He didn't want to know what would be there waiting for him.

"That's why it's so important that the power have a point to it. If you weren't picked, if you weren't *chosen*, then you're just some jerk with a power. It doesn't mean a thing. You were just lucky enough to get something you don't deserve, and I refuse to believe that.

They were at the bottom of the stairs now. There was nothing unexpected there, nothing waiting, nothing out of place. Nothing, except Darryl's face. It shone with newfound pride, a sense of place that he had been looking his whole life to find.

Suddenly Phil was seeing him, the real him, not the image of him he'd tried so hard to portray. He had lost weight, at least twenty pounds. Why had he not noticed that before now? All the signs were there: fresh fruit for snacks instead of candy bars, diet shakes instead of cheeseburgers. Darryl had hid his transformation, subtle though it was, beneath a baggy t-shirt. But now Phil could see past the disguise.

"You already know what I'm going to tell you," said Darryl. Phil nodded.

Darryl smiled, this time with his entire face, more confident, more collected than ever before. "Good. I knew I got that much right. Come on. It's right around the corner."

He led the way past the toys, the posters, the obsessions of a lifetime. Beyond them was a wooden door frame covered with a black sheet, something Phil had seen many times but never given a single thought to.

"You see, if this had just been some sort of accident, if I had been walking down the street and gotten hit by radiation or toxic sludge or something, I could just call it dumb luck. But it just happened, right out of the blue, which means that somewhere out there, there's a plan for me. And if there was a plan, I knew that some day, I would find out what it was, and before that day came, I had to be ready."

He drew aside the curtain

Beyond it was a room, but more than just a room. It was lit only by the light from three monitors, each large enough to dominate the space by itself, aligned one beside the other in a loose horseshoe. One was tuned to cable news, another to a weather station. The one in the middle was attached to a computer, and on it shone a map of the city, little areas marked out in red, others in blue. Before them was a desk, doing double-duty as a workbench. Clusters of wiring and ambiguous electronics lay strewn between stacks of paper. At its edge, an old sewing machine with a yellowed plastic housing clung to a length of dark fabric: the beginnings of a costume.

Phil wondered at once how many first editions, how many rare treasures had been sacrificed on this altar before him. He wondered how much of Darryl himself had been in those books, those irreplaceable items that he held so dear. He wondered how much of himself Darryl had left behind.

Then he noticed the smell.

It came at him all at once, low and earthy, like meat left out to rot. The air seemed weighed down by it, and it made Phil's stomach want to heave its contents out onto the floor. He kept it in check, but only barely. If Darryl noticed his reaction, or even the smell itself, he gave no sign.

"This is why I brought you here. You're my friend, and that means one of two things. You know how this works as well as I do. You know how these things happen. You can tell me what all of this is for. You can help me find the purpose!"

Darryl's eyes were wide, and as he spoke, he seemed to get taller. There was pride in his voice, but those eyes betrayed the insecurity behind his words. He was watching Phil, waiting for him to speak. But Phil had no words. It was all too much, this place, the idea that someone he had known for years could—

Then, at the edge of his vision, he saw something move.

It was in the deep shadows beyond the monitors. Phil's eyes were still adjusting to the darkness, but he could make out a deeper shadow at the edge of the floor, a crawlspace whose boundaries were lost in the distance. There, in the midst of that space, two glowing pinpoints stared out at him.

Then Phil realized all at once what had been missing upstairs, what he should have known right away. If he had seen it then he would never have come to the basement, that much he was sure of now. There should have been at least five of them underfoot, weaving their way among his legs, tripping him as he walked. But the cats hadn't been there, and Phil should have seen that and ran.

"The power's kind of tricky," Darryl said. "I haven't quite gotten the hang of it, but I will. It's all about precision, really. If you want to move something, you have to squish it down really small. The hard part is figuring out how to make it come back right."

The thing in the crawlspace was edging toward them now, and Phil could make out the whiskers jutting from its face. Something about the movement of it was all wrong. It seemed to lurch forward, hesitating as if some great weight was holding it back. Phil stared, not wanting to look, unable to turn away. A sound came from deep within the thing's throat, something between a wet gurgle and a purr. It made wet, scraping sounds as it dragged itself across the gravel floor, halting with pain at every step.

"She was my first try," Darryl said. "I managed to move her almost four feet, but she came back, well . . . The others didn't do as well. They're back there if you want me to show you."

"Darryl, this is—"

"I know. It's amazing. I tried making it work on other stuff, like a chair, an ashtray. But I couldn't do it. It needs a heartbeat. It needs a pulse."

"It's horrible."

"That's what I thought at first, too. It's too limited. I could go through hundreds, even thousands of tries before I figured out how to get it right. That's why I made this place. This city's a mess, Phil. Drug dealers, criminals, dregs of society; this place would be better off without them."

Phil looked at the computer screen again, at the map with the spots marked in blue. All the worst neighborhoods. All the places where Darryl should have been afraid to go.

"I've been there, Phil. I've gone at night to the places that most people wouldn't visit in the daylight. I've been close, so close that it would have been easy. All I would have had to do was reach out with my hand and they'd be gone, just like that. But I waited, Phil. I waited for you."

The thing in the crawlspace let out a low grunt, and Phil thought he could see something bubble and pop loose from its side.

"That's why I brought you here. You've read the stories the same as me. You know there's always someone close, someone to help figure out what it all means, what it's all for."

"Darryl, you can't—"

"I can! But I can't do it alone. There's so many choices, so many wrongs to right. They used to make fun of me. They tortured me all my life, but they wouldn't have if they had known. They would have been afraid. Not me! Them! But there's so many! And so many just like them! How do I know where to start?"

There was a wildness about him now, hatred mixed with a lifetime of fear. Yet, beneath it was a kind of confidence, a sense that that everything he said made perfect sense, that the confirmation he was looking for was almost within his grasp.

"Start?" Phil said. "You have to stop!"

The confidence drained down the corners of Darryl's mouth. "But, this is what I've been waiting for all my life."

"No, it's not, Darryl. I don't know what happened to you, but this isn't a comic book. It's not right. We have to call the police, get you to a doctor or—"

Phil stopped. Darryl's face had changed. Wild excitement was replaced with stark disappointment, fear with sadness. And beneath it all was a sense of grim determination. "Oh," he said. "It's the other way, then." As Darryl took a step forward, Phil realized what he had done.

"No, Darryl, don't."

"I wanted you there, Phil, I wanted you to see it happen. Now I'll have to do it alone." Another step forward, a fist clenched in the darkness.

"Darryl, please."

"I guess I was wrong, Phil. At least this way you'll still be helping me, even if it is only for a minute."

"This isn't what heroes do."

The fist opened into a hand, and in the palm, something began to swirl, like oil on a moonlit lake.

"Heroes? Who said anything about being a hero?"

The hand came up. It gave off a blue glow that lit the room, and Darryl held it stiff-armed in front of him. Phil knew he couldn't run, that there wasn't enough room, enough time. The hand inched closer, and he closed his eyes.

Then Darryl fell.

Phil heard the sharp crack of skull on concrete, the ragged gasps of fading breath. It was only when that breath stopped that he finally opened his eyes. Darryl's eyes were open, too, his last look one of surprise, perhaps even wonder. Where his foot had slipped, something new and wet was still flopping.

The thing in the crawlspace gathered itself and lurched out into the open. It found the flesh, the spot where it had been pierced by Darryl's boot heel, and began to feed. Phil backed away, not wanting to watch, not wanting to stay in that place one second more. As he turned for the stairs, the last thing he saw was the beast's ruined face, the fish in its jaws, retreating into the dark.

All For You, Sara Sue

Ken Goldman

The moment a child is born, the mother is also born. She never existed before. The woman existed, but the mother, never. A mother is
something absolutely new.
- Bhagwan Shree Rajneesh (1931-1990)

Would it mean anything now if I told you that I loved my
husband? I know that's hard for you to swallow considering what's
happened, but I do mean it. No woman could ask for a finer man
than my Elliot, least of all a woman like myself. Just look at the sac-
rifices he made for us. How could anyone with a beating heart not
love a man who would suffer for his loved ones like that? And we
did love our Sara Sue so much, you know, so very much.

Ever notice how in those Hollywood movies these beautiful
couples always manage to meet in real cute ways? Some Jennifer
Aniston type breaks her heal on the streets of New York and then—
Wham! This prince of a guy shows up to help her, he just material-
izes out of thin air for lovely Jennifer, and he's usually some beef
cake, or maybe he has this really charming accent every woman in
the audience immediately goes wet for. And of course, despite the
inevitable complications, love happens in the space of the next nine-
ty minutes, during which time for the women in the theater there's
not a dry seat in the house. Everything wraps so perfectly, just in
time to cue the syrupy love song they run with the end credits. Yeah,
those movies, they're always the same. Some boy wins some girl,
but then loses said girl or she loses him, and then—well, I've already told you the rest. My point is, everyone goes home happy.

I'd like to say that's how it happened with Elliot and me.
Yes, I'd like to, but I can't. Oh, we started happy enough during
one rainy afternoon when he sat alongside me at the Charlestown
Avenue Starbucks and didn't speak a word for ten minutes. See, it

was crowded, and that seat was the only one available. And when he finally did speak, he asked me for the time. I gave it to him, he thanked me, and . . . well, end of story. Almost. Because when I ran into him on the bus later that day, again only one seat was available. So I sat next to him expecting at most a smile of recognition. But no, that man spoke right up.

"Well, this must be *kismet*," that's what he said, and only then did I realize how attractive he was. Not movie star attractive, of course, but easy enough on the eyes. I'll admit I was startled the man said anything considering I sat there soaking wet and looked awful. I mean, look at me. Do I have the kind of face men would remember?

"What's that?" I asked.

"*Kismet*. From this 50s late show musical of the same name. It means fate, destiny. And I'd say there must be some kind of fate working here, sitting next to each other again like this, wouldn't you?" He smiled, offered his hand. "My name is Elliot. And who might your soaking wet self be?"

I smiled but didn't answer his question. The man seemed to be coming on to me, and that didn't happen often—or ever. So instead I said the first thing that came to mind, which was, unfortunately, something stupid.

"Elliot. That was my father's name. He's dead now."

Dumb, I know. But my hesitation didn't put that man off for one second. "It's not a name you can do much with. Too humdrum to shorten into anything. Not much wiggle room to do that. I mean, come on—El? Ellie? Try surviving the school yard when kids call you that." I smiled politely again, although I could feel my heart beginning to race. We seemed pretty awkward talking such nonsense, so I went for the save, leaning closer as if sharing a secret. It was a daring move for me

"My real name is Darcella Etheridge, but everyone calls me Darcy. I'm not sure how that started, but I'm glad it did. Anyway, you can call me anything you like." I had no idea what that meant, but Elliot seemed to think I had said something very clever. He grinned, leaned close too.

"So, you're suggesting I call you?"

It wasn't the stuff great romance stories are made of, I know. But that's how we began, and by the end of our bus ride I felt I had been talking with an old friend. No Reese or Julia or Jennifer meeting Hugh Jackman or Clive whats-his-name while Celine Dion warbles on the soundtrack. Attractive as Elliot appeared, I doubt anyone would mistake him for Mr. Jackman, or me for . . . well, I can name about a hundred movie stars to whom I bear no resemblance whatsoever. But to Mr. Elliot Hanover, that didn't matter in the least. And when he spoke my name my heart pretty much supplied its own soundtrack. I suppose I'm getting much too talky about that first day, so I'll go easy on all the love stuff that followed. Oh yes, there was quite a bit of that, in case you were wondering, but I'll skip to the serious parts you ought to know about, okay?

We married. It didn't take long. A woman knows when it feels right. Hell, I practically jumped into that man's arms when he asked me to be his. Somehow he managed to present me with a beautiful ring too, although to this day I couldn't tell you how he could afford such a thing working in the city mail room at the time. But we were both so young, and with youth comes foolishness. I've no doubt Elliot probably spent most of his life savings on what he placed on my finger.

Our wedding ceremony wasn't anything to make those English Royals envious and the small apartment we moved into fell considerably short of palatial, but none of that mattered. I knew this was as perfect a life as I'd ever hoped for, and only one thing could make it more perfect. Elliot felt the same, so we got to working on beginning our family right away. We were young. We didn't know . . . we just didn't know.

See, it wasn't really anyone's fault, my not being able to conceive, it just didn't seem in the stars for us. So after many months trying, we decided to find out if maybe we had been doing something wrong. Turns out it wasn't Elliot or me who got it wrong. No, nature herself had made that decision for us; it was what Elliot had called *kismet*. Well, fate can *kismet* my ass. Dr. Byron over at the County Medical Hospital, he informed us that my eggs weren't doing what a woman's eggs are supposed to. But that wasn't all. Because, see, Dr. Byron also tested Elliot, and . . . well, let's just say that Mother Nature decided to hit us with a double barrel. I must have cried myself to sleep for weeks.

"We can adopt," Elliot tried reassuring me. "I swear, we would love that child like it was our own, Darcy, I'm sure we would." But I knew it wouldn't be the same, not for me, and besides, we could never afford what those agencies were asking. Talk about a hard pill to swallow, and I really did try. But knowing that

I could never be a mother, that I could never hold my own infant in my arms, it was just too much for me to stand.

That's how Sara Sue came to be. She was Elliot's idea, and maybe at first I thought it seemed crazy. After I'd spent so many nights bathing my face in tears, one morning Elliot sat on the bed alongside me. He wore this huge grin, something I hadn't seen for weeks. Taking my face into his hands, he kissed me.

"I think maybe we're going to have that child after all. See, I've been doing some thinking, Darcy, and I believe you're going to give birth to our child any day now." I had no idea what he meant. Unless my new husband intended to kidnap some infant from its crib, I didn't see any child in our future. But doing something so wrong wasn't Elliot Hanover's style. I sat up, managed a few words.

"You want to tell me how that's going to happen, considering the doctor explained that a newborn coming out of me is as likely as one coming out of that old bowling ball of yours?"

Elliot's grin grew wider. He rubbed my stomach, then put his ear to it. "Why, I believe I've just felt that baby of ours kick. She's going to be a healthy one, our Sara Sue, I just know it. I'm so proud of you, Darcy. You'll be be such a wonderful mother." He turned serious. "Are you following me on this?"

"Not at all." I'll tell you right now that at that moment I felt certain my Elliot had completely lost his mind. Either that, or he had something up his sleeve I couldn't begin to guess. As it turned out, he did.

"Okay, then, I'll explain this only once, and after today I'll never say another word about it. You can either agree to it or not. Whatever you decide will be all right, but I'm hoping you'll see this situation the way I do."

I might have felt frightened had those words come from a man less rational than my husband, but I knew he was dead serious and that his feelings for me never had proved less than solid gold genuine.

Elliot took my hand, held it tight. His words sounded as if he had rehearsed them for hours. Likely, he had. But he spoke with such assuredness, such certainty . . .

"Our Sara Sue will be born in a few days. We'll need time to fix up the place, of course, maybe purchase an old crib at the thrift store, some baby clothes too. You'll deliver a little prematurely at home, and it may seem somewhat touch and go for a while, but I'll be there to deliver our child and it will be a perfect birth. And from that day forward, you and I, will watch our daughter grow every day, and we'll ask her how her time at school went, soothe her when she skins her knee, laugh and cry with her when circumstances call for it. Most important, we'll love that little girl every bit as much as if—"

He seemed to almost choke on the rest of that sentence. I finished it for him.

"As if she were real?"

Those words did not come easy. I looked hard into my husband's eyes to determine if maybe something had gone seriously wrong with his thinking to cause him to suggest something so preposterous. But I saw a clarity there that I knew meant he had earnestly weighed the pros and cons of his proposition.

"She will be real, Darcy. To us she'll be more real than anything else in the world." Elliot squeezed my hand, then kissed it. "Our Sara Sue will be the most perfect child a parent could want, and you—you will be the perfect mother."

I didn't know whether to laugh or cry. I did neither. What Elliot had suggested was possibly the most insane idea a man could propose, or maybe it was the most incredible demonstration of love of which any husband were capable. Knowing my man the way I did, I didn't have to question his reasoning for very long.

"Why Sara Sue?" I asked.

His smile reappeared. "You wanted a girl, right?"

I nodded.

"Well, then, why not Sara Sue?"

Thinking over what he suggested, I felt so much love for my husband I knew no other response would do. Elliot had found a way to give us our child, and I threw my arms around him, held him as close as I could. "I know our Sara Sue will be perfect," I whispered. "I know she will."

It was an amazing moment, all right. I was laughing while tears clouded my eyes. And Elliot and I, we held each other so tight for the next hour as if we were each afraid to let go.

And maybe we were.

* * *

Elliot proved true to his word. Never once did he imply that

Sara Sue would be anything less than our flesh and blood daughter. So I played along, even down to his providing all the skills necessary to make our imaginary child's imaginary birth anything but imaginary.

I'll spare you the details of that day, but I will admit that I screamed and pushed just as accurately as any woman going through the wonderful agony of childbirth, and Elliott stood by me the whole time wiping my forehead with a moist towel while coaxing my breathing. When it was over I felt exhausted, and I really was bathed in sweat. Moments later, there stood Elliot holding the most beautiful imaginary infant a new mother could ever hope to see. Yes, I knew that wrapped inside the pink blanket was probably a bag of flour, but I swear, for a moment I really did see our new daughter in her father's arms. And I'm telling no lie when I say my heart nearly burst with happiness when he handed Sara Sue to me.

In the days that followed when Elliott returned from work, his first words always were "Where's my little angel? What wonderful thing did our daughter do today?" And I would answer, I'd say "Oh, you should have seen her! She was so good, Elliot, the way she ate all her carrots, and without so much as a whimper the entire afternoon. She's fast asleep now. Come, look." But sometimes Sara Sue could be difficult too, and I'd complain, "Oh, God! I think I want to scream. That child just refused to eat anything today, and I must have changed her diaper ten times!"

During the night Elliot often would climb from our bed, tell me "I hear Sara Sue crying. You go back to sleep, Darcy. I'll take care of it." Other times I would sit for an hour rocking her to sleep and singing gently to her "Hush little baby, don't say a word . . ."

And so it went . . .

"Oh, Elliot! Sara Sue spoke her first word today! Mama— she said Mama!!"

"Look, Darcy! I think . . . Yes! I think she's trying to take her first step right now!"

"Hush little baby . . ."

"Who's Daddy's perfect little angel? Who? Who?"

"First day of school! Let's get going, munchkin!"

"Elliot, come see what our daughter drew in class today!"

"Love you . . . Love you . . ."

No there was nothing there to see, I knew that. But another part of me disregarded that empty space, and instead I saw the most precious girl child on this planet. And like a madly spinning carousel the years seemed to pass too quickly. . .

"Sara Sue got picked for head cheerleader today, Elliot. Head cheerleader!"

"Doesn't our daughter look beautiful all dressed up for the dance?"

"Tell her, Elliot. Tell her how boys sometimes can seem cruel like that . . ."

Sara Sue came laughing to us when she saw the first robin of spring, told how she caught lightning bugs inside a jar on the first day of summer, rolled in the autumn leaves or made snow angels in the park. They were such wonderful years. Sara Sue was our life.

No, that's not correct. She was more.

Sara Sue kept us alive!

But then, during the darkest days of winter, our old friend *Kismet* reared her ugly head.

Elliot came from our daughter's room. "Darcy, do Sara Sue's eyes look a bit swollen to you? She's been complaining about stomach pains and she can't seem to move. I think there's something seriously wrong."

Of course, I realized a child's illness was a problem all parents face. Our daughter was an adolescent now but never had she been sick, so some kind of illness seemed inevitable. I entered Sara Sue's room, looked into the empty bed and waited a respectable few minutes. Returning to my husband I told him "You may be right, she doesn't look so good. There's some fever too." Then I added the only thing a concerned parent would say, "I think maybe we should see the doctor."

I had barely got that sentence out before Elliot grabbed his coat, so I went for mine. But he told me, "No, Darcy, you stay home," always wanting to protect me from anything disturbing. Although my maternal instincts disagreed, I chose not to argue, certain that within the hour Elliot would return, explain to me that our daughter had just caught a bad virus, or something like that. I heard him tell Sara Sue to put on some clothes, watched through the window as our old Camry drove off.

For hours I waited but Elliot didn't return, and when I called his cellular he didn't answer. I prayed our Sara Sue would be all right, all the while realizing the foolishness of that prayer. I suppose when you believe in something hard enough, you make it so. That night I realized how authentic Sara Sue had become to both of us, understood the fear any mother would feel for her ailing child. Near dawn, Elliot appeared at the door. I could tell he hadn't slept, and the look on his face was one I had never seen.

"Sara Sue isn't with you?" I asked.

Without removing his coat he sat on the couch, just looked at me. "Darcy, I think you had better sit." Taking his hand I could feel his trembling. "It was her heart, Darcy. The doctors, they tried and tried, but Sara Sue just wasn't strong enough. She didn't make it."

The world stopped in that instant, and I couldn't form even the simplest rational thought. "That's . . . that's not possible, Elliot. She's just a young girl, hardly into her teenage years. A child's heart—our child's, it just doesn't quit like that. It can't! "

"Sara Sue's heart did. It just stopped, Darcy, like some busted watch. Just like that."

[She isn't real, Elliot. She never was. You know it. I know it. How can she die?]

But Elliot insisted our child lay in the morgue at County Medical. I heard growing anger in his voice and I reached for him, but he pulled himself from me, told me he needed to be alone for a while. I understood, or at least a part of me thought I did. I'm certain we never felt so lonely in our lives as we mourned the tragic death of our child, arranged for her burial, spoke of her funeral—all without leaving our apartment. We opened imaginary cards of sympathy from imaginary friends, shared them, answered imaginary calls. I guess after all those years I just got caught up in the pretending, and I almost believed our daughter's death to be so. I knew Sara Sue seemed real—but she wasn't! Still, the grief felt as real as anything I'd experienced, although what followed after weeks of mourning our loss . . . well, I couldn't have seen it coming in a million years.

Searching for answers, at first I believed maybe Elliot decided Sara Sue had to die hoping we might grow closer in our grief. But that didn't happen. We stopped talking, ate little, slept less. Sometimes Elliot disappeared for the entire night. I knew better than to ask where he had been because the alcohol on his breath told me. But that wasn't the worst of it. Often at night, Elliot would leave our bed and scream like a man gone mad. I could no longer suggest that our Sara Sue existed only in our imaginations. He would glare at me as if I had uttered something reprehensible, my words deserving no response beyond his complete contempt that I had suggested such a terrible thing. His misery grew so terrible that now it seemed I mourned more for my lost husband than for Sara Sue.

I should have seen it coming—I should have seen it!

He had managed to do it so quietly while I slept, I never heard a sound from the bathroom. I found Elliot in the morning slumped in a spreading puddle of his own blood, the razor's blade still in his wrist, a smeared note at his side:

I'm so sorry, Darcy. I just can't take the pain any more. I love you.

I won't go into the details of the awful scene I found. I really can't do that without bringing myself back to it. Seeing my beloved husband there on the floor, and the blood, so much blood . . . well, just talking about it, I'm sorry, but I don't want to say any more about that. I can't tell you how I felt either. I couldn't get my mind to comprehend what Elliot had done or why he had done it. I still can't. No matter how I look at it, it makes no sense at all. Well, maybe that's not entirely true. See, I always knew my Elliot was more man than a woman like me ever deserved, and I love him still despite the terrible thing he did. So there's one thing I do understand. It's been almost a year now since my husband and our Sara Sue have been gone, and that one thing rings pretty clear.

Loneliness, it does terrible things to a person's head—terrible things.

Yes, I know it wasn't right, my taking that infant from its carriage. But when I saw her at the Charlestown Mall left unattended for that moment . . . well, I just did what I did without putting much thought into it. That little darling looked so much like our Sara Sue, it seemed my hands developed a mind of their own when they snatched her. After I'd done that, all I could think to do was just run. So there I was, standing in the middle of that parking lot holding some strange woman's infant, having not the slightest idea what to do next. I found this large plastic trash bag in a bin, emptied it to put the infant inside. I wanted to hide her, that was all. I wasn't thinking clearly, you have to know that. I just wasn't thinking clearly.

Would it mean anything now if I told you how sorry I feel for all I've done? Because I do feel sorry, you know—so very sorry for whatever sorrow I've caused. It's just that I miss my family so much, even knowing our Sara Sue never really . . . she never . . . not really . . .

140

Damn! Oh damn!

Do you think you could turn off that recorder device now, please, Sergeant? I've told you all there is to tell, and I'm feeling so tired.

* * *

5th POLICE PRECINCT: CITY OF CHARLESTOWN
12: 47 a.m.

After a third replay of the recorded confession of the woman who called herself Mrs. Darcella Hanover, Sergeant Harry Servitto felt damned tired himself. Arresting officer Will McCormack poured two cups of coffee and spoke Harry's thoughts.

"She's wrong about that last part, Sergeant. There's more to tell, all right. A dozen witnesses saw her take that child, a dozen more claim there always seemed something not right about her. I saw that close up when we busted that woman's door and found her singing some 'Hush Little Baby' song to that stolen infant's corpse. Never looked up, just kept singing her damned lullaby like we weren't there, as if that dead baby was gurgling happily in her own mother's arms."

Servitto raised a pair of bloodshot eyes. "To that woman you weren't there, William. People see what they want to see. Maybe doing that, they goose up fate into being whatever they want it to be. She wanted a real Sara Sue. I guess she found one. But fate has her way of biting you in the ass. *Kismet*, like the lady said." He stubbed out his cigarette, stared at the ashes. "Christ, it's too late to be getting philosophical."

Looking as tired as his superior, McCormack sipped his coffee. "Go figure what crazy shit goes on inside a lonely woman's head to make her self-destruct like that, eh? Guess we'll have to let the court shrink decide that."

Servitto nodded agreement. "You find anything about this Hanover guy?"

The officer shook his head. "Not a damned thing, Sergeant. Elliot's her late father's name; Hanover's the family name of some local garage mechanic who says he took this Darcella to a movie once when she was about fifteen, and he hasn't seen her since. But there's no record of any Elliot Hanover in this woman's life, not a

141

signature on any document or canceled check, not one person in that apartment building who's ever seen a trace of the man. No one's ever seen her sporting any fancy ring like she spoke about, neither. She's never been anything but Darcella Etheridge. Court shrink's going to have a field day with this one."

Servitto forced a tired smile, quickly gave it up and reached for his coffee.

"Loneliness is one mean mind fucker, all right. A woman wants a family, she figures a way to have one. Imaginary dead children and husbands don't mean a whole lot, legally speaking. But now we've got a dead infant for real here. Write it up by tomorrow morning, will you? Go home and kiss your wife and kids." He glared into his cup. "Anything else, William?"

The young officer took a moment to consider the question. He shrugged. "Coffee's gone cold," he said.

Hi Ted

David Bischoff

The computer game company president read his next e-mail:

Hi Bill,

Okay, I think I found a goldmine. My public domain idea is working out, I think, especially since POWERDOWN flopped and you want another DIABLO-type fantasy build rather than sci-fi.

Story's called The Hoard of the Gibbelins by a guy named Lord Dunsany.

Read it.

Now.

Stan

Att. : Hoard.doc

The computer game president opened the attached file.

The Hoard of the Gibbelins
By
Lord Dunsany

The Gibbelins eat, as is well known, nothing less good than man. Their evil tower is joined to Terra Cognita, to the lands we know, by a bridge. Their hoard is beyond reason; avarice has no use for it. They have a separate cellar for emeralds and a separate cellar for sapphires; they have a hole filled with gold and dig it up when they need it. And the only use that is known for their ridiculous wealth, is to attract to their larder a

continual supply of food—Man. In times of fam-
ine they have even been known to scatter rubies
abroad; a little trail of them to some city of Man,
and sure enough their larders would soon be full
again.

Huh? thought the computer game company president. He
forwarded the message from the guy from Creative to a lower-level
flunky named Ted.

Hi Ted,

Summarize.

Bill

Att. : Hoard.doc

He then answered two more e-mails, sighed, and got up to go
for the meeting with Financial, taking a couple of Vicadin first.

When he got back, he took another, and he pulled a bottle of
Johnny Walker out of the bar and brought it to his desk. After a stiff
one, he checked his e-mail again.

Hmm. That flunky was fast! Sharp too. Knew C++ and an
excellent gamer. Just out of CalTech.

Hi Bill, said the e-mail.

Boy he's right! This is a good story.
So these critters, the Gibbelins. They're nasty
monsters. They've got this castle and it's just crammed
with gold and jewels. They use the gold and jewels to
lure human beings to the castle? Why? Because they
want to eat them.

Now get this paragraph. It's my favorite.

Here the Gibbelins lived and discreditably fed.
Alderic, Knight of the Order of the City and the
144

Assault, hereditary Guardian of the King's Peace of Mind, a man not unremembered among makers of myth, pondered so long upon the Gibbelins' hoard that by now he deemed it his. Alas that I should say of so perilous a venture, undertaken at dead of night by a valourous man, that its motive was sheer avarice! Yet upon avarice only the Gibbelins relied to keep their larders full, and once in every hundred years sent spies into the cities of men to see how avarice did, and always the spies returned again to the tower saying that all was well.

So Alderic. He's the hero. A knight, right? He's so now. Entitled, you know? He wants some of that Gibbelin stash and has a clever way of getting it, he thinks.

And it pretty much works. He extorts a dragon to help him and he tries a different way than the others who've gotten eaten by the G.s. He nabs a bag of emeralds and is about to snag more. Oops! There are the G.s.

And, without saying a word, or even smiling, they neatly hanged him on the outer wall—and the tale is one of those that don't have a happy ending.

I'm thinking of a great game based on this! Ideas to come!

Best,

Ted

———

Hmm, thought the computer game company president.

Ted. Ted. Which one was he? Oh right. That guy who thought computers were gonna save the world!

Yeah. Right. The guy who thought computers were gonna

take Man to the Stars.

Sheesh.

Bill, the computer game company president, was surprised to see, almost immediately, an e-mail from the guy at Creative.

Hi Bill,

Wow! I can't believe this! So I put the text into that latest device from the OZzone. You know, Magic SpellChecker?

And there's some kind of portal that's opened up! There's some cool colors . . . like gold and sapphire and diamond.

Gonna check it out.

The computer company boss saw that all these e-mails were from the previous day. He assumed that Stan was stoned or drunk or both and shrugged. Creative. So it goes.

He went to pee.

When he returned, he saw that there was a fresh e-mail from Stan, dated just moments before.

Dear Sirrah,

Greetings from Elsewhere.

We are happy to have employed your previous servant and absorbed from him certain details and knowledges. We believe we may come to a mutually beneficial relationship with your company. We are selective in our needs, and thought our previous predilections in taste no longer of value. This is no longer the case.

If you can provide one of your minions for our exclusive use and absorption, we in turn can promise a most rewarding computer game. Nor will the disappearances of its subsequent purchasers be many and those occluded by our mythic methodologies.

In return, we offer a product with a potential beyond your dreams of need.

We eagerly await your reply.

Most sincerely your servant,
Jasis, Lord of the Gibbelins.

The computer game company president looked around at the meager furnishings of his room. He thought about the many, many bright young people pumped out of the universities. He thought of the many, many, many and yet more punters eager for the latest adrenaline-tech.

He thought about his recent meetings with Financial. He thought about his need for a new Mercedes Benz and a vacation.

He sighed.

Well, geek, he thought. Maybe you won't save the world, but you just might save my ass.

The computer game company president started up the e-mail that would deal with it all:

Hi Ted . . .

Child and Guardian

Michael B. Tager

The moment Child's head touched the pillow, the guardian awoke, and when gentle snores reached her ears, she stood and moved about, waking herself thoroughly. She paid a long glance to the still forms of Child's other silent watchmen: the brown, soft form of the monkey with cheap-looking cymbals attached to its hands and the smiling form of a plush bear next to each other above Child's head. The guardian regarded them thoughtfully while it washed itself with a rough tongue.

Alert for any noise, the guardian padded with delicate care over every inch of the silent room. She ignored the howling of the wind outside and the normal sounds of the house: the ticking of the grandfather clock downstairs and the hum of electricity. The house was old and always made some kind of noise, but she would be damned if through her carelessness or inattentiveness, Child was harmed. The ancient, creaky hardwood floors made no sounds, no groans when she set foot ever so carefully on the scarred and scratched boards. She moved so slowly that the air was barely disturbed and no wisps of dust ever lifted more than a scarce inch from the ground.

When she reached the threshold of Child's room and made to enter the long, densely shadowed hallway, she paused and sniffed the air, alert for any hint of danger in the musty, dank-smelling corridor. After long moments of flared nostrils, the guardian lifted one paw beyond the doorway. She sighed internally for a long moment as she scanned. She glared with suspicion at the veiled window, able to detect the bright glow of the harvest moon just through the gauzy curtains. She thought to herself that of all nights, tonight might just bring the danger she expected. After staring long and hard at the innocuous seeming aperture, she decidedly dismissed it from her mind, readying herself for what lay beyond.

She continued, inspecting each segment and every shadow. She thrust her snout into each shadow and tracked each possible

148

movement, freezing whenever something that did not seem to belong intruded. When a tiny spider scuttled along one of the long grains in the floor, the guardian lowered her head to the floor and tracked the long-legged creature with huge, soulful eyes. Motionless save for her pupils, the guardian waited until the spider moved closer and, with a snap, ended the life of the hapless arachnid.

Wincing at the bitter taste and the hard crunching in her mouth, she moved on. A cobweb wafted from the ceiling, struck down by a sudden breeze. Suspicious, the guardian followed it and, when it lay motionless on the floor, pounced on it with all four feet, tearing it to shreds silently and viciously, the strands becoming tangled in her velvety-soft brown hair. As she savaged it, she looked down the hall and saw the window next to the stairs, the mirror to the one by the Child's room. What looked like a long, skeletal hand reached up to enter the open window and the guardian, disdaining subtlety for speed, flashed down the wooden floor and jumped with all of her might at the window, slamming it shut on the slender limb attempting to enter the house. There was a snap and a clatter as the branch fell lifeless to the ground.

Victorious, the guardian allowed her heart to settle from its rapid beating in her chest and dropped her body to the floor. Nose to the ground, she inspected the fallen, unmoving object. She felt a surge of shame when the image of the severed tree branch, apparently thrust into the window by the gale outside became clear to her. She sat on her haunches and wailed silently, when she heard a noise coming from downstairs.

She shoved down her embarrassment and firmed her resolve, moving her long, graceful legs down the padded wooden steps with no sound. She rounded the landing and ignored the window above her, moonlight streaming through the blue curtains. She could hear further movement close by, through the parlor and in the kitchen, by the back door. She plodded down the last step and dropped her belly to the ground, inching forward slowly. She ignored the pricks and slices of the jagged wood, so close to her body and lifted her small delicate ears to discern what she could.

When she reached the swinging door, she became perfectly still and lay in the shadow of the door. Her dark hair and deep pools of eyes blended perfectly in with the shadows. She trained her eyes on the white kitchen door and listened for the sounds from within. She could hear muttered speaking; a rough voice intoned like gravel crushed through a vise and a high-pitched twittering response. The guardian waited for long moments. Nothing, however, came through the door. The guardian closed her eyes and stayed motionless.

The only sound heard was the roar of the wind outside and the tick-tock of the grandfather clock. Occasional mumbles came through the cracks of the door and once, a muffled *thump*. Her ears perked and she rose slightly, tensing her leg muscles and baring her small, razor-sharp teeth. Her heart beat faster than a rushing river and what passed for adrenaline flowed through what resembled veins. She was ready. There was danger here to Child and she would not fail.

The door burst open, shocking the guardian with its suddenness. A shadowy form stood in the shattered doorway, outlined by a shimmering light. There was a rough outline to its face and it looked nearly human except for the single eye glowing red in the center of what should have been a face and the large, night-black tail that whipped around behind it. Fluttering around its head and garbed in light was what looked almost like a bat, if bats were made of purplish-green light and dripped a thick ichor from their wings. The two started forward, not seeing the guardian as it lay on the ground, watching them with half-lidded eyes. They were the stuff of dreams, nightmares. They were what every child feared lay beyond their closet door.

The guardian rose and opened her mouth, tongue lolling to one side. She spoke in a crystalline voice, without actually using voice or breath. "I am here."

The great shadowy creature froze and trained its one eye on the guardian. The fluttering light became frantic for a moment before alighting on the shadow's arms. They regarded the guardian and though they had no face, she could sense the hostility and anger emanating from them. She spoke again, "You are not welcome here."

"Madness," the light said. "We go where we wish." Its voice was glass scratching marble. "You are not one to deny us."

The shadow spoke in its gravelly rumble. "You should scamper off, little one. *You* are unwelcome. We are here for our prize, promised to us by the Dark Ones." They started forward.

The guardian lifted her hind legs and deliberately stretched before speaking. "None shall pass. Even if my life is forfeit, you will not claim Child." She opened her garnet eyes wide and hissed, lifting one paw and extending six razor-sharp claws. The two intruders paused and seemed to converse soundlessly before rushing forward. The shadow-creature's eye glowed red and liquid fire leeched out in an arrow, aiming at the guardian, who was no longer there.

The guardian, nerves wired, had launched herself the second the two started to move. She sprung straight at the light-bat, swatting it from the sky with one swipe of her paw and shrieked as searing heat lanced through her. She fell to the floor and tumbled before regaining her feet. She turned to see the light-bat flying at her in a dizzying zig-zag motion, specks of iridescent shards lancing from its body and carving paths in the wall and floor. One ray brushed the guardian's head and she moaned, not taking her eyes off the oncoming enemy, despite the pain radiating from her half-severed ear. The bat screamed as it approached, beams of fire lancing in all directions. Within seconds, it was upon her.

The guardian opened her mouth wide, a tearing sound at the corners of her jaw. The bat, surprised, attempted to stop its momentum, but as it slowed, the guardian leapt forward, engulfing the creature of light whole. She shuddered as she swallowed, feeling searing heat coarse down her gullet and set the depths of her to smoldering. She knew she had little time and whipped her head all about in search of the shadow demon. She could not find it. She frantically searched all over the smoking, dark room, before heading for the stairs.

Doing her best to ignore the pain rising in her, the guardian jumped several steps at a time in her haste to get to Child's room. She reached the top of the stairs and turned, skidding along the hard floor and slamming into the wall. She coughed in pain and vomited a mixture of smoke and ashes. She could feel her energy draining from her and knew her time was ending. Shoving the panic and terror down, she looked to the end of the hallway, seeing the shadow-figure regard the door in front of it. She shrieked internally as the one-eyed thing looked to her and, somehow, conveyed a sadistic sort of smile.

She strained herself and almost flew down the hallway toward the gloating creature. It awaited her, eye glowing fire-red. Just as guardian neared, the eye exploded its energy at her. She stopped suddenly, ducking and throwing herself to the floor, skidding along, energy missing her by inches and tearing the floor to shreds. She slid into the creature's feet, bounced up, and with one paw reached back, then drove her claws into its ankle with all of her strength. The thing roared in pain and reached down with one massive, black dagger-tipped hand. She scampered up its leg, using her claws like pitons, she reached its chest and neck. She looked at the creature as it trained its eye on her. She opened her mouth, tongue wagging in satisfaction and said, "Goodbye. You will not be missed," and made as if to cough up a hairball. The shadow-creature's eye glowed red and fire lanced out, only to be deflected and absorbed by the projectile expelled from the guardian's stomach. The light-bat, coated in some kind of viscous fluid, screamed forth, emitting light in all directions. The guardian was able to discern anger and disappointment in their screams before they met. There was an explosion and a flash of red and purple light and both the shadow and light creature disappeared.

The guardian, buffeted all about, fell to the floor in a heap. She could feel, as if through a dense fog, all the cuts and burns she had suffered and her life draining out of her in a torrent. She closed her eyes in front of Child's room. She was tired and Child was safe. That was enough. She was so tired . . . she would just rest for a short time. The night continued around her.

* * *

The guardian opened his eyes and saw that Child was safely asleep. He stretched his long arms and placed his shiny brass cymbals on the ground beside him before he moved his tail about, getting a feel for it. He could sense little amiss and thought a short circuit of the house would be enough. He stood from the foot of the bed and used his tail to swing to the floor. He stopped at the threshold and regarded the door. He put his hands out, inspected them and pushed ever so slightly—almost experimentally—and was gratified as the door swung open. He looked down on the ragged and burned stuffed animal lying on the floor, its garnet eyes closed in its feline face. The guardian walked over on his knuckles and inspected the remains. He nodded and made his way down the hallway, ready to defend what he had been made to protect.

Connection

Richard Farren Barber

"What does he want now?" Gail asked. She reached across the table and grabbed the phone before Jenny had a chance to pick it up. Gail turned the handset round. "What's that supposed to be?"

Jenny took her phone out of her friend's hand. The picture showed a grainy black image shot through with blurred red and silver lines. She shrugged. "There must be something wrong with Mick's phone, they've been coming through like that all day."

"He's doing it to punish you."

Jenny laughed, short and low. "What for?"

"For coming out tonight."

Jenny put the phone back down on the table where it joined the cluster of other handsets. She shook her head. "He was fine about it. He said so."

Helen picked up the phone and looked at the image. Shrugged her shoulders. "He's playing you, Jenny."

"He's worried about me. It was just a misunderstanding."

"Worried you might have a good time without him."

"He isn't like that."

"Look at him—a hundred miles away and yet he still manages to make sure that we're talking about him," Helen said. "I'm sick of his controlling ways. Let's talk about something else for a change. Anything else."

"I didn't mention Mick first anyway," Jenny said. She was aware of the strident tone of her own voice, her words just a little too sharp, too defensive.

"Let's make a pact," Helen said. "We don't mention his name again. He isn't going to ruin girl's tonight." A moment later the phone rumbled against the surface of the table as another text came through. For a moment all three of them stared at the handset.

"Leave it," Gail said.

Jenny ignored the handset and tried to follow the conversation. It was difficult; the phone seemed to suck her attention away.

Even while she listened, Jenny could feel the message on the phone calling to her, demanding to be read. But she knew that although Gail and Helen didn't say anything they were still watching her. For her own good, as they kept telling her. Mick is trouble, they always said. Even though they didn't know Mick, had never really given him a chance.

After ten minutes Jenny offered to get the next round of drinks; as she stood up, she swiped the phone from the table and then, while she stood at the bar waiting to be served, she quickly checked her messages. Another picture, just like the others: a black image with crimson and silver lines.

* * *

Jenny left the pub early, trying to ignore the telling glance that passed between Gail and Helen. She almost said something to them—that it wasn't because of Mick. That she was tired. That she had work in the morning. But in the end she stuffed her phone into her handbag and walked out of The Tavern without offering an excuse. They wouldn't have believed her anyway. It was the same as always, Mick did something and she jumped. Always. And her friends feared that she would never be out of his grasp.

She waited until she was beyond the reach of the gold light that seeped out from the pub windows before she dipped her hand into her bag. There was another picture waiting for her, just as blurred and pointless as the others. Her tired eyes tried to squint at the latest image. It didn't make sense, his messages always had a point—a demand.

She dialed his number—straight to voicemail.

Dialed again. Again. Again. Hanging up every time Mick's "sorry I can't answer you right now…" spiel began.

No answer.

On the sixth attempt she left a message. "Where are you? Are you okay?" and tried not to imagine what Helen and Gail would say if they heard her. They simply didn't understand.

Her phone chirped. Not a call, another message. She hoped— prayed—it would be a picture of Mick at home looking sad and apologetic. He'd done that before when they'd had the argument about a trip to Leeds. It had made her laugh. He could do that—and that was what Helen and Gail weren't able to see in him. The humor.

The fun. They just saw it as manipulation. His need to always know what was happening.

Her hands were shaking as she pressed the button to view the message. Just a blank screen.

Must be an error. An accident. The picture corrupted as it flew over the airwaves from wherever the hell Mick was. Or maybe he hadn't meant to send this one, just a random press of keys when the phone was in his pocket. Maybe that explained all the photos she was getting from him.

She looked again at the image—not completely black, a few freckles of deep red and dark blue. As if there was a proper picture hidden just beneath the surface.

Jenny pushed her phone back into her handbag and hurried home. She needed to get some sleep. She was going to be knackered in the morning.

* * *

Jenny woke late, tired and confused and blaming the alarm clock for not waking her. Or maybe for not keeping her awake. She had a hazy memory of turning the thing off because it had been too early to think about getting up when it rang at six.

She showered, ate and dressed in a chaotic rush. Stupid things like trying to eat a piece of toast as she pulled a jumper over her head and inside her mind she was chanting, *I'm late, you're late, I'm late* like some crazed March Hare.

Jenny caught a taxi because no way would the bus be able to make up for her lost time; she ran through the office, switched on her computer and put on her headset a full two minutes before they tripped the switchboard over. Gail parked a cup of scorching hot, black coffee by her elbow.

"Are you okay?"

Jenny took a sip from the mug and then pulled her phone out and put it under a pile of papers at the edge of her desk.

"If Liam sees that he'll murder you."

"It's on silent," Jenny said. "Mick still hasn't called. Hasn't answered any of my messages."

"Good," Gail said. There was a hard finality to the word that made Jenny shiver. "Maybe he's finally found someone new to bully."

155

"He's not like that." Jenny heard the wail in her own voice and stared down into the mug. *He's not. He loves me.*

And then the switchboard was coming on; phones flashing and the huge dot-matrix sign at the end of the room flickered on with "Good morning, you have . . ."

A pause, and like always Jenny could feel the room holding its collective breath in anticipation. Less than 100 was bad for the company—more than 200 meant you were going to spend the next seven hours chasing the backlog from Chonqing.

. . .

The dots pulsed.

"You okay?" Gail whispered again.

Jenny shrugged, not sure what okay was anymore. The pair of them looked back to the switchboard.

. . .

329 calls waiting.

Jenny groaned, but smiled too as her body dumped the first load of adrenaline into her system. Worked faster than coffee.

She heard the familiar hum of the line close to her ear and then clicked the button to pick up her first call.

329—it felt like a personal mission, Jenny Furnen needed to clear that backlog before they handed the switchboard over. She knew it was stupid—focusing on that to avoid having to think about Mick. But it worked; she could concentrate on John from Clapton shouting at her because they were late again and if she thought they could be proud of such a crap service . . . or Mrs. Elly Maine from Portsmouth who was awfully sorry but the engineers seemed to have cut through her water pipe.

The first text of the new day came just after ten. The phone clattered against the desk and Jenny picked it up without pausing in her spiel about getting an engineer out to see if the bird's nest really was a fire hazard.

Another image. No accompanying text. No explanation. Just a dark screen with a couple of pale lines running through it.

Jenny thumbed in the response—ARE YOU OKAY?—while she let Mrs. Bird's-nest chatter on about whether the little things might be endangered, and Jenny had to stop herself from absently telling the woman: *They'll be endangered once our lot get onto them.*

She put the mobile back down and tried to concentrate on typing the fix code into the bird lady's account. Nothing about birds' nests or animal homes, so she stuck it under MISCELLANEOUS with a little note attached.

Her mobile phone rang—causing the picture on her monitor to tremble. She felt a flare of anger, Mick knew she couldn't take personal calls at work. It was almost as if he had chosen the timing deliberately, knowing she would be sitting there with her headset on and the mobile blinking insistently . . . answer! Answer? ANSWER!

She picked it up. When she saw NUMBER WITHHELD she felt sick.

Jenny took off her headset and dropped it onto her desk, pressed a button to cancel the call and cut the customer off mid flow.

"Phone's gone dead," she told Gail. She grabbed the mobile and ran across the floor, pressing answer once she'd passed the last of the calling stations. She reached the door to the stairwell and pushed it open.

"Where are you?" she snapped as the fire door fell shut behind her.

No answer. Bad line. Just the crackling of static—like a connection not quite made.

"Mick, is that you?"

Jenny paused. It was silence . . . just those pips and crackles of static, the sort of thing she was used to from spending every minute of each working day hard-wired into the telephone system. Except it wasn't the same . . . there was somebody's voice buried deep beneath the static.

Jenny tried, but couldn't make out any of the words. If she concentrated on the voice it seemed to melt away.

Something about the voice, and the constant pop and hiss of the telephone line. Something very wrong about it. She wanted to hang up, but another part of her owned a horrid fascination.

"Jenny."

Her name spoken so softly she wasn't sure that she'd heard it—probably just her imagination, so desperately wanting to hear from Mick.

"Mick?" she asked.

"Jenny."

It *was* Mick. The line was so poor and crackling, but Jenny was sure she recognized the voice calling her name, that it wasn't just her imagination.

And the line went dead. A steady hum in her ear.

157

She dialed Mick's number immediately.

Liam's scrunched up face appeared in the glass panel of the fire door. He didn't look happy. In fact it was obvious he was shouting even before the fire door cracked open to release his voice—no pops or crackles to distort *that* message.

" . . . hell are you doing out here?"

Someone answered the call, it took Jenny a moment to realize it wasn't Mick. Thinking she'd rang the wrong number she glanced at the screen: Mick mob. The man on the other end was talking, but Jenny couldn't hear him—not with Liam jabbering away at her about disciplinary and rules and whatnot just a couple of inches from her ears and bouncing off

" . . . Michael Whalley . . ."

the walls of the stairwell. She waved her hand at Liam to try and shut him up, but that just seemed to make him worse.

" . . . A23 . . ."

He started to go red in the face which made Jenny think of Tom and Jerry cartoons where steam would blow out of Tom's ears (or was it Jerry's?). Even though she knew she should be listening to what the man talking on Mick's phone

" . . . your full name, Jenny . . ."

was saying and just tell Liam to leave her alone, she couldn't get away from the distraction of this stupid pillock flapping in front of her face like some demented

" . . . died . . ."

chicken and so it took her a while, she didn't know quite how long, but a while, before she realized that the man

" . . . car . . ."

on the phone was trying to tell her that Mick was dead.

That he'd been dead for the last 13 hours.

* * *

Jenny sat in a corner of the stairwell, looking up through the spiraling railings above her to the tiny white square of light that came down through the sunroof. She was probably going mad. No, she was *definitely* going mad. But really she knew—as soon as she heard she knew it was true. It made sense of all those phone calls and messages she'd left for Mick that he hadn't answered. In some prosaic, no supernatural-bond required way, as soon as she heard

158

that he was dead it felt true. Horrific, but true.

She couldn't recall the details—the man on Mick's phone had explained but Jenny couldn't hold onto his words. It was like trying to catch a waterfall in her fingers. Everything just seemed to slip through her.

Something about a car crash. Down near Brighton. And something about . . .

The door creaked. Jenny looked over and saw Sharon's face floating behind the glass pane. They'd been doing that a lot since Liam had gone back inside—like ghosts appearing and fading, standing silently on the other side with that mournful, pitying look. Nothing to say.

Liam flitted back and forth. "Do you want a cup of tea?" "Is there anyone I can call?" and although his intrusions were clumsy and annoying, she could tell that he was trying to do the right thing. Jenny assumed the *Introduction to Supervisory Management* course he'd taken a few months ago probably didn't have a section on how to respond when one of your staff learns that her boyfriend has been killed in a car accident.

Jenny sat in the stairwell because she didn't know what to do. She looked up at the door. At least the latest ghost at the window had gone. Bad enough to have ghosts phoning her without them floating around the place too.

Gail came to the glass paneled door, but unlike the other ghosts, she pushed it open and sat down in the stairwell beside Jenny.

"How are you?" she asked.

"Bad day. Some old biddy's got a nest full of Starlings wedged down her chimney and my boyfriend's lying dead in a Brighton morgue."

"I'm sorry," Gail said.

Jenny looked at her. For a moment she couldn't remember who the woman standing in front of her was.

"I know we gave you a hard time about Mick, and I'm sorry."

Jenny shrugged. It didn't seem important now. Nothing seemed important.

She started to stand up, crawling her hands up the wall. Her legs were numb from sitting down for so long. Shards of broken glass ran up and down the nerves in her calves. There was a moment, just as she got to her feet, when the stairwell flipped and spun and she thought she was going to crash down onto the floor. But when she stood she was only swaying slightly.

"Do you want me to go home with you?" Gail asked. "Make sure you get there okay? Liam won't mind if I finish my shift now, he'll probably agree to anything you ask."

"I'm going back in," Jenny said.

"I can pack up your things if you want; avoid all these people gawking at you."

"No. I'm going back in. What's the point in sitting at home going mad? At least while I'm here . . . "

"Are you sure?" Gail asked. "You've had a shock. No one expects you to work, not even Liam."

Jenny walked over to the door. Now it was her turn to stare through the little glass window, out onto the call floor. All she could see were people hunched over their computers, tapping away at keyboards. For some reason she was struck by the image of battery hens—rows and rows of them clucking and pecking, grain in and eggs out. Not so different here.

It was crap, but then so were most of the jobs, and at least in this one they paid her to talk. And Mick had always said that any job in which Jenny was paid to talk was perfect for her.

Mick had said. Past tense—now everything about Mick was going to be in the past tense: he said, he did, he heard, he . . . died.

You spend too long thinking like that it's going to drive you mad, Jenny thought. She pushed the door open and walked through.

The constant babble of voices hit her, as it did every time she walked onto the floor when it was live. A couple of people turned around, but no one paused in the conversations they poured into their headsets.

Jenny walked over to her own booth and let Gail fuss over her for a couple of seconds before shooing her away. She looked up at the board, almost 500 calls waiting; she'd never seen the number so high—someone's balls were in the vise over this. She imagined all the managers in their little pre-fab cubby-holes watching the figures rising, loosening ties, beads of sweat on their foreheads. For sure, someone was going to get it today.

She put on the headset and felt an immediate rush of relief at the familiarity. The warm cushion against her ear, the slight press against her temple. She didn't know what to do about the mangled wreckage of Mick's Nissan somewhere near the bonny blue sea of Brighton, but she could answer the telephones.

She took a deep breath and then flicked the switch. The screen in front of her immediately flooded with the caller's details. The line was poor—crackling with static. Somewhere buried deep below it was a voice.

"I'm sorry, can you speak up," Jenny said. She scanned the details coming in. The call was from Newark, only 20 miles away. She'd probably be better off with a piece of string and a couple of tin cans.

" . . . need you . . . "

The only words she could make out, but nothing surprising with them—they all needed help. None of them ever rang up just for a chat. Well, except that guy down in Worthing.

"I'm sorry, but I'm having great difficulty hearing you," she tried to explain. The voice carried on chattering beneath the static, drowning under pips and crackles.

" . . . Jenny!"

Her name, screamed through the white noise, puncturing the static.

Mick.

She pulled the handset free from her ear, dropped it curled across the desk like a black snake. Even now she could hear the static rising up from the earpiece.

Jenny backed away from the desk, horrified.

Leave me alone.

The coil of wire looked as if it might start to twitch, might strike out at her. Images flickered in her mind of the grainy, dark photos Mick had been sending her. Where was that?

She turned away from the desk and ran. Across the calling floor. Hurried between corrals of desks. Past everyone with their heads bowed. She hit the door with both palms. Slammed it against the wall as she made her exit. The phone in her pocket began to ring.

By the time she reached the street her phone was quiet. It chirped one final time to tell her that she had a voice message. Jenny took the phone out of her pocket and turned it off.

She walked through roads lined with identical red-brick boxes, the offices only differentiated by little plaques and logos beside entrances. The best thing about these soulless industrial estates: She could walk through them in the middle of the day, bawling her eyes out, and there was no one around to see her.

It took Jenny nearly an hour to walk home.

She unlocked the door to the flat—it didn't seem noticeably different to how she'd left it that morning; the half-filled mug of coffee on the windowsill; faded knickers drying on the radiator, *The Time Traveler's Wife* open and face down on the arm of the sofa. The book made it obvious that Mick wasn't around. Whenever he came across her latest tented novel he would slip in a scrap of paper to mark her place.

No, not he *would*, he *had*. Now all her paperbacks would have broken spines.

Like him? A flash of his body in the car wreck—crumpled and crushed. Jenny collapsed onto the sofa, trying to banish the image, but every time she closed her eyes it was waiting for her.

The telephone began to ring. Jenny realized she was holding her breath, waiting for the answer machine to trip on.

She walked across the room, listening to her own recorded voice.

" . . . can't be bothered to answer . . . "

And faintly she could hear Mick's laugh in the background and she could remember when she'd recorded that message. Her sitting on the edge of the sofa, glass of wine in her hand. The alcohol adding a soft burr to her voice that Mick claimed was sexy. Mick beside her, suggesting what she should say on her message.

" . . . after the beep . . . "

He was all around her. Not just in the photos or his laughter floating at the back of the message, he *haunted* the room.

She walked over to the phone, like so many other times, ready to pick it up if it was Mick, or her brother, or . . .

The long beep and then a crackle. White noise.

"Need you . . . "

Mick's voice through the static.

Jenny picked up the phone. "Mick."

"I . . . need . . . you."

She could hear the effort it took him to speak.

"What do you need me to do?" she asked.

"I . . . need . . . you . . . " his voice so strained.

Yes, Jenny thought silently, encouraging.

" . . . you . . . to . . . come . . . "

Okay. Okay.

" . . . with . . . me."

Jenny screamed and slammed down the phone.

Her whole body was shaking. She sat down on the floor. She could still hear the hum of the white noise and the hypnotic babble of Mick's voice. He couldn't mean it. She must have misunderstood, because he couldn't mean . . .

The phone started to ring.

"Leave me alone," Jenny screamed.

It rang; three, four, five times until the answer machine clicked on. Then a long, drawn out single tone, like a car horn sounding after an accident.

Jenny heard the soft crackle and pop of static on the line and could feel the person at the other end of the phone—as if *he* was listening to her. Waiting for her to make a sound.

Stupid, she knew that, but no more ridiculous than the idea of Mick ringing her after he had died, or sending her photos on a mobile that, the more she thought about those pictures, represented what his dead eyes saw: a marbled darkness.

"Jenny? Jenny are you there? Pick up if you're around."

"Oh." She actually sobbed with relief; a proper voice—Helen.

Jenny grabbed the phone. "I'm here."

"I just wanted to check if you were okay. Gail rang me up and told me about Mick. I don't know what to say. I'm sorry."

"He won't leave me alone," Jenny blurted.

Silence. She wondered what Helen was thinking.

"He keeps calling me."

Helen's voice came back, soft and neutral. The calm voice she used with customers to explain that the contractors couldn't be on site in the next ten minutes.

"He's dead, Jenny."

"My phone. You saw the pictures."

"Mick is dead. He can't hurt you anymore."

"I heard him, Helen. I heard him on the phone. He wants me to . . . to . . . " Jenny heard emotion crack her voice, then it rushed like water through a broken dam and she was sobbing.

"I'm coming over," Helen said.

"Please," Jenny said. She couldn't be alone, better to have the house full of screaming, chattering people than cold and silent as . . . well, silent as the grave.

She shuddered.

"I'll be right over," Helen said and then carried on talking but Jenny couldn't hear her, because instead all she could hear were the noises in the background—soft and subtle.

"Need you, Jenny," Mick breathed. "Need you to come with me."

She bit down on the scream.

"Leave me alone!" she shouted over the voice (Needyou, Needyoutocome, Comewithme, Youwithme). She was aware Helen was talking but the other voice was too loud and Jenny couldn't tell which voice was Helen's and which was Mick's.

"Sorry." She slammed down the phone and silence rushed in like a storm.

The phone started to ring. Jenny could hear the voice over and over in her head. Is this what it feels like to go mad?

Ring-ring

Needyou.

Ring-ring

Come with me

She reached around the back of the cupboard, pulled the phone out of its socket. The last ring faded away and then the phone lay on the desktop, dead.

A door slammed. Next door. Jenny screamed in fright. Music bled from The Tavern at the far end of the street—it sounded like a different world; a world where you didn't scream and piss yourself with fear at every loud noise or every time a phone rang.

From inside her handbag her mobile phone chirped: another message. She thought she'd turned it off, she thought—it rang again, another message. The thing shuddered with urgency. Call after call coming through. She wanted to ignore them but it was impossible. Jenny went across the room and opened her handbag. The phone lay inside, shaking as another and another and another message came through and the display screen lit up with: YOU HAVE 17 . . . 18 . . . 19 MESSAGES. The numbers just counting up.

She picked up the phone. It showed the first text: NEED U. And then another black photo. Another photo, lighter. Coming out of the darkness into—a clear image now—the pavement in front of The Tavern.

Jenny screamed and threw the phone away. It smashed against the wall, dented the plaster and then broke. The battery, the front and the back all separated.

The phone rang! No battery in the bastard thing but it still rang, and then the house phone, the phone Jenny *knew* she'd just unplugged, started to ring too.

The radio clicked on in the kitchen—a burst of static and then the voices rising up from the white noise: needyou, needyou. The husk of the mobile phone on the floor shuddered as another message came through. The TV turned on, the screen filled with a speckled display of black and white dots and the speakers pushed out a rising hum. The picture cleared, changed to a sepia image: slightly blurred but definitely the path to Jenny's house. Through the windows she was watching an image of herself staring down at the TV watching herself watching . . .

She jerked her head upwards, stared out of the window. Expecting to see Mick, but there was no one. The path beyond her door was empty. Jenny looked back down to the TV screen.

He was inside the house. In the hallway.

"Needyou," the voice crackled through the static. No hiding the desperate hunger in his voice. On the screen she could see her hallway. The blurred image turned and looked through the door at Jenny standing in the middle of the room staring down at the television.

"Needyou," the voice called and she could feel the cold, dry breath on the back of her neck.

Jenny wanted to scream 'no!' but she couldn't form the word. It struck her then—she couldn't *ever* remember saying 'no' to Mick. She flinched, braced herself for the slap. Mick had never hit her, she wouldn't have stood for *that*, and yet she realized now that the threat of violence had always been there, simmering beneath the surface.

"No," but the word was too weak.

The screen darkened: a blackness freckled with spots of deep red and dark blue. And then Jenny realized it wasn't the screen—it was her. She couldn't see.

She felt Mick touch her—pressing against her arms, her legs. Pressing onto her and then into her and heard his cold voice: "Needyou" the words spoken aloud through her mouth. Cracked and stilted on her dry tongue. Felt him inside her, clamoring for each fragment of warmth within her body.

She gave in—as she always did with Mick. Controlling to

165

the very end.

"Needyoutocomewithme—forever."

And she did.

The Balancing Act

Lawrence Conquest

I've always been afraid of violence. I guess most people do their best to avoid it, but the very thought of confrontation sends me into a state of panic.

The trouble is I empathize too much. If I hear about something awful on the news I'll brood over it, casting myself in the role of the victim, vicariously replaying the scenario over and again in my mind. An incident that may have lasted only a few minutes in real time can disturb me for days.

And what must it feel like to be stabbed, I wonder? To be beaten, maimed, killed? How can a person live with the memory of so much pain? How can they cope?

I'd sooner run than get caught up in violence. Confrontation just isn't in my nature. I'm a coward and proud of it.

So I'm having a little difficulty working out what's gone wrong with my face. It bears all the hallmarks of violence, yet I remain ignorant of the cause. I reach up and my fingers come away tacky with blood. Worse, when I touch myself I can feel the sensation only in my fingertips. My face is numb, as though the nerves beneath the skin have been severed. My features are puffy and bloated to the touch. It feels nothing like me and everything like a badly made mask.

I walk slowly towards a nearby shop window. Early evening street lights reflect off the glass, transforming the substance into a ready-made mirror. I fail to recognize the figure that stares back. His face is beaten and bruised, a jagged tear across his hairline leaking some kind of crimson paste. I step closer. My shadow blots out the light and my own reflection is replaced by the view of the shop interior. It is a budget supermarket, one of those new ones specializing in cheap foreign brands. I recognize it instantly, and walk inside.

The store is nearly deserted at this hour, with barely a handful of late-night shoppers browsing its aisles like hungry ghosts. You are behind the till, flicking through a gossip magazine and idly twirling one finger through your long, blonde hair. You look up as I approach. You are young, petite, with striking Slavic features. I think I might find you attractive, were it not for the strangeness of the situation.

"Excuse me," I hesitantly say. "I know this must sound odd, but I think that something has happened to me. Only I'm not entirely sure what." My words sound strange. Unnatural. More like lines of scripted dialogue than real conversation.

You look both shocked and slightly afraid. "God! Are you alright? What happened? An accident, or—?"

I wish I could answer you, I really do. I wish I could put your mind at rest, smile and tell you that it's all just an elaborate joke. But the fact remains that I have no memory of how I came by my injuries, or even how I came to this place. I suddenly realize that I cannot remember my name, or where I live. The facts seem elusive, and slip out of my clumsy grasp like wriggling fish. It's utterly ridiculous, and yet somehow it's true.

You call the manager and he leads me away. He takes me into a stockroom and tells me to sit. I feel like an intruder, sat here amongst the pallets of baked beans and toilet paper. I shouldn't be seeing this. I'm a customer, not an employee. Why is everybody being so nice to me?

A paramedic arrives fifteen minutes later, and casts an expert eye over my wounds. Nothing broken, as far as he can tell. Concussion is probable, he says. Either way, hospital scans are required. The paramedic leads me out of the shop and towards his waiting car. As I pass you, I offer a sympathetic smile. I'm sorry to have disturbed your evening. I don't know what's going on any more than you.

I still feel like a fraud, an actor in a badly-written play. Amnesia is such a cliché. And yet despite the concern in other people's eyes, I feel no pain myself, only a dull sense of numbness. The long dreaded moment of violence has been and gone, and yet I remain oblivious of the fact. The irony is not lost upon me.

God must love me. Only later do I realize how much.

* * *

The next evening I revisit the supermarket, ostensibly to buy food, in reality to see you. It strikes me that I may have alarmed you with my gruesome appearance the night before. I thank you for your assistance and assure you that I am much recovered. We shake hands and I tell you my name: Lawrence, spelled with a W, not a U. You tell me your name is Grażyna. After some gentle probing you reveal that it is Lithuanian for 'beautiful.' I smile. Your parents picked an appropriate name. You smile back.

Feeling confident, I ask you out for lunch. You say yes.

The scales are rising.

* * *

"Do you remember what happened?" you ask. "Has it come back to you yet?"

"Some of it, yes," I reply. "Not to put too fine a point on it, I was beaten up by a gang of kids. Well—I say kids, they were probably about fifteen-years-old, but there were enough of them that I didn't stand a chance."

You look shocked. "But why did they attack you?"

I shrug. "No reason. Stupid, really. I'd gone down to the local newsagents and this kid was loitering in the doorway, getting in the way. Just making trouble, the way kids do."

"What did you do?"

"I asked him to move. That's all. And when he didn't, I brushed past him. He started having a go at me, so I told him that if he was going to stand in doorways he should expect people to push past. I don't normally go in for confrontation, but there was only one of him and he was a scrawny looking kid.

"Trouble was, it turned out he wasn't alone. When I left the shop about a half-dozen of his mates turned up out of nowhere. They started following me and I knew I was in trouble. I tried to run, but one of them tripped me up. I was sent sprawling on the pavement and that was it. The last thing I remember is them coming towards me. After that, nothing."

"Nothing?"

"A complete blank. The next thing I *do* remember is finding myself outside of your place, and wondering just what the hell had happened. I still can't remember the details of the assault itself."

You shake your head. "That's terrible."

I laugh. "I think it's pretty amazing actually."

"What?"

"Just think. Maybe I fought back. Or maybe I didn't. They could have done anything to me, anything at all. Maybe it was all over in one punch, or maybe they tortured me for a while. Perhaps they jumped up and down on my head and used it as a football for half an hour. The point is, *it doesn't matter* what they did because I can't remember it. The only outcome of the whole incident has been a good thing: meeting you. They did me a favor, if you think about it."

Your voice is raised, angry. "But what if one of them had a knife? They might have killed you!"

"True, but so what if they had? Would it have mattered to me? After all, if I was dead I wouldn't be around to remember whatever pain they inflicted. Violence only matters if you can remember it. Thankfully, I can't. It's like being sedated before an operation. Who cares what the surgeon does while you're unconscious?"

"Well, do be careful. They must be local. What will happen if they see you again?"

"Oh, don't you worry on that score—I'm planning on it."

* * *

The next time I'm not quite so lucky.

I take to hanging around the newsagents, waiting for the gang to strike again. I see them most days. Old enough to skip school with impunity, yet young enough to get away without working, the youths seem to congregate around the parade of shops as though drawn by magnetic attraction. And yet, despite my best efforts, they don't want anything to do with me. Maybe the sight of my slowly healing injuries gives them pause. The bruises have turned an alarming rainbow of colors, a vibrant reminder of their physical abuse. Possibly they think I am mad, or just setting them up for the police. I taunt them on street corners, calling them every name under the sun. They look suspiciously at the nearest CCTV cameras, crane their necks back into their hoodies like bashful tortoises, and studiously ignore me. They just don't care.

Or at least that's the impression I'm under, until they break into my flat.

One of them must have followed me home without my noticing. One minute I am asleep, the next I am awoken by the sound of the front door being kicked off its hinges.

170

The beating is more serious than before. I end up with two broken ribs and a collapsed lung. I also lose a part of one ear and several teeth. Again, I have no memory of the actual assault. It is as though the incident has been erased from my mind. All I am left with are the after-effects.

I am hospital-bound for the best part of a month. I have to stay off work another two. The good news is that during this time I see a lot more of you. The beatings seem to bring out the caring, mothering instinct in you. You spent every spare moment at the flat, nursing me back to health and generally doing your best to care for me. By the time I am recovered you care for me enough to tell me that you love me. Within a year we are married.

Every cloud has a silver lining.

* * *

I know you wonder why. I'm *telling* you why.

I know it's going to hurt, believe me. But it won't last forever.

Listen. Can you hear it yet?

* * *

I suspect about your affair, though I never actually find any proof. All the signs are there, though. You appear distant, cold. I go to kiss you, and you turn your head and present me with your cheek. You start spending more time with your friends. You come home late, some nights not at all.

I cannot blame you. Things haven't been good recently. We seem trapped in this dead-end town. You with your supermarket work, on minimal pay for all hours of the day. Me with a trade where the opportunities are withering in a shrinking economy.

And yet, for once, my luck seems to turn. My firm gets a commission to renovate part of the local hospital. It will only last a few weeks, but I'll take any work I can get. I'm grateful to be working. Focused. Happy.

So I'm not sure how the accident happens. To be honest I'm not even sure if it *is* an accident.

One minute I'm cutting lengths of oak flooring on a table saw, the next minute I'm lying in a hospital bed with you by my

171

side. When I awake you smother me with kisses, telling me how lucky I am to be alive. Your eyes are red from crying. I wonder what I have done to gain such affection.

You tell me that the details are vague, but apparently something happened at work. Somehow I got caught in the table saw, and before I could hit the emergency stop it had taken away most of my hand. Three fingers had been partially severed, with the tendons chewed so badly that the doctors say I'll never be able to make a fist again. They say I should consider myself lucky. They say the fact that I'm even alive means someone up there must like me.

But was it an accident, or was it deliberate? To be honest I can't remember. I do remember looking at the blade as it tore through the wood like a shark through water. I remember wondering if my life would ever improve, or if I'd be stuck scraping a living from this trade for the rest of my life. And then—nothing. Once again, the actual moment of violence seems to have passed me by. The doctors tell me this is not unusual. Moments of extreme trauma often cannot be recalled by the recovered patient. It's the mind's self-defence mechanism, apparently. It doesn't need that information to survive.

I want you to remember this. It's important. The pain will pass.

Anyway, I'm feeling pretty low after the accident, but it doesn't last long. My near-death experience only brings home how much we truly value each other. Recovering from the trauma, our love seems to grow that much stronger. Violence brings us together. It's like breaking a bone to reset it. Sometimes you have to hurt the better to heal.

Of course, my career in the building trade is pretty much finished after that, but the three-quarter of a million pound payout helps cushion the blow.

* * *

Apparently there is some sort of device you can fit to a table saw these days, a sensor designed to stop precisely the sort of accident occurring that happened to me. Of course my employers were too tight-fisted to have fitted one. They claimed that the accident was down to my own negligence, and that the saw was perfectly safe.

The judge disagreed. Balance is restored.

172

For every action, there is an equal and opposite reaction. Isaac Newton once said that, and it is my considered opinion that he was right. Good and evil will always balance out in the end. Harmony is the natural state of the universe. All things will equal, given time.

I thought we had reached our perfect balance. We were happy, you and I. The move into the country removed us from the stresses of modern day life, allowing us to focus only on each other. Of course we had the usual little ups and downs, but the scales continued to balance themselves as was their due.

And then came the greatest gift of all: Joanna. Our beautiful daughter, radiant, unique, she turned our every day into a shining moment of bliss.

I should have known there'd be hell to pay.

* * *

Our poses are not by chance. I have arranged our splayed out forms with great care. When the train hits, our bodies shall be as nothing before the force of its industry. Its wheels will cut through our flesh like butter, paralyzing and quartering, slicing our spinal cords just so. The jutting stumps of our arms and legs shall be pruned back like the limbs of overgrown trees. Extremities removed, our lives will be cut to the quick.

We sprawl across the tracks like murder victims. All that's missing are chalk outlines and the flash and pop of a police photographer's camera. I imagine a surrounding frieze of puzzled faces, as the accident investigators try to work out just how such a terrible tragedy could have occurred.

Perhaps this is a vision of what is yet to come. Perhaps we shall die here, our bodies divided into a grisly jigsaw that only a team of skilled pathologists will be able to piece together.

Or perhaps the driver will see us in time to brake, to ensure that our wounds are merely crippling instead of fatal? Perhaps the drugs I administered will wear off earlier than intended, and one or both us will drag ourselves to safety?

I leave it in the lap of the Gods.

But we have to *try*. Some risks are worth the taking. A gambler's winnings will only match the strength of their initial bet. We have to place our very lives in hazard for what we truly cherish. Only then may the scales balance again. Only then might Joanna's leukaemia enter remission, her tiny body recovering from its internal trauma as our own bodies lie broken beneath the soil.

Good luck must follow bad. It is all a matter of balance.

So do not struggle, my darling. Our thoughts must be pure. The Ancient Egyptian's believed that they would be judged upon their deaths. That their hearts would be weighed against their sins upon the scales of *Maat*. Law. Morality. Justice. Soon the cutting wheels will free our own internal organs from the shackles of the flesh. Our hearts will burst forth from our chests like bright red birds, lighter than the air. Lighter than our sins.

Do not cry, Grażyna. The drugs that have slowed our reactions will not lessen the pain before us, that much is true. That agony is inevitable now. But we will suffer together through it, you and I. Should we survive, our minds will of necessity forget the searing moment of torment. For the memory of such pain would surely be unbearable. Such memories will live on only in the healing scars of the flesh, not the eternal now of the mind.

But listen. Can you hear it? The train is fast approaching. I can feel the track vibrating beneath us. Judgement is swift.

Whatever happens next, pray God we shall not remember it.

Somebody's Daughter

Angela Bodine

Her name was Tami. She was beautiful and curvaceous, with legs so long and smooth that any pervert with half a brain could imagine how silky they must have felt. Exposing her lightly-tanned skin—draped, stretched, arched—across the magazine covers, Tami was the definitive object of desire. She was youthful. She was alluring. She was erotic.

She was somebody's daughter. She was mine.

* * *

It was foggy that night. It should always be foggy when your child dies. Much better than a blue sky full of sunshine, because whatever the weather's like, it's always going to remind you of that night. That horrible night your whole reason for living was extinguished. A blue sky full of sunshine, so much more common than fog, would have only been a mockery.

The sun had been out when I got the call. "Mom, I need you. Can you come?" Just like when she'd been a baby, leaning against the railing of her crib and reaching out with those chubby little arms. Only now, instead of a hallway separating us, it was a continent.

The plane ride was the worst, sitting there in that seat, trying to be calm despite the fact that my baby was out there waiting for me, crying for her mama. It gave me plenty of time to think about what had gone wrong though; think how the chubby, little cherub I'd once known had grown into the kind of woman who would sell glimpses of every inch of her body to millions of strangers.

I had tried to do everything right. Sure, I'd let her wear make-up when she was thirteen ("but, Mom, all the other girls are wearing it"), but I absolutely, positively *refused* to let her have a boob job for her sixteenth birthday. Okay, so maybe I let her get the implants just one year later, but I'd known she was nearly a legal adult and I didn't want us to become estranged. Other than that, Tami was an

175

exemplary child. She'd done fine without a father. Honor roll, no drugs that I knew of, kept her room clean; she was an ideal child and teenager. Hearing my girlfriends talk about the hell their own teenagers were putting them through, I'd felt lucky. No, not lucky. Proud. Proud because I was a good parent and that was reflected through my child's pristine behavior.

I stopped talking to those girlfriends the day I spotted Tami's left breast exposed to the nipple in a grocery store checkout line. It took about two years of pleading and begging and yelling before I stopped talking to Tami, too. And when I finally did hear from her, it was "*Mom, I need you. Can you come?*" Those words reverberated within my entire body throughout the plane ride, every nuance of every syllable coursing through my being until they were transformed into "*Help me! Help me!*" But I could only sit for excruciatingly endless hours and listen to the words in my head, feel them in my soul, as I waited for the plane to deliver me to my baby.

When the plane finally landed on the east coast, the sun had had set, allowing the slinking fog to garnish my memories of Tami's death night: vaporous and surreal. I have no recollection at all of how I got to Tami's house. Have you ever been through any kind of tragedy or trauma? Have you ever received *that* call while you're at work, going about your mundane tasks when suddenly they're cruelly interrupted, and aterwards all you want is nothing more than the mundane again? It's dizzying, disorienting. Like suddenly you're drunker than you've ever been, but you haven't had a drop of alcohol. How I was transported from the plane to Tami's front door isn't just a blur to me, it's a complete blank. I don't know if I walked, ran, hitched. Hell, for all I know, I could have been carried piggy-back on a priest's shoulders. I only wish what came after was so vague. But, no, unlike the fog that had kindly descended on my most unhappy of nights, my daughter's death is remembered with complete clarity. The blood. The screams. All of it.

And now I'm going to tell it to you, so that you can carry the horrible images with you through your daily mundane tasks, the way I do. So that the next time you see a fog bank, and you squint your eyes just so, you might see the shapely outline of an alluring vixen who used to be somebody's daughter. You're not starting to feel a bit squeamish, are you, knowing what's coming next? It's not pretty. Nothing like the curves and folds you're used to staring at in the magazines.

So, there I was, standing before Tami's front door, the fog swirling behind me and the fear swirling within me. The brass knocker on the door was in the shape of a nude woman. It might have been classy—placed there in the opulent house with more stories than I'd bothered to count—if I could've stopped picturing Tami's face on the object. Throughout the entire plane ride (and presumably during my unexplainable journey to her house), I had been overwhelmed by the urgency to reach my child. But now that I was there, I was overcome by dread. Dread that I was too late. Because sometimes, call it maternal instinct if you will, but sometimes a mother just *knows*.

I knocked.

The nude knocker was cold and moist from the weather, and I wiped my hand on my jeans repeatedly, trying to rub the dirty feeling off of it. I was still rubbing when the door opened wide.

A servant was standing there to greet me. It struck me as absurd that my daughter, only a few months over the legal drinking age, should have a servant, but the thought was quickly overridden by the twenty-foot tall atrocity that loomed in front of me. Honestly, I couldn't even tell you what the servant looked like, even what color her skin was, because I was so taken aback by the portrait that hung in the entryway of the house. It was the worst, the absolute worst picture that I'd ever seen of my daughter.

It was the picture that had fueled our last argument before we'd stopped talking to one another. It had been on the cover of a well-known fashion magazine, I can't recall exactly which one, and it was even more appalling in its twenty-foot hideousness.

I remembered how Tami had defended the photo of herself: "*Mom, get with it. It's just the next wave. Models and singers are showing more and more of themselves. It's the evolution of the fashion industry. The more you expose, the more exposure you get.*"

I looked up at Tami's picture in the entryway to her house, saw my daughter in a skimpy pink shirt that was more of a bra with the fabric removed so that her entire areolas were exposed, and felt nauseated. It didn't help when I realized that, in the blown-up photograph, her nipples were bigger than my head.

"This way, ma'am. She's been waiting for you."

I followed the servant (God, I can't remember at all what she looked like), trying to look anywhere but at that damned picture.

Upstairs, I was led down a hallway and left alone. I stood

before a door that was cracked open, so just a little bit of golden light spilled through. I was taken back to all those nights ago when I had peeked through the door into Tami's nursery, wanting to check on her but not wanting to disturb her. I thought of how she use to fall asleep on my shoulder, cradling her face in the crook of my neck, so content and secure. It had been heaven.

I took a breath, slid the door open, and entered hell.

I can see that room in my mind, even now, with complete clarity. Oh, how I wish that the window could have been opened to let the fog creep in and obscure the scene! The golden light that I had seen seeping through the crack in the door had come from a large fireplace, its crackling luminescence the only light in the room. There was a bearskin rug laid out before the fireplace, the empty carcass of a proud animal that had once roamed the country only to be killed and gutted and turned into a furnishing. The hardwood floor flowed out and away from the bearskin rug, leading to a large canopy bed directly across from the fireplace. The canopy, a dark burgundy like rich wine or spilled blood, was drawn shut.

It didn't occur to me at the time that this was the same room Tami had often dreamed about as a child. I've spent many nights and days thinking about it since, seeing that room over and over again. Just three items in the huge empty space: a fireplace, the bearskin rug and the canopy bed. Tami, with all of her ill-earned fortune, could have furnished the room with just about anything. Sculptures. A Jacuzzi. Expensive paintings and furniture. But, no, she had only those three items in her bedroom. I realized it after many nights and days of seeing the room in my mind. The canopy bed was a grown-up version of the 'princess bed' she had always wanted as a young child. The fireplace was a grown-up manifestation of the innocent concern she'd once had that *'Santa Claus can't come in and leave me presents without a chimney.'* And the bearskin rug? Well, once he had had a name. It was Fluffy, and he had lived on the pillow of one little girl's ordinary bed, there to protect her and soothe her from her bigger-than-life childhood fears.

The room of my daughter's dreams had become real, and it had become my nightmare.

"Mom?"

The voice that came from behind the canopy was weak, barely discernable. It sounded as if it was muffled by the heavy fabric, but I would soon know better. I approached, feeling the heat

178

from the roaring fireplace at my back. I stopped at the edge of the bed, hesitating.

"Tami?"

The canopy before me parted, like the curtains on a stage, revealing a show. *Ladies and gentleman!* It was dark within the bed, and it took my eyes a moment to adjust to the gloomy shadows. *Feast your eyes on tonight's attraction!* The bed was large, my daughter small in it. *Tonight we have a grand surprise for your amusement!* Her body was covered by heavy blankets, despite the heat coming from the fireplace. *We are uncovering something that will amaze you!* Her face seemed to be covered with blankets as well, but as my eyes adjusted I realized that there were no blankets at all. *It will astound you!* Bandages. My daughter's entire body was covered in bandages. *Ladies and gentleman!* The bandages were not white, but red, a deep burgundy like rich wine, or—*feast your eyes on the amazing*—spilled blood. There was not an inch of her body—*the incomparable*—that wasn't covered in bloody bandages, except—*the beautiful, Tami!*—for her eyes.

I knew those eyes. Somewhere beneath those layers of blood-soaked dressings was my daughter.

I think I whimpered. The eyes flinched slightly. Not much. Not enough.

"Mom?" The voice was weak, and now I knew why it had sounded so muffled before.

I reached out for where her hand should have been buried in the bandages. I didn't recoil at all from the blood. Moms aren't repulsed by a little blood (or vomit, or diarrhea), if it comes out of their kid. One of the glories of being a mother, I suppose.

I tried to ask her what had happened to her, but all I could manage was another whimper, this one a little stronger than before. My eyes grew teary (another side effect of motherhood) at seeing my daughter in that condition.

Finally, I managed to speak. The words that came out were not the ones that I had intended to speak, but at least it wasn't just a whimper.

"Does it hurt?"

Does it hurt?! My daughter's entire body was bloody and bandaged, and all I can think to ask is the only question that I already knew the answer to!

The eyes I knew flickered within the blood-drenched mask.

179

"Not so much. They have me on a lot of painkillers, the good stuff."

"Good." *Good.* Nothing about that was good!

"I need you to see, Mom, now, before, before you see somewhere else."

I wondered how many painkillers they had her on. I wondered what it was she needed me to see. I wondered where in the hell the sweet, chubby baby that had once clung to my finger had gone.

"Take the bandage off, the . . . the one on my face."

Remember earlier, when I told you it wasn't going to be pretty? Remember how I told you there would be blood and there would be screaming? Well, the blood was my little girl's.

With shaking hands, I obliged, simultaneously curious and terrified. For all the blood, the bandage came off fairly easy.

And the screaming? The screams were all mine.

With perfect clarity, the image of my daughter's eyes set in the face of a monster will always haunt me. The blood and the gristle. The exposed muscle and bone. The gore and the horror. A mother can only take so much.

Tami spoke again—I *saw* the jaw bone lift and fall—but now her words were not muffled by bandages but by my screams. Yet I still heard what she said. And with those words, my daughter died.

"It's the . . . the next step, Mom. The newest trend. The clothes, they got smaller and smaller. More and more flesh exposed. But what's left, when, when you've already shown everything?"

I kept screaming until I'd left behind my daughter in her childhood dream room and even the fog that had marked the death night of my once-cherubic Tami. I kept screaming long after I stopped making any noise.

* * *

There's a girl on all the magazines with my daughter's name and body, but her face is that of a monster. Girls all over the world are trying to imitate her, and hundreds have already died at the hands of back-alley butchers. She's nothing more than a murderer, this thing, and they say she has a face only her mother and a camera could love.

Now I Lay Me Down to Sleep

Matthew S. Dent

Pam awoke to the darkness. She had the distinct impression of having been awoken by *something*, but she was still too sleepy to pinpoint precisely what it had been.

Sitting up, she saw through her open bedroom door that the bathroom light was on. Its pale light spilled out and illuminated the hallway.

Donna, her mind realized, groggily

Her daughter hadn't been sleeping well lately. She'd developed a habit of getting drinks of water in the middle of the night but unfortunately, hadn't taken to turning the light off afterwards.

Hearing a sudden creak of the floorboards, Pam guessed that the light hadn't been on long. Donna could only just have returned to her room. With a deep breath, Pam threw off the heavy duvet and swung herself out of bed.

The hallway was cold, and Pam's thin nightie wasn't really appropriate for the middle of a winter night. Shivering, she turned towards Donna's room. The bathroom light could wait until after she'd checked on her daughter. The extractor fan hummed away in the background, like a giant insect on the toilet.

Donna was in her bed, sitting up against the headboard with her knees tucked into her chest. Her plastic cup—translucent pink, with ponies prancing around the edge—was clutched tight in her little hand. Her teddy, the one with the missing arm, lay on the pillow.

"Donna, honey!" Fussing, Pam drew her daughter's duvet close around the little girl. She set the cup on the nightstand and lay Donna back down. "You'll freeze if you don't keep covered up."

Pam silently cursed the central heating system which had chosen the most inopportune moment to seize up. It had taken three days of persuading, cajoling and threatening for her to get Neil to wire her the money for repairs. Then, British Gas had told her that unfortunately, all of their technicians were too busy, ma'am, and an

181

engineer couldn't get to them until the next day. So Pam and Donna had to survive a little longer without the warmth their aching bones craved.

"Sorry, mummy," Donna said timidly. "You woke me up and I was thirsty."

"*I* woke you up?"

"You were talking. Is daddy home?" Excitement leapt in Donna's voice, and for a moment guilt overwhelmed Pam's confusion. Her daughter smiled a gap-toothed smile up at her, with a corona of reddish brown hair surrounding the pillow.

"Talking? No, I wasn't . . . " she said, confused. "No, honey, daddy isn't here."

"Oh." Donna tried her best to hide her disappointment. "Well I heard talking, mummy. Honest I did."

"It's okay, sweetie," Pam reassured her, gently stroking her hair. "I must have been talking in my sleep. I'm sorry I woke you up." She forced a smile. "Do you think you can get back to sleep now?"

"Yes, mummy." Donna smiled, finished her water, and lay back down. Pam tucked her in tightly with a kiss on the forehead. "Goodnight, mummy!"

"Goodnight, Donna."

Leaving Donna's room, with an irrepressible smile at the simplicity of Donnas view of life, Pam turned off the bathroom light. The buzz of the extractor fell into the lurking silence, which rose up out of the darkness and haunted her as she passed the third bedroom on her way back to her own.

Through the open door, she could see the silhouettes of the still mobile and the empty crib, bathed in the moonlight. She looked away quickly, but it was too late, she had seen it. The sight exacerbated the sting of Donna's comments, opening up a festering wound that had never really healed.

Donna must have been in there. Pam would never have left *that* door open. But she was too tired and drained to dwell on it.

She returned to bed tearful and eager for sleep—sleep which eluded her as her pillow dampened.

* * *

The following night, Pam was up late. The heating had been

fixed that afternoon, and the house was pleasantly warm—toasty, even. When the clock radio displayed 1:00, she was still awake, reading a collection of ghost stories in bed.

She sighed, and placed the book down on her lap. She wasn't a fan of ghost stories, but the book had been on the shelf downstairs—one of Neil's no doubt—and had looked interesting. It wasn't. And now, after a few unimpressive tales, she found herself weary of it, but not yet tired.

Donna was tucked in bed, fast asleep. She hadn't stirred so far tonight, for which Pam was very grateful. It had been almost a year and Donna was only just getting back to sleeping through the night. Pam shifted uncomfortably, her eyes were drawn to the third bedroom, the doorframe dimly visible through the open door of her own bedroom.

The door was closed again. It was the only thing she could do to take the edge off the painful memories inside. Memories that she would never be able to forget.

She sighed, reaching for an orange plastic bottle on the nightstand. She popped the top off and tipped two pills onto her hand, before throwing them into her mouth. They were difficult to swallow without water, but she wouldn't allow herself a drop.

Grief should be painful, something inside her insisted. It should be difficult. It should be unpleasant. It should *hurt*. The only way that Pam could take the antidepressants was to force them down over a period of hours.

She lay back down, returning the little bottle of Fluoxetine to the nightstand, and prepared for the long descent into sleep. But no sooner had her head touched the linen, than she heard something out in the hall.

She turned to the door, threw off the covers, and got ready to get up and check on Donna. But she froze halfway up. The bathroom light illuminated the hall, and the extractor fan was once again humming away. Pam didn't remember it starting. Had she fallen asleep?

And there, silhouetted in the yellow light, was the dark shape of a little girl.

"D-Donna?"

The child didn't respond. She stood there in her nightdress, a disfigured teddy bear dangling loosely by its solitary arm, one woolen foot scraping the floor. Pam couldn't see her daughter's face. She suddenly wasn't sure that she wanted to. The secrets veiled in the shadowy darkness were perhaps better kept secret.

"Donna, honey." Pam forced herself to keep her voice steady, but it still came out thin and reedy—a tiny sound in a chasm of nothing. She shivered. Why did the sight of her own daughter unnerve her so much?

"Donna, what are you doing awake? Are you alright?"

Donna didn't answer, she just kept staring. Or at least, Pam assumed she was staring. Her eyes were lost in darkness, so there was no way of being sure. But Pam's skin crawled like she was being watched.

The silhouetted child raised her empty hand, pointing an outstretched finger at her mother. Pam's stomach tightened. Her throat was dry.

Forcing herself to swallow, she placed the ball of her foot lightly on the carpet. The bristles felt warm to the touch. Donna didn't move, just continued pointing at her mother with one hand; the bear dangled wordlessly from her other hand.

"Donna, what's wrong?" Pam gathered confidence from the success of her initial move, and stood up. She took a step towards her daughter.

Donna turned immediately back towards the bedroom from which she had come. As she did so, her face turned into the light from the bathroom and Pam saw her face. Her eyes were closed. Not scrunched, as if she were pressing them shut, but lightly, with the slight movement of her eyes flittering beneath betraying the fact that she was asleep.

Sleepwalking? Pam was surprised. It wasn't, she knew, an uncommon reaction to grief. She'd read all the informative literature on mourning that she could lay her hands on. But actually seeing it was startling nonetheless.

Donna had never walked in her sleep. In fact, She'd never witnessed *any* of the classic grief reactions in her little girl. Other than waking up thirsty in the night, Donna seemed perfectly fine.

Slowly, but without hesitation, Donna walked back in the direction of her room. Pam followed, but by the time she reached her daughter's bedroom, the little girl was tucked back into bed.

Pam faltered. She was sure Donna hadn't had time enough to arrange herself so neatly. It was like she had never been gone. But she had seen Donna's face. She had definitely seemed to be asleep. Pam paused for a moment in the doorway, unsure of whether to inspect closer.

No, she decided eventually. No, Donna was asleep now, safely in bed. Whatever had happened, Pam could speak to her about it in the morning. There was no sense in disturbing her now.

Pam turned back towards her room, once again turning off the bathroom light along the way. But in the remaining silence, Pam found herself tossing and turning, unable to rest her racing mind.

* * *

The next morning, Pam poured milk into her cereal as Donna watched the cartoons dancing across the television. Her eyes were fixed on the screen, watching the characters play out their parts. She didn't look tired. She didn't look like she'd been up in the night, scaring Pam half to death.

"Eat your breakfast, sweetie," Pam told her with a tired smile. The skin felt tight and drawn around her eyes. "You're going to be late for school." Donna didn't respond. "Donna!"

She looked up. "Sorry, mummy." She shoveled a spoonful into her mouth. The sugary puffs floated on a brown lake of chocolate milk, just how she liked it. She would eat about half of it, maybe more. But there would still be a little pool of milk in the bottom, a mound of cereal lurking like a sickly, sweet iceberg just beneath the surface.

"Donna, did you . . .wake up last night?" she asked, uncertainly.

"I don't think so. I don't remember waking up, mummy."

"Not even for a drink? Or to go to the toilet?"

Donna thought for a moment and shook her head, her reddish-brown locks bouncing. "Nope," she said, looking up with almond-shaped eyes. Her father's eyes. "You weren't talking last night. You didn't wake me up."

Donna smiled an innocent smile, and turned her attention back to her breakfast, slurping at the milk. Pam gave another smile, and put a hand to her daughter's head, burying her fingers in her red hair.

* * *

Pam awoke with a start, sucking air deep into her lungs. It was cold and tangible, an anchor to the real world by which she

185

could pull herself out of her nightmare. She was soaked with sweat, her nightie clinging to her damp body. After holding onto the breath for a moment, she relaxed and allowed it to rush out of her in a cleansing sigh. She fell back onto the pillow with a soft thud.

Jesus . . .

She still had the nightmares. Three nights a week, if she was lucky. But it was getting better. She didn't think she'd ever be rid of them, but she was grateful for the nights she didn't wake up heart racing, weeping. The hope of quieter nights to come was what got her through.

It took her half an hour to calm down. She sobbed as quietly as she could, trying not to wake Donna—not immediately noticing that the extractor fan was buzzing again. Donna was already awake.

Pam cursed, wondering if she had interrupted her daughter's sleep. But listening carefully, she heard no signs of activity outside. Donna had probably just gotten herself a glass of water, and gone back to bed.

Pam sighed, gently rubbing her sore and salty cheeks. Her throat was dry and she reached for the glass of water on the night-stand. But as she brought it to her lips, she caught a whiff of a strange smell. She paused. It was the water. Moving it away, she sniffed it. It had a chemical aroma, burning in her nostrils. It certainly wasn't water. Dipping the tip of her finger into it, she felt the skin start to fizzle and burn, and swore aloud.

Bleach! She shook the droplets off her fingertip. How the fuck was there bleach in her drink?

Then the realization hit her and the glass tumbled to the floor. Its toxic contents spilled out onto the carpet. If she'd drunk it . . . But how could it have gotten into her water? Unless . . .

Pam was up in a flash, running through the door and bounding down the stairs like a madwoman. Crashing to the ground, she seized the front door handle and rattled it with paranoid desperation. It was safely locked. The back door was the same, and dashing around the house she found no open windows.

Pam sat on the kitchen floor. She was panting from both exertion and terror, and could feel the tears begin to flow. What was happening? It had *definitely* been bleach in the glass. But the doors were locked, with no sign of a break-in. The possibility that it might be Neil had occurred to her, but she had changed the locks a few months after his disappearing act.

Air hissed out of her in a protracted sigh, and she slumped like a deflating balloon. Idle, frustrated curiosity seized her, and she reached over to the cupboard beneath the sink where she kept the cleaning products. The bottle of bleach sat there staring at her. It was leaning against another of the bottles, as if it had been hurriedly replaced. And there was a trail down the side of the bottle. She picked it up, examining it more closely. A hair was caught in the cap.

A long, reddish-brown hair.

* * *

It took Pam a few hours staring at the phone before she worked up the courage to dial the number. She had a silent breakfast with Donna, watching the little girl with concern and fear. She hadn't slept after her discovery. Three consecutive nights without proper sleep had taken their toll.

Donna had seemed perfectly fine. She hadn't noticed any of her mother's strange behavior. She had been far too absorbed in her morning cartoons. Once she had left for school, Pam turned on the radio to escape the quiet.

She knew what she had to do. There was only one person she could ask about all this, only one person who could have any understanding of her situation.

Too bad he was the bastard who had run out on her a year earlier, in the deepest chasm of her grief. She wasn't looking forward to this.

The tone sounded. *Ring ring.* Pam squeezed the plastic handset until it creaked. *Ring ring.* Her teeth were on edge, and a light mist of sweat glistened on her forehead. *Ring ring.* She wished he would just answer, the stupid—*Ring click!*

"Hello."

"Oh, um . . . hi," she stammered, her nerve melting at the sound of his voice. "Hi, Neil. It's me."

"Oh." The reply was less than enthusiastic. "Hi Pam. I can't talk long, I have to get to work."

Irritation flared. Less than ten seconds, and he was already trying to shake her off. And to think, she'd loved this man, married him. Had his children . . .

"Just listen for a minute, Neil, this is important. It's about Donna." That worked. He waited for her to continue. "She's been acting . . . strange."

"Strange how?" Neil's voice was breathy and deep. Hearing him now, it was hard not to remember the better times, those romantic times, when the family had been all together. She blinked back tears. She tried to form a dam, a barrier made out of all of the bad memories of Neil. She wasn't convinced it would hold up.

"She's started . . . sleepwalking," Pam answered. She realized that she had so far avoided trying to rationalize her daughter's behavior. "And saying strange things."

"She's been sleepwalking for years," Neil said, as she'd expected. "You just never believed me. You were always asleep, but I could hear her walking around at night."

Pam sighed. She didn't know what to think anymore. She was all alone. "You shouldn't have left, Neil," she said in a small voice. "I shouldn't have to deal with this on my own."

"Oh, fuck off," he snapped. "I had to deal with it alone. With you and everyone else telling me I was going crazy, that I was being unfair."

"You *were* being unfair!" Pam shot back, old anger dredged up clouding the waters of fear and depression. "Neil, whatever problems she might have, she's still only a little girl."

"Then how do you explain it?" He waited, but Pam didn't answer. "Billy was healthy. He was fine. There was no reason for him to simply stop breathing."

"That's why it's called Sudden Infant Death Syndrome, Neil! The coroner found nothing suspicious. My little girl couldn't do anything like that."

She heard the sharp intake of breath, air rushing through her estranged husband's teeth on the other end of the phone. It was a familiar sound. It was how Neil bit back all the angry remarks he didn't want to escape. But she'd witnessed his acid tongue against other people, and the whistling sound of breath passing his teeth was just as hurtful as any remark he could make. Well, almost any.

"The coroner's verdict was inconclusive. That's why it's called SIDS, *Pammy.*" That stung. She hadn't been called Pammy since he left. She'd used to like it. Now it sounded patronizing and insulting. It made her feel like a silly, little girl.

"Look, I know what I saw and heard. She was moving around at night, ever since Billy was born. At first I thought it was sibling jealousy or some shit. But she'd say odd things, when she was out

188

of it, when she was asleep or tired. Strange things, disturbing things. And then Billy stops breathing in the night? And you know the baby monitor was off that night? I didn't turn it off. Did you?"

"Neil!" Pam cut him off. "That's enough! Donna *has* been up in the night, and strange things *have* been happening. But that doesn't mean she killed Billy!" She closed her eyes, tears squeezing out of the corners, and her voice choked.

"What has she done then?" Neil asked.

She didn't want to say it now. She was angry and upset and wanted nothing more than to hang up the phone. But then what would have been the point of calling in the first place? No, she was worried enough about her situation to call Neil, and that wouldn't go away unless she asked him about it. Of course there was no guarantee that it would, even if she did tell him, but . . .

"I was nearly poisoned!" she said, in a hurried rush that blended the sentence into one long word. There was a tense silence.

"What?"

"I was nearly poisoned," she repeated, more slowly, wincing at how ridiculous each word of it sounded. "Last night."

"I thought that was what you said," he responded. There was a sigh. "Nearly poisoned? How?"

"My glass of water. By my bed. It had bleach in it. I nearly drank it," she shuddered. The memory had taken on a hazy quality, but the thought still disturbed her.

"Bleach?" He chuckled, and Pam's anger surged. "Are you sure you didn't just pick up the wrong bottle?"

"This isn't funny, Neil!" she shouted. "If I hadn't been as awake as I was . . . If I'd drunk that . . . "

"Shit!" Neil's voice was filled with concern now. "You're serious? Donna tried to poison you?"

"I don't know that it was her, Neil, I just—"

"You suspect," Neil finished for her. "Else you wouldn't have called me."

"She's been waking up in the night," Pam began, feeling it all start to rush out of her, knowing that she couldn't stop it. "She has since . . . But I saw her sleepwalking the other night. I'd never seen that before. And then last night, I woke up thirsty and . . . and there was bleach in my water!" Her voice had risen to a shrill, hysterical shriek, but if Neil was trying to calm her, she couldn't hear him. "And I came downstairs and all the doors were locked but the bleach had been used and there was a red hair caught in the cap and it was Donna's I'm sure and . . . and . . . "

She gasped for breath, tears running down her cheeks, leaving her red-flushed face shining. She was trembling. It was all she could manage to keep the phone pinned to her ear. She wept, baring her soul to the man who she should have been closest to, but who was the furthest from her in the world.

"Shhh," he soothed. "Don't cry, Pammy, it's gonna be alright. Listen to me, I know you didn't believe me before, but I believe you now."

"You never should have left us, Neil," Pam whispered.

"I didn't leave you," he replied softly. "I left her. I never left you."

"She's your daughter, Neil!"

"No!" His voice was cutting and final, with an air of hard decisiveness that was rare for him. "She is not my daughter. That ... that *thing* murdered my son."

"You selfish bastard!" Pam spat.

He was about to reply, but she hung up, hurling the phone across the room. Alone and isolated, she slumped to the floor, sobbing.

* * *

That night, Pam gave in. She was exhausted, and had spent the evening in a daze on the sofa. When she finally did get Donna to bed—the little girl not commenting on her mother's strange behavior—she found herself some old sleeping pills in the medicine cabinet and chased them down with a glass of wine. She didn't trust even the water she ran from the tap herself.

The pills worked like a charm, and she soon found herself in a drugged, deformed sleep. Her dreams were twisted and mutilated; falling, then suspended in a liquid smelling of bleach. It flooded her lungs, covered her face, but it didn't burn. She hung in the misty liquid, like a fetus in the womb.

She was asleep. The realization rolled and echoed all around her, sounding into the deepest recesses of her consciousness. She smiled. She was asleep, and everything would be alright.

All of her worries had been washed away. This sea of unconsciousness had borne her up and over the grief which had been dragging her down—like a millstone around her neck—for the last year. She sighed, and was lifted higher on a liquid thermal. It was beautiful.

But something was changing. The liquid became dark and turgid, and she could feel some force or current moving her against her own will. She struggled against it, but it was too strong. She felt lethargic, anaesthetized.

What was happening? Was this a nightmare?

It wasn't like the nightmares that had plagued her since Billy's death. It wasn't like any dream she could recall. It was abstract. All representation and sensation. Vague, not definite.

She clutched her hands to her chest, and then her throat. Her lungs were burning. The water filled her lungs like balloons, burning from the inside out. She gagged, but it made no difference. The pain was unbearable and getting worse.

Feeling like she was going to explode, Pam flailed for the surface. She had to wake up. It was all a dream, a terrible dream. If she could only wake up, everything would be okay. WAKE UP!

But as she crashed out of the abstract sea of her dream, into the cold air of reality, her lungs still burnt with a need for air. Her mouth, desperate to oblige, was denied by something pressing down over her face. Pam tasted linen. And as her eyes fell upon the familiar slumbering face of her executioner, revealed in the dim light from the bathroom, she felt raw terror.

She kicked weakly, but she was lethargic and easily overpowered. The combined effect of sleeping pills and alcohol were present in the haze of her mind, and juvenile arms with unexpected strength held her fast. She was slipping away. Her heart pounded, but her muscles cried out for more oxygen than it could supply. As her brain starved, her hand fell limply onto the bed, knocking the one-armed teddy to land on the pale, bleached patch of carpet with an anticlimactic thud.

* * *

Donna sat quietly in the corner of the room, playing with teddy. This room was larger than any in the house she had lived in with mummy—and daddy too, before he left. This house was much bigger, and had so many more nice things.

But she wasn't allowed to touch them. She had to sit in the

191

corner and play with teddy.

She missed her home. She missed mummy. But mummy had gone to be with baby Billy now, the lady had said. And Donna had been sent to this nice house, with the nice people who had lots of nice things.

But she hoped she wouldn't be here for too long. She was on her own most of the time. Lonely.

"—probably nothing, but she's been up in the night a lot... I know her mother and baby brother died . . . " The voice drifted through to Donna from the kitchen. "They really ought to find her father . . . I know . . . It's just that, well, she's been sleepwalking, and saying odd things . . . Yes, I saw her last night, in my doorway, just pointing . . . I'm sorry, it just . . . scared a little . . . Yes . . ."

Donna carried on playing with teddy, oblivious to the subject of the phone call in the other room. The lady couldn't mean her. Donna had slept wonderfully last night. Of course, she *had* heard the same voices that had talked to her at mummy's home; she always heard those voices at night. But they never bothered her sleep, really—just told her things. Things she should do perhaps or maybe what . . . problem was she didn't know; Donna could never remember what they said once she woke.

Oh well, she was sure they would go away, eventually. Teddy gave her a knowing look, and she smiled contentedly.

Worms in the Walls of My Mind

G.K. Hayes

PATIENT #B39-66-08/PED-NEC. TRANSCRIPT DATE, 04/10/2023.

This transcript was obtained through the use of the Ulmer Neural Implant and Translation System (UNITS). Random and superfluous thoughts have been filtered to reinforce dominant patterns resulting in a representative approximation of higher thought processes usually associated with speech.

This information is of RESTRICTED USE and CANNOT be transmitted to other vendors or agencies outside UNITS CORP. without express legal permission.

* * *

The worms have started wiggling out of the walls again. Around and around in that crazy, spasmodic dance, like someone or something behind the wall is slowly unscrewing strange, bent, rubbery, flesh-colored screws.

When they first started coming out of the walls, it really freaked me out. But after several hours of watching them wiggle out and around, I became more relaxed. Now I find that it's actually soothing in a grotesque sort of way.

In one of my earlier sessions, I actually dozed off. I slipped into that strange world of half-sleep where you can't tell if you're dreaming or awake. I'm guessing that it took the worms at least an hour to crawl up onto the bare mattress where I lay. Then another twenty or thirty minutes to inch their way up my body.

I remember first feeling their cold little bodies touching, exploring my face, much like the fingers of sweet little children. In my dazed state, I found it actually quite pleasant.

Then one of them, a most adventurous soul, smelling of rich, black earth, wiggled into my nose. It felt like cold snot slowly sliding up and up. I can remember the sensation clearly. He tickled my nose hair and wormed around until he pushed his way up through my nostril and into my right sinus cavity. It was fascinating and awful and gross and wonderful all at the same time.

But the feeling of that worm burrowing up into my head suddenly nauseated me so that I came fully awake. I tried to pull him out, but even as big as he was, there was only a little bit of him sticking out. He was slick and slimy and difficult to get a good grip on so I used my shirt-tail to grab onto him. It felt strangely erotic pulling that long, fat worm out. It was almost like I was pulling out parts of my brain. Like the worm had eaten some of my more abhorrent memories, areas of black cancer evil, that infect my mind.

I started blowing my nose, over and over, trying to get the smell and the feeling of wet earth and slime out. I kept blowing and wiping and digging until the snot ran red with blood.

I am more careful now not to fall asleep. Now, I flick them off the mattress as they raise their searching heads. I sit here and watch them crawling around and over each other for hours, ever watchful.

The thing that bothers me though, is that I know the worms are supposed to mean something, something important. That's why the Keepers put me down here. I know that it's some kind of therapy, but I can't . . . I just can't seem to . . . it keeps flashing around in my brain but I can never get a good hold on what it's supposed to mean. They want me to associate the bad things I've done with the worms so that when I think of doing bad things again, I'll think of the worms and remember how disgusting it is and eventually, someday, I'll be cured.

And I do want to be cured.

Sometimes, when I've been down here a long time, I run old movies in my mind. Horror movies are my favorite—particularly zombie movies! Something about the walking dead has always fascinated me. But you know something you hardly ever see, something that would be deliciously scary? . . . a zombie child emerging from the grave!

Just imagine . . . you're walking in the woods late at night with a full moon overhead. Then suddenly, you stumble over a fresh mound of black earth with five deathly-white, little fingers peeping through. Then suddenly, they start to wiggle, around and around, like worms searching for a way out!

Children can be frightening, but oh, so loving. Their little hands and fingers on your face or digging in your pants for candy. Ahhhh . . . .

The worms are almost touching the mattress again, little fingers waving in the air. Soon they'll be touching me again too if I let them.

I think I've had a good session this time. The Keepers will be happy. I just wish I knew what it all means.

In The Shadows They Hide

AJ Brown

"Why are you so afraid of the dark?" Sarah asked. She stood across the room, near the door that separated us from the rest of the world. Beyond that door was the hallway that led to the stairs that went down to where the foyer and hall split off into several rooms. At that moment, it was just her and I in the house, me the fourteen-year-old boy who had never been in a room alone with a girl that wasn't my mother or sister and she, the girl two years my senior, her low cut shirt showing more breasts than I had ever seen, even in my dreams.

"I'm not afraid of the dark," I said, nervously glancing down at my dirty sneakers. When I looked back up, a smile had spread across her face, showing hints of teeth and signs of mischief. To her right was a light brown dresser, two stuffed teddy bears side by side sharing an ice cream cone sat in its center. Directly behind her was the door. To her left . . . to her left is what had me fixated at that moment. The light switch was the color of sand and less than a foot from her left elbow.

"Come on, Spencer," she said and gave a giggle. "Everyone knows you're afraid of the dark."

She was going to test that theory. I could see it in her green eyes, hear it in her drippingly sweet voice, feel it in the sweat beading along my forehead. My stomach groaned, rolled and knotted up. It tugged on the muscles of my groin, shriveled my nuts to raisins and sent electric pulses throughout my body like tiny shockwaves dancing along my nerves.

"It's not the dark I'm afraid of," I said, my voice a weak whisper. I cleared my throat and repeated, "It's not the dark I'm afraid of."

Sarah raised her eyebrows. "Really? Then what are you afraid of?"

How do I explain my fears without sounding like a nutcase that should be in an asylum? I didn't know, so I shrugged and looked

196

back down at my dirty shoes.

"Are you afraid of me?" she asked. She took several steps, stopped in front of me and leaned forward. I looked into her eyes, passing over the open portion of her shirt that showed her breasts in all their glory, nipples included. My face grew hot. I'm sure she did that intentionally to frustrate me. She succeeded.

I stammered through my answer, barely getting it out without dripping a glob of slobber out the side of my mouth. "No, Sarah. I'm not scared of you." That was a partial lie. I wasn't afraid of her, that much was true. But, I was terrified of Bobby Jenkins, the typical football stud who was the size and shape of a brick wall and Sarah's boyfriend.

She gave a smile, one that said she knew I liked what I saw and that she would use that against me if she could. Sarah stood straight. I exhaled, glanced around her room at all the things that teenage girls have: posters of rock stars or movie stars missing their shirts, make-up cases, cute little outfits hanging on a hook on her closet door, which was slightly open. I could see a swath of darkness peeking out at me. If I looked hard enough I could have probably seen it wink at me, a smile on its gray face. But that fear made my head swoon and I turned back to Sarah. She stood at the light switch again.

"It's hard to explain," I said and glanced out the window. The purple curtains were pulled to the side. When did it grow dark out? My skin crawled as if a thousand hands ran their fingers along it. Outside, in that type of dark . . . I could feel them waiting, hisses on their tongues, clawed fingers longing to sink themselves into my ivory skin.

"Try," Sarah said.

Why do girls do these things? Why do they hold boys captive with their sweet eyes and pouty lips; their curvy bodies? I didn't want to look at her, but I couldn't help it. She was fifteen feet from me. I could smell her cinnamon perfume, or maybe it was the unlit candle on the night stand by her bed. I don't know, but the scent was intoxicating, much like I imagine getting a little drunk would be.

I stood and went to the window, putting a few extra feet between us. It was cruel what she was doing, playing with my fear. But, she was a girl—and not just any girl, but Sarah Poe, a blonde, a junior in high school, one of the more popular girls. And we were alone in her bedroom.

How was this so? We were nothing alike. I was chunky—not fat, just a little overweight—with dark hair that sported constant cowlicks, even when I used gel or hairspray to hold it in place. Brown eyes and that hauntingly white skin that made me stand out, even in the dark. I think that's why they like me so much—not people, but *them*, those things that hide in the shadows. How did I end up a few feet away from every wet dream I had ever had, with her parents gone for the better part of the evening? And why wasn't Bobby Jenkins here instead? The books on the bed reminded me: the guise of studying. Certainly, her parents trusted the geeky kid who had no chance of getting into their daughter's panties. Would they have trusted Bobby so easily?

"Why am I here?" I asked, glancing out the window. A streetlamp on the corner came alive, casting a yellow glow in a circle a few feet in every direction. I saw the first of them flee the glare, its black tendrils pulling away as quickly as the light flooded the new night. In the dark, gray objects moved toward the house. Hairs stood on the nape of my neck. My eyes watered. I closed them and forced back tears.

"You know why you're here, Spencer," Sarah said and walked over to me. She put one of her arms around me and pressed her breasts to my back. My breath caught and my jeans grew tighter around the crotch. She kissed the back of my neck. I shivered and moved away from her. My hands shook and my breaths came in short bursts. I tried to slow my breathing, to keep from hyperventilating, which would have been bad, so very bad in front of Sarah.

Just outside her window, the motion sensor lights came on. Most people would glance out, see nothing and switch them off. I knew better. I wanted to look, to see how many of them were there pacing the shadows, waiting for me. Instead, I moved further away, focused on shoving my books in my bag. I would call my mom and wait for her in the living room with all the lights on.

"Don't you like me, Spencer?"

A false hurt spread across her face. It had to be fake, with her eyebrows lifted and that bottom lip poked out.

"Y-y-yes, I like you . . . a lot." I hated the tremor in my voice.

"Then why won't you talk to me?"

"I have been," I replied.

I could almost feel her eyes rolling. When I looked at her, that expression of hurt was still there. Maybe . . . No, it had to be a lie—a girl like Sarah wouldn't dig a guy like me. She liked them hunkier, better looking. That's why she and Bobby had been an item for the last few years.

"Spencer, what are you afraid of? If not the dark and not me, what is it?"

Why did that question sound so wrong in my ears? If she wanted to talk, why not ask me what my favorite color is or what I like to do on the weekends when I'm alone or why not ask me about the weather? Why ask about my fears?

"Is it being touched by a girl? If so, I can help you—"

"No, that's not it." It was a lie. I was afraid of being touched, more because of how I looked with clothes off, not the actual physical contact. But, that wasn't what she was getting at. I knew it and I should have asked for the phone. I should have finished packing my bag and called Mom and . . . "You won't understand," I said. "No one understands."

She turned me around and we stared eye to eye. She was inches from me. My face grew warm again. "Try me," she said. Her breath smelled of spearmint.

I licked my lips and took a step away. The backs of my legs hit her bed and I sat. I looked at my shaking hands, then up at her. "It's called Sciophobia."

"What?" Her face scrunched up and one side of her mouth lifted in a confused grin.

"Sciophobia—the fear of shadows."

"You're afraid of shadows?" she asked. I could hear the laughter in her question. "Like that?" Sarah pointed to just beneath the clothes hanging from her closet door, at the gray, boxed-out portion beneath them.

"No, not quite. Those are normal shadows. This room is bright—the shadows that . . . bother me are not like that at all."

"Then what do you mean?"

I looked over her left shoulder to the window. Was that lightning I saw? Was it supposed to storm? I listened for a few seconds until I heard the faint rumble of far off thunder. Tears tickled the corners of my eyes. They liked storms, the way the lightning flickered for less than a second, casting the room in white or yellow with hundreds and thousands of black shadows dancing along the walls and floors. At those moments they were free to roam, only hampered by the electric bolts and then only for a mere second or two.

She put her hand on my chin and lifted my face to meet hers. "Help me understand."

The closet still sat slightly open. The blackness within dripped with malice. They were in there, biding their time. "Your closet," I said. "Do you leave it open all the time?"

"No," she said with a shrug. "I keep it closed at night."

I went over, put one hand to the side of the knob and shut it. "There are shadows in the darkness," I said. "You can't see them when the lights are on. You can only see them when it's dark, when there is just enough light to give them life."

"You're not making any sense."

Outside lightning flickered across the sky. Thunder followed a few seconds later.

"I need to get home. There's a storm coming."

"Don't worry about the storm, Spencer. Mom will take you home when they get back."

There was no comfort in her words.

"You don't understand, they like storms. They—"

"Who does? Who are they?"

"The shadow people."

"Shadow people?" Sarah let out a long breath. This time she did laugh. It was the sound of disbelief; the sound of a girl wondering why she had a geeky, fat kid in her room and not the hunky jock. It was the sound of a girl who just realized she has wasted her time on something or someone that she thought would be worthwhile. It was the sound of a lie.

"Sarah, there are things in the shadows, kind of like the boogeyman, but so many more of them than just the one monster under your bed."

"You believe in the boogeyman?" This time she rolled her eyes. "Seriously?"

I looked at the tops of my shoes. One of the laces had become untied somehow. I pulled my feet onto the edge of her bed, lifting them away from the darkness beneath it, where small hands could swipe at my ankles or tie my laces in knots.

"I told you, you wouldn't understand. No one does." I stood, shoved the last of my books into my backpack and slung it over my shoulder. "Can I use your phone?"

"Wait," she said and grabbed my arm. "Don't get all panicky on me, Spencer. Just relax and tell me about this . . . about this boogeyman."

"They're shadow people," I snapped.

"Okay, whatever," she said and shook her head. "Who are these shadow people?" Another roll of the eyes and sarcasm filled her voice.

Lightning flashed. Thunder rumbled. I groaned.

My muscles quivered, stomach knotted, released, knotted again. Those short breaths were back, this time worse. My head grew light and for a moment I thought I would pass out. I pinched my right cheek, forcing the world to even out.

Concern filled Sarah's face—for me or not, I don't know, but when I regained myself, she looked worried.

"Are you okay?"

"No," I said. "I need to get home. Can I please use your phone?"

"Sure," she said and grabbed her purse from the floor by the bed. She rummaged through it until she pulled out a pink cell phone. Sarah extended her arm, but pulled it back when I reached for it. "Tell me about the shadow people first."

I wanted to scream. I wanted to cry. I wanted to run from the room and down the stairs, find one of the house phones and call my mom—anything but sit there and wait for them to come get me.

"Sarah, don't do this. Please, just let me use the phone."

"Tell me about the shadow people and you can have the phone."

Another streak of lightning was followed by a louder boom of thunder. I pushed by Sarah and practically ran to the window. Outside, they gathered. With each flicker of lightning they drew closer, their lithe bodies bleeding into the darkness.

"Who are they?" she asked again.

I turned to her. Tears fell down my cheeks and I felt like the wimp she was sure to tell everyone I was. But, she didn't look as if she were enjoying my shame. Maybe she *did* like me. Maybe she *did* want me instead of Bobby Jenkins. Maybe . . . maybe a boy's heart can lie to him when his fear is heightened.

"They're not really people," I said quickly. "They're not really anything. They're shadows that live within shadows. They wait for the lights to go out at night and come crawling from the darkness. You see them as clothes hanging from your closet door or the teddy bears on your dresser, just average things that aren't so average after all. They want you to believe they aren't real so they cling to the stuff that is and if they want you, they just wait until you're asleep and tear you to shreds. They're not like any other creature out there."

"That's crazy, Spencer."

"Is it?" I asked as lightning flashed beyond the window. The rumble of thunder shook the glass.

"Yes, it is," Sarah said. "There's no such thing as shadow people. Or the boogeyman."

"Then why do you close your closet door at night?"

She shrugged, that confused expression spreading across her face again. "I don't know. I just do."

"You don't just do something without a reason," I said. "Someone either told you to keep it closed or you figured it out on your own. You've seen the shadows in your closet, haven't you? You've felt that pit in your stomach as you stared at the open door, trying to get up enough courage to jump out of bed and close it."

Her mouth—such a beautiful mouth—hung open. This was no lie. She had seen them, she just never realized it.

Rain pelted the window, a *rat-a-tat-tat* that resembled mobster movie gunfire.

"You're crazy, Spencer, just like everyone said you were."

"What?" I asked. The lies came clean in that instant. I was crazy? That's what they said?

"You're a freak, Spencer. Bobby was right. You're a checkup from the neck up."

My heart sank. Not only was there a storm tilting toward full blown outside, inside there was the girl of my dreams calling me a whack job. The brief glimpse of her nipples would surely be the last I would see until I was well into my adult years. I would live the rest of my teen years as the butt of many jokes. In that moment, I thought of the shadow people, of my fear of them. Were they real or was Sarah right? Was I crazy?

Sarah went to the door. A lump formed in my throat. She was going to hit the switch and plunge me into the blackness of a stormy night. The lights flickered before she reached the switch. I saw her look up, saw the fear in her eyes. Everything went dark.

Lightning lit the room briefly. They were there with us, crawling along the floor, clinging to the walls and ceilings, their bodies long and sharp. I ran for the door, stumbled on the rug and crashed into the wall. I grabbed the door knob and tried to turn it, but it wouldn't budge. I fumbled for a lock I couldn't find.

I looked back. In the flicker of lighting I could see them closing in, crawling through the closed windows and scurrying over one another. The closet door had swung open. One shadow, much larger than the others and somewhat more three dimensional, came at me. I smashed my hands against the door and screamed, "Let me out. Someone help me. Let me out."

Its hands wrapped around my waist and lifted me from the floor. I was in the air, arms and legs flailing. The weight of my backpack spun me around and I landed hard on my bottom.

There was laughter—a deep baritone that sounded familiar. In the cacophony of thunder and hisses and my own screams, I couldn't make it out.

"Spencer," the voice said. "We're going to eat you."

They knew my name?

I was as good as dead.

The lightning came quicker, giving the room a strobe effect. In those flashes I saw them—so many of them. And there was the other one, so unlike the rest it seemed wrong. Its body stood out among them, not blending with the furniture or the walls but more concrete. And it was laughing . . .

It grabbed me again, this time by my head. Its hands weren't clawed like I thought, and it was very much a physical creature. I swatted at it, a feeble swing of my left hand, but it caught the side of its head and . . . its head? I was able to strike it? It cursed and shoved me to the floor.

I can't say I didn't see this coming. Deep in the back of my mind I had known all along. I scrambled backward, putting a little distance between us. When the lightning lit the sky next I saw Bobby Jenkins' face as he approached me, arms outstretched.

"I'm going to kill you, Spencer," he yelled.

I braced myself for his fist, my arms over my face and knees pulled up to my chest. I screamed, the sound of a little girl scared of a rubber snake dropped in her lap.

No punches came. No kicks, either.

Just laughter.

The light came on. I looked through the gap between my forehead and arm. Bobby was doubled over, his face red, and tears streaming down his cheeks. He sounded like a crazed hyena.

Sarah stood by the door, her hand on the light switch. She, too, was laughing, her face as red as Bobby's.

"Help me. Someone help me. Let me out." Bobby mocked, his hands near his face as if he were screaming for his life—much like I had. "Geek, you should have heard yourself."

Sarah put a hand to her face and pointed as tears spilled from her eyes. Her lips were pulled back, showing her beautiful teeth. But, they didn't look so beautiful. At that moment nothing was beautiful about her.

Heat flushed my cheeks and water touched the corners of my eyes. I bit my lip trying to keep the tears at bay.

Sometimes the world slows, just like in the movies during a critical scene where the hero is in grave danger. That's what happened then. Everything dropped to a crawl. Bobby was on his hands and knees. I thought he would throw up from laughing so hard. Sarah had moved from the door and was holding tight to one of the bedposts. She clutched her stomach.

My dream girl had become my nightmare and at that moment I hated her.

Lightning still flashed outside and the house shook with thunder, but inside the storm was so much worse. I could hear their laughter, their words barely recognizable as they tried to breathe.

I thought I would die. I wished I would . . . and then I noticed it. The closet door still stood open. Bobby had been in there with them and they had not hurt him. But, something was wrong. Something . . . something had changed and I saw it in the darkness within the closet. I *felt* it.

The world sped back up and through the laughter and thunder and the trip-hammer that was my heart pulsing in my ears, I heard their hisses and felt their malice seeping from the open closet.

My legs shook as I stood. Bobby and Sarah were both on the floor by then. She had an arm around his shoulders and they still laughed. I think she wiped her eyes of the tears in them.

I looked to the closet door, ready to give myself to them, to give up the fight and end the misery of my life.

Piss ran down my leg and my shoulders sagged. I didn't want to die, but I didn't want to live either. I turned back to Bobby and Sarah. Her shirt was pulled down on one shoulder, the breast fully out. It was white and the nipple was erect.

"Why me?" I asked and looked back to the closet. "What did

I ever do to anyone?"

Their hisses became frantic, like rabid dogs set loose on a fox or a squirrel . . . or a little kitten that could never escape those damnable jaws of certain death.

I was the victim . . . always the victim. Why couldn't something happened to the bullies for once, to the popular and rich and the good looking who pick on the weak, the poor and those of us not as attractive enough to fit in with them?

Maybe they knew what I was thinking. Maybe they felt it the way I felt them. I don't know. What I do know is I looked into the dark and I said: "I'll trade you. Both of them for me." It was a long shot. What if they took them and then came back for me? Or what if the shadow people were like Bobby and Sarah and only preyed on the weak?

Through their hisses I heard the question. "What are their names?"

"B . . . Bobby and Sarah."

Again, the hisses grew more intense. I saw the shadows moving, as if they were trying to break free from the darkness, but the light held them back.

I thought it was an answer. I grabbed my backpack and slowly backed up to the bedroom door. I looked at the light switch. Was I really going to do this? Let the shadow people take them both and hope it was enough to make them leave me alone.

Then I looked at Sarah's face and felt her stinging laughter. The answer was yes. I flipped the light switch off. The room swam in blackness and their hisses drowned out the thunder. The shapes in the dark spilled from the closet. Like a swarm they went after Bobby and Sarah. Along with their hisses and growls came several voices calling out, "Bobby . . . Sarah . . ."

I'd like to say that Bobby and Sarah stopped laughing long enough to realize the danger they were in, but I can't. Honestly, I don't know if they heard their names being whispered by the gravelly voices. I didn't wait to find out. I swung the bedroom door open and ran through it, making certain to slam it shut behind me.

In the hall—the brightly lit hall—I heard their screams, Sarah's panicked and terrified, Bobby's sounding every bit as feminine as mine had surely sounded to him.

Something thumped against the door and the knob turned. I held it tight, not letting the door open. Sarah screamed and I think I heard a 'Please help me,' from somewhere within that room. I pulled on the knob, afraid to let it open. Or was I really afraid? Maybe I just wanted them to suffer.

I thought of Sarah and Bobby, of the prank they played on me. It had been mean, but did they both have to *die* because of it?

"Spencer, help me," Sarah said. Her voice was weak. I started to let go of the knob, to help the girl I thought I loved. The knob turned in my hands. Her pulled back lips and bellowing laughter again resurfaced in my mind. I tugged the knob hard. It snapped off in my hands and I fell back against the hall wall. I looked at the knob, then back at the door. The darkness spilled through the hole where the knob had been.

Hisses and growls came from the room, but the screams had ended. My chest grew tight when one of the black tendrils spilled from the knob's hole. I tried to stand, but my body didn't respond.

"Spencer."

The sound that came from my throat was a squeal . . . a purely terrified squeal.

"Spencer."

The door opened, the hinges creaked. A pale hand fell from the darkness. It was Sarah's and her fingers were bloodied where her nails had torn free from trying to fight off the shadow people.

"No," I said.

There was a laugh, deep and hearty.

"Thank you, Spencer," it said and Sarah's arm jerked away. The door slammed shut.

I got to my feet, and ran. The laughter followed me down the steps and to the front door. I ran out into the night, no longer concerned that the shadow people hidden in the blackness outside. They were in Sarah's room and they were eating and laughing.

And they knew my name . . .

Until I Come Again

Justin Gustainis

All the whores were frightened—and who could blame them, with doom stalking the avenues and lurking down every fog-shrouded alley?

But skittish or not, they still went out to ply their trade. After news of the latest depredation, some might stay inside for a night or two, cowering like rabbits in their holes. But eventually, they would venture forth again. They had needs, after all—whether for drink, or drugs, or feeding hungry children, or simply putting bread on their own tables in a world where a poor woman's choices were often reduced to either the scullery or the street, and maid work being damned hard to come by.

Sooner or later, the whores always came back.

Robert counted on that—had done so from the very beginning.

He stood in the shadowed doorway of the closed apothecary shop for a long time, watching the street. Midnight came and went, then one o'clock, but the area remained abustle with drunken sailors, slumming toffs, pickpockets, beggars—and whores.

Finally, he spied one who interested him. Tall, she was, with reddish hair reaching nearly to her waist. He studied her for several minutes, then made up his mind. Waiting until she was facing the other way, he stepped from the dark doorway and headed toward her, assuming the pace and posture of a tired man on his way home. Not too fast, not too slow, that was the ticket.

As he drew near the whore, he let his eyes dart her way for a moment then looked to the front again. He slowed his walk, but only a little. A direct approach had been effective with the first few, but now the strumpets were wary. Let her come to him.

And that she did. Stepping forward a little she said, "'Allo, darlin'. Interested in a bit of fun this evenin' are we? Only twenty shillings."

He stopped and turned to face her. "Well, I don't know—I

mean, I was just going home, er, Miss." He strove to convey shyness, unease, and more than a hint of lust. Henry Irving, the great actor, could hardly have done it better.

"Home, is it?" she said with a toss of her head. "Then why not kiss the missus with a smile on yer face? I knows *all* the tricks, luv, you'll see." There was something in her voice and manner that spoke to him of Ireland.

"Well, um, yes, all right," he said, with just the right combination of eagerness and embarrassment. "Is there somewhere we might—"

"Oh, ta, I got a room, a nice one. Not far from 'ere." She stepped up to him boldly and took his arm, just as if she were a decent woman. "Shall we be off, then?"

They went together, and if she noticed the valise he carried in his other hand, she made no mention of it.

"What's yer name, luv?" she asked, sounding as if she were actually interested.

For a moment he was tempted to say 'Jack,' just to see what she would do, but squashed the impulse. This was not an occasion for levity. "Robert," he told her. "And what might yours be, my dear?"

"Oh, you just call me Mary," she said, laughing lightly. "All the lads do."

* * *

Her wretched little room actually *was* close by, in a little byway called Miller's Court. He stayed there with her for a little more than an hour. His work did not usually take him so long, but the unaccustomed privacy prompted him to linger, to do a really thorough job, his best so far. Most of his cleansings had taken place in semi-public areas, alleys and courtyards, with the danger of discovery always prompting him to hurry. But not tonight.

Finally, he was finished, cleaned up, and ready to face the world again. He blew out the single lamp before opening the door, so that no one passing when he opened the door would catch a glimpse of what he was leaving behind. But Miller's Court appeared deserted at this late hour.

As Robert pulled the pocked and warped door shut behind him, he noticed the building number for the first time: 13. His mouth twitched in something like a grin.

An unlucky number, people say. Well, sometimes people have it right, don't they?

Before venturing further into the street, he made a quick mental inventory. After a moment he nodded to himself. Everything he had brought into the room with him was back in his valise. Plus one additional item—a little souvenir of the occasion. He took in a breath of the cool night air and started on his way home.

The stupid police could search in vain for their 'clews,' and be damned. They would never catch him. Not the peelers, or the Baker Street Wonder, either—yes, the papers said *he'd* been consulted, bad cess to him. And certainly Robert had nothing to fear from that drug fiend inspector from the Yard, the one they said had actually been having visions of the killings. Visions, indeed!

They could not stop him, and the work would go on, until he had cleansed Whitechapel, then all of Spitalfields, then the whole of East London of these filthy trollops. They were all of a stripe, just like the slut who had given the pox so many years ago to his father, who had then unknowingly passed it on to Mother. The old man had slowly gone mad from the disease, screaming denunciations of the dirty whores to the very end. Mother had been unwilling to face such a fate for herself. Father had been in his grave less than a month when she was found in her bed, the empty bottle of laudanum beside her, the note to her son reading only "Forgive me." And of course he would, how could he do otherwise, but not the whores though. Oh no, *they* were responsible, *they* had destroyed his family, his life, forced him to be raised and used and abused by his hateful uncle and aunt, and he would go on making *them* pay, the filthy sluts, until—

His head came up suddenly, eyes narrowed to slits. He felt his heart began to pound, faster than it ever had while he'd been dissecting the whore's body.

There was someone standing in the road.

* * *

He was a tall man, and strongly built, by the look of him. He wore clothing so dark that it looked black in the uncertain light of the street lamps.

A bobby? No, he wore a gentleman's top hat, not the helmet of the Metropolitan Police. Scotland Yard? A detective? But they never worked alone, surely. Robert thought of turning around, walking off the other way, but that would only draw attention. So he continued straight on, just another professional man on the way home after working late.

As Robert drew closer, he saw that the man was older than he'd seemed at first. The hair was white, as was the great mustache that curved down and around the mouth.

But his eyes, there was something about his eyes beneath those massive brows, the way they seemed to catch the lamplight and hold it with a glow of their own.

Robert thought about the razor-sharp implements in his valise, wondered how quickly he could produce one if he needed it.

"Good evening, my young friend," the man said. His deep voice was accented, the intonation strange and unfamiliar.

"Good evening." Robert nodded, curt but polite, and kept walking.

But the stranger held up a languid hand, palm outward. "A moment, if I may delay you."

Robert found that he had stopped, without consciously deciding to do so. "The hour is late, sir, and I am weary. What do you want with me?"

"Only to express to you my . . . admiration."

Robert blinked. "Admiration? I fear you have mistaken me for someone else. You do not know me, sir, nor any admirable deed that I might have accomplished." His right index finger went slowly to the latch of his valise, ready to flick it open.

The stranger smiled, but without humor. His teeth were white and sharp looking. "I do not make mistakes. I know your name—and also that other name, by which you are so well known to the common people. I have read of it in your newspapers—indeed, they write of little else, these days."

Robert tried to sound impatient. "I repeat, sir, you have mistaken me for another. I have not the slightest notion to what you are referring." He thought the big autopsy scalpel was near the top of the valise's contents and could be reached quickly. He would have to use it left-handed, which would be awkward. And he had never killed a man before, let alone a gentleman like this stranger seemed to be. But, if his freedom was at risk, there was no option.

The old man seemed almost to read his mind. "Fear not, my friend. I am not some common policeman. I am not even English—

but you discerned this at once, by my speech. Did you not?"

"Well, I had noticed something of an accent, it is true." For quicker access, he lifted his right hand, the one holding the valise, just a little. The sequence was clearly laid out in his mind now. Flick the clasp open, reach across with his left hand, grasp the scalpel, then slash a vicious backhand from right to left, disemboweling the man and leaving him open to the killing stroke across the throat. *All right, then. Ready, steady . . .*

"You may put down your case." The stranger's voice seemed to reverberate within Robert's brain like an echo, and the eyes, the red-rimmed eyes were impossible to resist. "You will not require a weapon now."

His hand opened, seemingly of its own volition. The battered leather valise dropped to the cobblestones, its contents clanging faintly.

"It is true that I have the speech of one not native to your people," the stranger said, as if he had not interrupted himself. "But that will change. Nay, it *must* change before I may think to make this land my home."

"Home? Here?" Robert spoke as if from a dream.

"Such is my intent, yes. My own country has grown stagnant, its people pale and listless. But even from many miles away have I read of the crowded streets of your mighty London. And now I have seen for myself that all those accounts were true. The heart of this great city beats strongly, full of activity, of vitality, of . . . blood."

He stepped closer, and now Robert could see how extraordinarily pale he was, except for those incredibly red lips, and the eyes, the eyes . . . .

"I was myself once a soldier, nay, more—I commanded armies," he went on. "Well do I know the value of what you English call *reconnaissance*. And in this brief visit I have learned much. Now I return to my own land for a time, to make my preparations. And then in a year, two at most, all will be in readiness, and I shall return."

He placed his hands atop Robert's shoulders. The fingers gripped like the teeth of a steel trap, but the voice was soft, almost purring, and utterly compelling. "But even when I have made my new home in England, I may still require assistance of one who has knowledge of the local customs, and who can move about freely, in

211

both day and night," he said. "I had despaired of locating a man who was suitable to my needs—but then, at long last, I have found you." He nodded in satisfaction. "Rare it is, to encounter someone who is not … *vlkoslak* … but yet understands the vital importance of blood, who revels in the blood of others, who knows deep in his heart that the blood is the life."

The red eyes bore into Robert, and his sanity, what little was left of it after years of abuse and four murders, began to crumble and fragment under the terrible onslaught of the old man's will. "The blood is the life," Robert repeated softly. "The blood is the life!"

"Ah, you do understand!" The stranger nodded again. "It is well. You will wait for me, then. Here, in London. And when I return, you will be my right hand, my good and faithful servant, and I will be your *boyar*, your Lord, as is only right and proper for one of my noble blood. I will summon you again when I return. In the interval, you will slay no more harlots, lest you be apprehended by the authorities and hence become useless to me. Do you understand? No more 'cleansings'—for now."

"Yes, my Lord!" Robert said, nodding wildly.

"And if you serve me well, I will repay your loyalty with the greatest gift of all. Do you know what that is?"

"No, my Lord. Please, will you tell me?"

"The answer is in your own Scripture, Mister . . . Renfield." The man tapped his own chest with one sharp-nailed finger. "You must have faith when I say to you that *I* am the resurrection and the life, and he that believeth in *me*, even though he die, yet shall he live." The stranger gave vent to a singularly humorless laugh that seemed to echo through the empty, squalid street for a long time before it finally died away.

"The blood is the life," Robert said eagerly. "The blood is the life!"

"Indeed, it is so." The stranger let go of Robert's shoulders and stepped back. After a moment the man's body seemed to grow indistinct, as if he were somehow becoming one with the fog that swirled around them. But his voice was still clear as he said, "Remember, Englishmen: no matter of how long it may be, you will wait—as your Scripture also puts it, until I come again."

And then he was gone.

Robert stared into the mist for what seemed like a long time. A thread of spittle ran down one corner of his mouth, but he made no effort to wipe it away. After a while, he picked up his satchel, containing the set of operating knives, some bloodstained rags, a nearly-empty bottle of distilled water, and, wrapped in waxed paper, the heart of a prostitute named Mary Kelly.

Robert Renfield settled his coat around his shoulders and staggered off into the night, his brain afire from the glory that had been revealed to him. He would wait quietly, as instructed. He would be a loyal servant, and would earn the reward that his Lord and Master had promised him.

As he walked the dark streets, he muttered to himself, as lunatics often do. "The blood is the life," he said, over and over. "The blood is the life."

A bat flew overhead, casting an immense shadow over London as it passed before the full moon. But Robert Renfield did not notice. If he had, it is doubtful that he would have cared.

The Boy in the Well

Danny Rhodes

The snow came yesterday, tiny white crystals so delicate and yet so determined. In a few hours the neighborhood was hidden under a blanket of white. Once again, between bouts of splintered sleep, I was forced to think of him.

I was nine-years-old when the bad winter came. I'd seen snow before, a few inches each year that came and went, brief and playful bouts that added a touch of magic to the Christmas holidays and then melted quickly to nothing. But the bad winter was different. The snow fell and settled. More snow followed, snow piling on snow. There were huge drifts on the hills, great expanses in the streets. The first time I went out to play in the snow that year I became disorientated. All the distinguishable features of the world I knew were buried from my sight. There was just a wilderness of white. My mother had to come out into the street to fetch me in.

I had a dog at the time, a cocker spaniel called Snap. I'd had him three years and he was 'my' dog. I called him Snap so that all the other kids would think twice before giving me any trouble but in truth he was softer than soap. He liked tearing around the yard with me at dusk and sleeping on my bed at night. He loved to sniff out every nook and cranny he could find when I took him for walks, which I was allowed to do on my own as long as I only went as far as Nonsuch Park, as long as I was back at a certain time and as long as I promised that I would never, under any circumstances, enter Cheam Woods. My father said the circus families, who sometimes hitched their trailers there, used the woods for all sorts of business and that I had no calling to have any dealings with them. My mother simply didn't like the woods at all. My parents were protecting me I suppose, as all parents protect their children, keeping me away from a life that was unpredictable and dark in ways that I would never have understood at that age.

My walks with Snap were predictable and safe. I kept him on

his lead while we were on the avenue and then let him off when we entered the alley behind the high school. He'd tear away from me then, down the alley and out into Nonsuch Park. Together we'd skirt the park's edge so that Snap could forage in the undergrowth and I could avoid running across the older boys who played football in the grassy middle, or the teenage gangs that huddled together on the swings, smoking and laughing. The walk took me forty-five minutes, an hour if I dawdled, which I did when I had chores to return to or if my parents were arguing and I wanted to stay out of it all.

It was January of the bad winter when my mother packed her bags. My parents had argued all through the Christmas holidays. With only new snowfall and insults marking one day off against another, a type of cabin fever overcame us. In the end my father delivered my mother to her mother's in the center of town then came home and explained himself. It was just for a few days, he said, just while the snow was a problem. By staying closer to town my mother could get to her job. She wouldn't be stuck in the house day after day. He said it would be better for everyone, that it would let the air in.

But my mother never came back.

Her absence had a peculiar effect on me. I experienced a new found freedom because of it. My father was busy and did not have the time to watch over me as my mother did. He did not guard the fridge or the pantry or watch the clock in the evenings while awaiting my bedtime. He let me stay up and watch TV shows I had never seen before. He stocked up on snacks, bought in take away food and let me munch away to my heart's content. He didn't ask me to tidy my room once, and he promised that if I stayed out of trouble for the rest of the holidays he'd take me to see Wimbledon FC play at home when the season next came around, something we'd never done together.

Perhaps I got complacent about my father's rules. Perhaps I lost some respect for him. Perhaps if my mother hadn't gone away I would never have found myself with Snap that cold afternoon, trundling through fresh snowfall, the sun weakening in the sky, no snow falling then but the promise of more and more to come. I was following a set of footprints, letting my imagination carry me away, tracking a fugitive through the wilderness with my trusted companion at my heels.

When I got to Nonsuch Park it was deserted and as still as

215

death itself. There was just a clean blanket of snow covering everything except the single set of footprints I was trailing, unusual because the person had been carrying something alongside them as they walked. In my mind it was a rifle, the outlaw I was following using it to prop himself up, tiredness setting in as the unrelenting chase went on and the inexorable hero hunted him down. I followed the tracks around the edge of the park while Snap bundled his way through the snow, his breath forming in bursts of vapor, his black fur sprinkled with white flecks. The tracks went on and on, skirting Nonsuch Park as I liked to skirt it, never wavering or altering, just two clean footprints set at an even distance and the regular spike of the implement marking the way. And then, quite unexpectedly, the tracks turned into Cheam Woods.

I hesitated.

I stared after the tracks as they disappeared into the trees and I think I knew, somewhere deep within myself, that my life was about to change forever. Snap waited at my side, anxious to enter the place I had always denied him, turning his head upward and then looking back at the trail in perplexed wonder. Were we actually going to go in there? I stood motionless for several moments, staring after those tracks, wondering who they belonged to, wondering where they might take me, my brain calculating the fact that if I followed the tracks in I could turn around at anytime and follow the tracks back out again. There was no risk of getting lost. And so, for the first time in my life, I defied my father.

The blanket of snow made it difficult to stay on the path. I could only make out its existence by calculating the space between the trees and searching for the curious footsteps. Snap tore around regardless, to one side of me and then the other, at times disappearing from view completely so that the only signal of his companionship was the distant cracking of twigs and branches as he barreled past them. The tiny movements of the trees in the gentle evening breeze added further creaks and groans. In those isolated moments of loneliness my mind invented monsters to accompany each sound. Snap would reappear, panting and breathless. For a moment he was my trusted companion again and then in a blast of energy he was off once more, back into the trees, following some scent that no human would ever have knowledge of.

I concentrated on the trail and fought to keep my mind off monsters by thinking instead about the owner of the footsteps. Was

216

it an old man with a walking stick, disorientated and lost? Might I come across his frail, frozen body in the snow?

I followed the trail for another ten minutes, these thoughts busy in my head, forever calculating that it would be okay to go just a little further, just as long as it didn't snow again, just as long as the light held. And I would have gone on forever perhaps had I not suddenly reached a clearing amidst the trees, a place where the snow lay like newly sprinkled icing sugar, so perfect and delicate. I resented the footsteps that marched right on through that clearing, oblivious to the picture they had spoiled. Or perhaps they hadn't spoiled it. Perhaps there was something magical about a single set of footprints leading across a snowy clearing in the trees, the sort of footsteps that might appear in a Robert Frost poem. My teacher sometimes read his poems during break times. She sat with the book in her lap, the pages spread open, her palm pressed against them and her words carried us to faraway times and places.

'Whose woods these are I think I know'

Remembering those words I felt a cold dread run through me. For the first time I considered who else might own those footprints and what they might do to a young boy on his own in a wood where even the virginal snow itself would help muffle a scream of terror. It was getting late. It was time to turn for home. At some point my father would think of me and begin to wonder.

Snap did not fear anything though. He was racing around the clearing, sending snow high into the air in great swirls. Each time he landed there was a puff of white behind him. I watched him, jealous of his innocence and vigor. I wanted to be enjoying the blanket of snow. I wanted to be tearing about after him, but another part of me could only repeat that line of poetry over and over again.

'Whose woods these are I think I know'

The words would not leave me. And I felt something watching us.

Suddenly I heard Snap yelp. I turned in time to catch the briefest sight of him as he disappeared into the snow. He didn't come out. Stillness descended on the clearing. I waited. For a long time there was nothing, just the tiniest creaks of the trees as they swayed immeasurably to and fro, and then I heard Snap whining. He sounded somewhere far off. He was calling his master. I raced across the clearing, my feet kicking up snow. Twice I stumbled forward into it, twice I got back to my feet, the snow caked to my clothing, but the

217

third time I fell was a blessing. That was when I discovered the well. The undulations of snow had hidden it from my vision and my fall had prevented me dropping headlong into darkness.

For a moment, teetering on the brink, I thought about Snap dying there in the well, his black body tumbling through the void, landing with a dead thud in the bottom, his skull breaking open, the blood coloring the snow that lay there. I was almost ready to leap into the well myself and try to save him. But then I considered how I was going to explain any of this to my father and I stopped myself. What excuse could I give to him for leading Snap to this place, for being in Cheam Woods alone? Why had I disobeyed him?

These thoughts were running around my head when the voice called out to me across the clearing.

"Wait!" it cried. "You're too close to the edge!"

It was a soft voice, as molded as a drift of snow. He came out of the trees, a boy like no boy I had ever seen. He was dressed in a ragged pair of jeans. He had a checkered lumberjack shirt on his back. He wore brown moleskin boots. His hair was long and moppish and it fell in front of his face each time he moved his head. He was tall, too tall for his age. He was carrying a walking stick and he limped across the clearing towards me. Each time he took a step he leaned on the stick for support and as he drew closer I realized it was his tracks I had been following through the snow. I stood transfixed as he approached, unaware of what to say, momentarily lost in some fantasy in which the stranger and I camped out in the woods, built traps and dens, sat huddled against camp fires while the world continued on its merry way. Then I heard another whine from deep in the well and it brought me to my senses. Snap was still alive down there and I had to get him out.

"My dog," I said. "I have to save my dog."

I crept towards the edge of the well, not knowing where was safe and where was not, inching forward on fresh snow until some of it broke and fell away.

"If you fall you'll die," said the boy. "Dogs are tougher than people."

"But I have to save him," I said.

The reality of the situation was catching up with me. I found myself choking up. I would have cried too, if it wasn't for the presence of the boy. I couldn't let myself cry in front of him because I just knew that he would never cry. He was stood beside me now. His skin was mottled and toughened but somehow his face still looked cherubic, as though he were blessed with knowledge and understanding beyond his years. Closer up, his hair looked lank and wiry. His fingernails were caked in dirt. There was a tough determination behind his eyes. I wondered how that could be, how a boy could be so many things.

"I can save him," he said.

There was something in his face, something in his eyes that made me trust him. I put my faith and the life of my dog in his hands.

"We're going to need some things," he said. "In my den."

"You have a den?" I asked.

The boy nodded. When he saw my eyes begin to widen with expectation, he grinned. Two of his teeth were missing. One looked to be broken at the base. I didn't care though. I was flitting between two states of being, half worrying about Snap, the other filled with the fascination of discovering a new friend who lived in a den in the woods and spoke about saving dogs from wells like he really knew how to do such things.

"We'll need rope and a basket," he said. "I've got both. I know the rope's long enough because I've been in the well before."

"What for?" I asked.

"To see what's down there," he said.

"How many wells are there?" I asked.

"In the woods? Loads. And caves and tunnels."

"Will you show me?" I asked.

"Let's save your dog first," he said. He set off across the clearing, limping along with his cane.

"What happened to your leg?" I asked.

"It's always been like this," he said.

His den was hidden in the folds of a great tree and it was impossible to see until we were almost upon it. He pulled on a rope and a ladder fell to greet him. He clambered up it, an expert acrobat despite his disability and disappeared. A moment later he was back. He was carrying a wicker basket and a rope.

"Do you live here?" I asked.

"Sometimes," he said.

"Don't you have any parents?" I asked.

He didn't answer me.

Despite his disability I struggled to keep up with him as we hiked through the snow. I had no breath for conversation.

It was almost dark when we reached the well again. The boy slung the rope around a tree, fixed the basket to one end and lowered it into the darkness. Then he gripped the rope and leaned back on it before descending. A minute later the rope slackened and he called up to me.

"Your dog's okay," he said. "I'm putting him in the basket. Haul him up."

I gripped the rope and pulled with all my might, my feet slipping in the snow, my hands burning each time the basket bumped against the side of the well. Snap was heavier than I expected but I couldn't allow myself to fail so I pulled and pawed through gritted teeth until the basket turned at the lip of the well and Snap jumped from it into my arms. For a few seconds I was glad just to hold him and pet him. He barked furiously and leapt down into the snow until I started to worry that he'd fall right back in the hole I'd dragged him from. I almost forgot about the boy in the well.

"Now tie the rope to the tree and send it down," he called.

I untied the basket and was tying the rope as instructed when I heard my father calling my name. Panic gripped me. I thought about my footprints in the snow. Had he followed them? What if he discovered me in Cheam woods? All of my new found freedoms would be lost. I'd lose face in front of the boy if my father scolded me, look like a spoiled child. I would never be able to visit the woods again, never learn of the secret caves and tunnels, never get to sit out in the wilderness or hide myself away in the boy's magical den. I had to get back to Nonsuch Park without my father spotting me. I had to make up a story to fill the hours I had been absent. There could be no woods and there could be no boy. Without thinking, I dropped the rope, turned and fled across the clearing away from my father's voice, into the trees and shadows, Snap racing at my heels.

When I thought about the boy again it was much later. I was in bed, my hide sore from the tanning I'd received as my excuses had melted to nothing under my father's questioning. It was snowing out. On my father's radio, which I could hear through the thin walls, the presenters were talking about the coldest night in decades. I regretted that I hadn't thanked the boy for saving Snap and I pledged to return to his den to do exactly that but my father kept me in the house for a week and when I was allowed out again I always feared entering the woods in case my father was testing me

220

and keeping an eye out. So I didn't pay the boy a visit. I did look for him in Nonsuch Park though, and I took detours past the circus camp whenever it was inhabited in case he was there, though I could never pluck up the courage to enter *that* world. I would stare at the rash of caravans and wonder. I was looking for a tall wiry boy with a cherubic face, moppish hair, dirty fingernails, and yellow teeth. I looked every day to begin with, then a few times a week, then occasionally, then never. Other things came to replace thoughts of the boy: sports, girls, my father's second wife, my mother's death, high school, college, marriage, my father's death, children of my own, divorce, a life of repeated patterns.

I forgot about the boy in the well.

But when it snows like this, hard and heavy, I'm forced to think about being in Cheam Woods with my old friend Snap. I think about the childhood I had before my mother left home, how I grew up so quickly when she did leave, how there was no room for a child in my father's world, only a trustworthy, independent son who would learn to face the world without faltering.

And I did learn not to falter, for a long time, until a day of snow, when my own children took *their* dog to Nonsuch Park and didn't come home; until I started to wonder where they might be as twilight threatened. Until I set off for the park in my boots, leaving my estranged wife waiting by the phone for news, my chest constricting with the longing only a parent has for their children; following the tracks of the three, the two children and the dog, to where they converged with another set of tracks, a set of limping footprints, a walking stick falling at regular intervals between, following them into Cheam Woods to a clearing dusted with virgin snow.

But my children were not there.

There were interviews and news reports, sightings and suggestions. There was talk of circus families and kidnapping, but nobody knew where my children had gone and nobody knows where my children are.

Sometimes at night I hear them crying, calling out from a deep, dark place and I think I might be able to find them if I follow their muffled cries. But each time I do, the boy in the well begins to cry too and then he screams his own muffled screams and when he does my children's screams are lost. The boy in the well screams for

221

help, screams for someone to come to his aid on a freezing night in Cheam Woods, screams for somebody to reach down and catch the rope, the rope that sent him crashing to the foot of the well when I let go of it in panic. In the darkness I see his black fingernails clawing and scraping at the walls, the blood thickening beneath them. I hear those fingernails break.

Each Autumn when the circus comes to Nonsuch Park and the big top is buffeted by the winds, I find myself wandering amongst the caravans and canvas awnings, searching for a glimpse of my own flesh and blood. Each winter, when the circus has moved on and Cheam Woods is buried in snow, I spend my nights listening for the sound of the boy in the well calling for help.

I hear the boy's screams and my children screaming for me in the blackest of places and I scream too.

I lie awake screaming.

Letting Out the Heat

Nicky Peacock

Her bedroom door creaked open for the third time that night; the thin corkboard was no match for the sucking draft of her open bay windows. This time Zoe just left it ajar, it was far too much effort to get up and push it too, and closing the window was not an option. Apart from the slight breeze fighting the suffocating summer heat, she was finding the jiggling net curtains both hypnotic and seductive; they made her feel like she was sleeping in a Mills & Boon novel, and that any moment a white shirt clad hunk would swing in and make her not care about sleeping anymore. But there was no hunk, and she did care about getting to sleep, she had an early start in the morning and already the heat had stolen her last three nights slumber.

The heat wave that was swaddling the city had turned from a pleasant temperature rise birthing picnics, sundresses and tan lines to an overbearing annoyance far too quickly. Like a house guest overstaying its welcome. Summer flowers lay dried and dead amongst the picnic tables, cotton clothes clung mercilessly to sweaty burnt skin and, at night, homes felt like gummy, tight prisons where sleep was just beyond your grasp, leaving everyone irritable and drained.

Zoe closed her eyes again and tried to clear her mind but the day's events kept skipping through it like selfish merry children. She tried imagining that it was the dead of winter and that the cozy warm sheets around her were not wrung with sweat and the faint smell of coconut sun cream, but even that bore no sleeping fruit. Taking a deep breath she opened her eyes and focused on her bedroom wall; on it was her favorite picture, a water color of her old family dog Bastion. A playful Red Setter, his tongue permanently dripping from his mouth and dark eyes filled with the kind of mischief that drove him to bury all her left socks in the garden. Though the picture at night took on an all together less inviting aura that sucked his fur of color leaving him sallow and his eyes black, like coal that would never be lit.

223

Without comfort she turned over, plumped the pillow, and after another painful twenty minutes crept by, Zoe finally forced herself into an uneasy sleep.

Her dreams led her down a twisted path bordered with heavy hedges the color of dead Christmas trees. She was dressed in a long, tacky white nightgown that billowed behind her like a B-list actress in a Hammer House of Horror film. At the end of the path lay a big wooden door partly covered in a coat of thin red paint. An old brass sign hovered above the door frame that read: LETTING OUT THE HEAT. She moved her hands over the wood and found the paint wet and sticky, it smelled of old metal, like the shed at the bottom of the garden that scared her as a little girl.

Pressing on the door, she pushed it slowly open; through it was a four poster bed with long trailing white curtains that shimmered in a breeze that seemed to swarm around the room. She couldn't see the window where the breeze had come from but her clammy skin welcomed it, so gratitude overrode logic.

She moved closer to the bed and noticed there was something still and rigid nestled between the sheets. Edging closer she found herself staring at an outline of a large animal. Zoe's fingers danced around the edge of the sheet and little by little she tugged it off. The body was that of a Red Setter dog, it was Bastion. She gasped as her eyes trailed from his lolling tongue to the open wound that slit his body from throat to belly. His matted auburn fur was scabbed with blood and his rib cage was cracked open like a pearl-less oyster. The sheet below was sodden with blood and feces and a heavy smell of rot and splintered bones wafted from Bastion's remains.

I need to wake up, she thought, I need to wake up. Her legs suddenly buckled beneath her and she awoke with a slight start, as if she had tripped over. Zombie-like, she turned over and was instantly sucked back into sleep, only barely hearing the raspy breathes coming from the shadow lurking in the corner of her bedroom. Back to sleep she fell, back through the red door, back to the side of the bed, to the breeze laced with death.

"Careful you might hurt yourself," a voice came from beneath the bed.

"Who's there?" she pulled at the bed clothes to try and get up, but the bed was poorly made and so the bottom sheet just fell on top of her bringing down what was left of Bastion to crumple like a wet sweet wrapper beside her. She gasped and threw the sheet back on itself to cover up the corpse.

"Are you hurt?" asked the voice.

"Who's there?" It was more of a scream than a question, but it got an answer anyway.

"I'm Gobble."

That was when she saw him. His eyes were black, but not the black that holes and deep darkness claim, no it was a black just devoid of light, missing all colors and capturing nothing; a dull and unreadable black, its only job that of allowing the small, spindly creature they were attached to to see. It jimmied itself from under the bed and sat crossed legged in front of her.

"Why are you here?" it asked.

"I came for my dog."

"I see," he hotched closer.

"I want to wake up now."

"What dog?"

She pointed at the lump of mismatched meat beneath the sheet.

"Oh, what was his name?"

"Bastion."

"What a lovely name," Gobble remarked as he stood up. His limbs were long and impossibly thin, but his belly protruded from his frame, large and round like he'd swallowed a pumpkin whole. His head was as large as his belly making him appear almost child-like. His skin was the shade of lavender long after it's dried and crushed.

"We had to get the heat out of him; poor thing was so hot with all that fur."

Zoe felt the color bleed from her skin, even her sunburn paled.

"You don't look well," Gobble whispered and placed a thin hand on her arm. It was cold but not uncomfortable, she did not pull away, instead she yawned and crawled onto the bed.

"Sleepy now," Gobble soothed as he began stroking her skin with his twiggy fingers. He edged his free hand beneath a nearby pillow and pulled out a thermometer. Gently he slipped it into her mouth, read it and then shook his head. "Your temperature is too high, we have to cool you down."

"Yes, I do feel hot, and I need to sleep. I have an early start in the morning."

He climbed onto the bed with her.

"Not long now," he soothed. "You'll feel better once the heat's out." It felt as if he was telling her a bedtime story. Memories of fairytales flooded her thoughts, knights and princesses, kings and queens. Stories where the righteous always prevailed and monsters were always slaughtered. Peril was just a prelude to a happy ending and the damsel was always saved in the nick of time.

She didn't really feel him cut into her stomach, but she did feel her body's inner heat escaping from her cracked torso and the warm blood that now soaked the bedding beneath her, those hot sensations were what shook her from her fairy tale. A cry escaped Zoe's lips, soft and laced with blood, she tried to put her hand to the pain yet found herself unable to move.

"Don't worry," said Gobble. "I've severed your spinal cord, you can't move and fall."

With that he eased his gangly hand into her stomach and pulled at her liver. She felt something snap and pop, then more blood oozed out. Wake up, she thought, please wake up. Slobbering noises made Zoe look up; Gobble was perched on her chest devouring her liver. He took great lusty bites from it, chomping and gnawing, his mouth extending enough for her to see her precious organ being mashed and skewed by his pointy plentiful teeth.

"Please stop . . ."

He pulled his free arm back and plunged it into the hole again. Pain shot through her like wild electricity, his black eyes staring as he pushed up through her rib cage. She felt a tug under her left breast and then gasped for air as he pulled out a lung. He discarded what was left of the liver and used both hands to turn the lung and lick the blood from the deflating organ.

Gobble grinned and then reached for his thermometer; he pushed it into the yawning red orifice in Zoe's chest.

"There," he said. "You're much cooler now."

Zoe's breaths became shallow and quick, the cavity where the fleshy bag had been ached with its absence. Pain clouded around her making the room go very dark. Her eyelids fought like dying butterflies. The last thing she saw was Gobble's teeth ripping through her lung and her final thought was that, at last, she was waking . . .

* * *

When the police arrived, they found Zoe's body strewn across the bed naked and cracked open. A policeman, staring at her remains, explained the situation to the coroner.

"We think he got in through the bay windows. A Mr. R. Gobs, an escapee from Moon Crescent Mental hospital for the criminally insane."

"Well," the coroner sighed. "I can tell you straight off she's missing her liver and at least one lung. Trophies?"

"No," replied the policeman mopping his brow. "He's an eater."

"How the hell did he escape?"

The policeman cast his eyes down and shuffled his feet around.

"The guard fell asleep and Mr. Gobs crawled out an open window."

"Dear God, man, what happened to the security?" The coroner shook his head trying to shake loose the thoughts of who else might have slipped away into the hot night while guards slept and windows beckoned.

"It's the heat, everyone is so exhausted and it would be inhumane not to crack a window for the prisoners."

The coroner's eyes widen. "Have you found him?" he asked.

"No, not yet, but he can't have gotten far . . . not on a full stomach."

The faces of all in the room blushed with a greenish tinge.

"We better get a photo of him out there, alert the media, and get the public more security conscious."

The policeman sniffed, the funk of new blood and an old murderer filled his nostrils. "I doubt anyone is gonna close their windows in this heat." He then remembered he'd left his own windows wide open back home. In a summer like this you had to let the heat out.

Tap Tap

Gregory Bastianelli

Marie entered the science building hoping to get some quiet time to study. She knew the building was being renovated during the day and several areas were off-limits to students, but the workers were usually done by this time in the evening. And truth be told, even if they were still working, construction would have been easier to handle than the noise back at the dorm that her roommate and her friends were creating.

As Marie walked down the second-floor hallway, Professor Stevens came rushing up to her, his face flush with excitement, his voice stammering.

He wasn't making much sense to her at first, just babbling that the construction workers had discovered something hidden behind a wall in the old resource room.

"What? What did they find?" Marie asked.

"Come," and he took off, Marie hustling behind to keep up.

"We're expanding the resource room," he said as they strode down past classrooms. "You know, house more books, students. But when the workers took down the paneling of one of the interior walls, they found another wall—like an alcove."

Professor Stevens ushered her into the dusty resource room, arms gesticulating with excitement.

It was a long, rectangular room, all four walls lined with deep bookshelves. The west wall—the wall that was going to be torn down to expand the room into the adjacent space—had three tall arched windows that looked out onto the tree-lined quad of the campus. The table closest to the west wall was piled with books removed from the shelves.

The wooden shelves had been removed from this wall and stacked into a corner. About one-third of the paneled wall behind the bookcase had been removed. In the darkened space inside the wall, Marie could see another wall recessed behind the original. There were shelves lining the alcove—old shelves—and on the shelves

228

were several glass jars covered in a thin film of dust. The containers were about two-feet tall, like old-fashioned pickle jars, and seemed to be filled with a brownish liquid substance.

"Just look at that," Professor Stevens said, shaking his head.

Two construction workers stood on either side of the opening, looking back and forth from the professor to the opening in the wall, not sure what to do.

Marie adjusted her glasses and stepped closer.

Beyond the dust covering, a warped face floated in the brownish liquid.

Marie gasped, bringing her hand to her mouth, and turned to the professor. She removed her hand and tried to speak but couldn't force any words out. She turned back to the jar and the small, grayish body with the large head and small arms and legs floating inside the container. She scanned all the shelves. There must have been at least two dozen of the jars and each one held a tiny body of various size and development. Human bodies. Babies.

Her stomach churned and she thought she might be sick. She turned away, her face pale, her head dizzy.

"What?" was all she could mutter.

"Fetuses," the professor answered. "The largest one can't be more than twenty-eight weeks." His face held an expression of marvel and wonderment.

"But . . . " Marie said, trying not to choke on the words. "What on earth are they doing here?"

The professor folded his arms and shrugged. "Who knows? The real question is how long have they been here? This part of the building hasn't been worked on in at least fifty or sixty years." He shook his head. "They must have been donated and used in some type of study. But why they were just left behind the wall or where they came from, I have no idea."

Professor Stevens walked up to the shelves and lifted a jar off the wall. He rubbed his sleeve against the glass and held it up to the light, peering in at what could have become a living human being. He carefully placed the jar back on the shelf.

"I've got to find Professor Brown and tell him about this. He's head of the science department; he's been here the longest. Maybe he knows about them, or at least has an idea what we do about it."

He turned to Marie.

"I need you to stay here."

"Huh?"

"The workers were kind enough to stay while I tried to find someone but they're off the clock." They muttered some words of agreement. "I would feel so much better if the room wasn't left un-attended while I contact Brown and the Dean. This find is too valu-able. I need someone to stay, just until I return."

Marie shook her head, "Oh no, I couldn't."

"Come now, Marie, you were coming here to study anyway."

"But not with those," she pointed at the opening in the wall.

"It should only be a little while, the phone is on the first floor; I can call Professor Brown and then return." Stevens turned to the workers and thanked them, and they left the room. "Please be a dear," he said. "Don't worry, it's not like they can hurt you."

She tried to utter another protest, but he was already patting her arm and then rushed out of the room and down the hallway. Ma-rie exhaled a deep breath. She turned back to the room and slowly walked over to one of the study tables, purposely not glancing at the opening in the back wall. Then, just as she began pulling a chair out, she did look over at the glass jars neatly lined up on the shelves, and the tiny bodies floating within them.

She shuddered, sitting down with her back to the wall. She flipped open a book and uncaringly stared at the jumbled words on the pages, not really focusing on the sentences and paragraphs. Dig-ging into her knapsack, she took out a notebook and a couple pens.

She glanced over her shoulder.

All the faces in the jars had their eyes closed, yet their heads seemed to be turned toward where she sat—as if staring at her through their dead, closed eyelids. The jar Professor Steven's had rubbed was the clearest now, and she could see the large head above the small body, its tiny nose and mouth. The fingers on its small hands were pulled together into tiny fists.

Of course the eyes would be closed, she thought. They hadn't even been born. And wouldn't be.

The pit of her stomach tightened and she turned away.

No, they wouldn't be born, because they weren't alive. May-be at one time, but something happened, and somehow they ended up here.

"It wasn't your fault." Marie was surprised she had spoken aloud. Her voice seemed lost in the empty room.

But was it *her* fault? She was young, her studies were important to her. It was her future she had to worry about. That may be selfish, but she had to worry about herself first. Maybe if she had taken better precautions. At the beginning she denied it had happened. Refused to believe it, even though the strange feeling inside her told her otherwise.

But she couldn't tell anyone, not even her roommate. What would she think? What would her friends think? She wasn't about to alter her life. She was a college student, and that's all she wanted to be—a college student, just like everyone else. So she didn't pay attention, just kept going to classes, kept partying, drinking, smoking and eating the things she wanted to eat.

When her body started to change, Marie just wore baggier clothing and no one noticed. Didn't all college kids put on a little weight? It was expected.

She twirled her pen around on her notebook. It was no use, she wasn't going to get any studying done, not with those *things* there in the room with her.

Is that what they were? Things?

Marie started to turn but stopped herself. *Just don't look at them. Pretend they're not even there.*

Isn't that what she had tried to do? Pretend it wasn't there, even as her belly grew? Could she really keep hiding it? And what was the point? Eventually she would have to face the truth and do something about it. Wishing it away wasn't going to work.

One day the sensations in her belly stopped. Maybe she had imagined it all. It gave her hope. Then the bleeding came, and she couldn't put off going to a doctor. She could no longer pretend nothing was happening.

Marie wished someone else were in the resource room with her, someone else studying. But with all the construction work that had been going on in the building the last few weeks, most students stayed away and went to the main campus library to do their work. That's what she should have done. Why did she have to come here tonight of all nights?

Tap tap.

It was a faint sound, and she sat straight up in her chair listening quietly. *What was that?*

She looked over to the windows. Maybe a tree branch bending to the glass in the wind. She ran a hand through her dark hair

231

and gripped her pen, doodling on the blank page in the notebook. She wished the professor would hurry. It was too damn quiet in this building.

Tap tap.

There it was again. She got up and went to the windows, looking out into the dark night and the students below walking to and fro on the paved pathways.

Oh to be out there with them and away from this desolate room, she thought.

She looked at the trees on that side of the building, but none of their limbs seemed close enough to the windows to brush against them.

Marie looked over at the opening in the back wall. No matter how hard she tried, she couldn't help staring at them. She didn't want to look at them, but there they were, always pulling her gaze back. She wished she could put something over them, a blanket or curtain, to block her view.

She thought for a moment, then walked over to the doorway and flicked the light switch. The room descended into darkness. She closed the door to keep the hallway lights out and blindly felt her way back to the table. She folded her arms on her book and lay her head down on them.

Just rest, she thought, until the professor gets back. Don't even think of looking behind you. If you can't see them, they're not there.

But they were there. Right behind her. And if she turned, would she be able to see them in the darkness. No, she thought. She had turned off the lights.

Marie raised her head and glanced behind her.

Light from the streetlights out in the quad spilled through the window casting a block of light directly on the back wall.

The opening looked jagged in the darkness. The liquid in the jars glowed almost green in the diffused light. The bodies seemed to bob in the liquid, like buoys on a dark sea—like boys in a jar. Tiny boys and girls. Little bodies, little arms. Eyes closed but staring at her through the murk.

She put her head back down.

Please hurry, professor.

She remembered the doctor scolding her. Her baby was still-born, and they would have to induce labor so she could still deliver it. Maybe it was the lack of nutrition, the fact she hadn't taken care of her body. They may never know the cause, but she certainly didn't help it any by her actions. Maybe she had inadvertently willed it. She hadn't wanted a child at all.

Tap tap.

Her head jerked up. Could there still be some other construction going on in the building? No. They weren't supposed to work at night.

She felt a chill and rubbed her arms.

Tap tap.

The sound came from behind her.

She slowly turned her head and looked back toward the opening in the wall. The jars glowed in the sickly block of streetlight, taunting her.

Marie got up from her seat and took a couple slow steps toward the back of the room. Her eyes scanned the rows of the jars, from one to the next to the next. She nervously moved even closer, till she was just a couple feet away from the wall.

Each of the little fetuses floated in the liquid, suspended in its tiny little prison. The soft flesh was gray, with tiny wrinkles where the limbs met the abdomen and around the bend of the knees and elbows.

They're so small and frail, she thought.

And helpless.

Just like in the operating room, when she pushed and pushed and the doctor finally pulled the lifeless thing from her body and she glanced down between her legs and caught, just for a second before they wrapped it in a sheet and took it away, the small, grayish, mucous-covered body with the large head and the closed eyes that looked like—

Just like the one in the jar whose dust the professor had wiped clean. A tiny little thing who couldn't even open its eyes to look at her. And what would it have thought if it had looked at her? What would those eyes have held in them?

She turned away from the wall.

Tap tap.

She stopped in her tracks. Her body pivoted slowly, and she looked back at the glass jar in front of her. The fetus' tiny right hand, fingers clenched, rested against the inside of the glass jar.

Not possible, she told herself. The hand was close to the

body before.

She wanted to back away, but couldn't force herself to move. They all seemed to be looking out of their jars at her. Even with their eyes closed, somehow they were seeing her, piercing into her soul.

She quickly glanced at the bottom shelf. Did something just move? Did the tiny figure in the middle jar shift? Of course not. She closed her eyes and tried to clear her mind.

Tap tap.

Her eyes shot open and looked at the jar directly in front of her. The knuckles of the right hand still rested against the glass.

She reached up and lifted the jar off the shelf. It was surprisingly heavy. The liquid sloshed and the fetus shifted, rolling over to its left. A small bubble rose to the surface of the liquid and burst. The fetus' left hand floated forward, bouncing against the glass.

Tap tap.

Marie shrieked and let go of the jar, watching it drop to the floor. It shattered on the wood, splashing her feet and legs with brown, wet muck. A rank odor wafted up at Marie, gagging her. The fetus flopped over onto its belly, its hands outstretched on the floorboards toward her feet.

"NO!" she screamed. She ran back to the table and threw herself on top of its surface. Still screaming until her fingers wrapped around a heavy textbook.

She stood, staring at the remaining jars on the wall, gripping the book.

"It wasn't my fault! There was nothing I could do!" she screamed.

Marie raced forward, gripping the book tightly and raising it over her head. She lunged forward, swinging it into the jar on the far right of the top shelf. The glass shattered against another jar and the liquid cascaded down the shelves, the limp body of the fetuses flowing with it, flopping from one shelf to the next till it reached the bottom. She continued swinging the book, busting one jar after the other, screaming as the frail bodies slid from them and dropped to the floor with fleshy thudding sounds. The stagnant liquid pooled up around her feet, the noxious fumes rising up around her and choking her.

Marie slid down to the floor, crying and sobbing, staring at the carnage around her feet. She sensed something above her and looked up.

Professor Stevens and Professor Brown, along with a campus security guard, stood there looking at her with horror. Marie's face was a tangle of hair streaked with sweat, tears, and formaldehyde. She could only imagine what she looked like to them.

"It wasn't my fault," she muttered. She continued muttering the phrase and nothing else as they hauled her away. An Ambulance eventual arrived, the medics sedated her, and Marie slipped into unconsciousness.

She awoke groggy, in a small dark room, on a hard bed. She reached her hand out and felt a soft padded wall. She looked around in the darkness and noticed a small source of light.

An oval window in the middle of a narrow door let in light. She got up and approached it. The door was locked. Wire mesh was imbedded in the thick glass window and she looked out into a well-lit hallway.

Down to the right she could partially see a nurses' station and a young woman in white sitting behind the counter bent over some paperwork. She cried out to the woman, but the room was soundproof. There was nothing the nurse could have done anyway. It wasn't *her* fault Marie was in there.

Marie slowly reached up a slight shaky hand, curling a couple of fingers and brought her knuckles against the glass.

Tap tap.

About the Authors

Desmond Warzel is the author of some two dozen short stories, including *The Elephant in the Marble* from the initial volume of Night Terrors. This past year, his work has appeared online at Daily Science Fiction and Tor.com, in ear-pleasing audio at Escape Pod and Cast of Wonders, and on genuine dead tree in I*t Came From Her Purse* (Sam's Dot Publishing) and *Candle in the Attic Window* (Innsmouth Free Press). He lives in northwestern Pennsylvania, where every day he wages a pitched battle against distraction and sloth, all to give you something new to read. Isn't that nice?

John Peters lives with his wife, their five children and an ever-changing number of assorted creatures (both domesticated and untamed) in the mountains of Southwest Virginia. He is editor of a small daily newspaper, and his fiction has appeared in the Stoker-nominated Horror Library Vol. 3; The Middle of Nowhere: Horror in Rural America; Midnight Echo; Spinetinglers; Dark Recesses, and elsewhere. When not writing, editing, or chasing the children (or their pets), he spends his time coaching a high school varsity ladies basketball team.

Madhvi Ramani grew up in London and lives in Berlin. Her short stories have appeared in Underground Voices, PARSEC Ink's Triangulation: Last Contact anthology and Tindal Street Press's Too Asian, Not Asian Enough anthology among others.

Amber Keller is a writer who delves into dark fiction, particularly horror and suspense/thrillers. Besides having finished two horror novels this year, she has numerous short stories available on her blog, and is fortunate to be a part of two anthologies. She is a member of the Horror Writers Association, and also contributes to various websites and emagazines, including horror and science fiction movie reviews. When not at her laptop, she can be found looking for things that go bump in the night.

Patricia Russo has had stories published at Fantasy, Chizine, Daily SF, and many other publications, online and print. Her first collection, *Shiny Thing*, has recently been released by Papaveria Press.

Jason Andrew lives in Seattle, Washington with his wife Lisa.

236

He is an associate member of the Science Fiction and Fantasy Writers of America and member of the International Association of Media Tie-In Writers. By day, he works as a mild-mannered technical writer. By night, he writes stories of the fantastic and occasionally fights crime. As a child, Jason spent his Saturdays watching the Creature Feature classics and furiously scribbling down stories; his first short story, written at age six, titled 'The Wolfman Eats Perry Mason' was rejected and caused his Grandmother to watch him very closely for a few years. You can find out more about Jason at:
www.jasonbandrew.com.

Amanda C. Davis is an engineer who loves horror movies, gardening, and irony. Her work runs the gamut of speculative fiction and has appeared in Shock Totem, Redstone Science Fiction, Goblin Fruit, and others. You can follow her on Twitter (@davisac1) or read more of her stories at: http://www.amandacdavis.com.

Matthew Fryer was born and bred in Sheffield, England. He studied English at university, but now works in a subterranean medical facility and probably doesn't get enough natural light. His fiction has appeared in publications such as *Murky Depths*, *Living After Midnight*, *Necrotic Tissue* and *Full Fathom Forty*. As well as books, he enjoys loud music, Texas Hold 'Em, Indian food, English beer, and watching reruns of *The Wire* with his very patient wife. They have a deranged cat that looks like Hitler. Visit his cheesily-titled website 'The Hellforge' at:
www.matthewfryer.com

Brad C. Hodson is a writer living in Los Angeles. His first novel, DARLING, will be released in April of 2012. He also co-wrote the award winning cult comedy GEORGE: A ZOMBIE INTERVENTION. When not writing, he's usually dragging heavy sleds and throwing sandbags in the park while pretending he's a Viking. The mead helps. For random musings on the horror genre, life in Los Angeles, or to find out other books to find his short fiction in, please visit: www.brad-hodson.com.

Maria Alexander has committed a number of literary crimes as an author of horror, suspense and humor. Her deeds have appeared in award-winning anthologies and magazines beside greats such as Chuck Palahniuk and David Morrell. Praised by disreputable rags like Rue Morgue and Fangoria, she atones for her vices by being an award-winning copywriter for Disney's websites. For the full literary rap sheet, visit her website: www.mariaalexander.net.

Jason V Brock has been widely published in magazines, comics and anthologies such as Butcher Knives & Body Counts; Calliope; The Weird Fiction Review; Black Wings II; Like Water for Quarks; Fangoria and other venues. He is currently finishing several novels. Brock served as coeditor/contributor to the award-winning Cycatrix Press anthology The Bleeding Edge: Dark Barriers, Dark Frontiers with William F. Nolan (Logan's Run). Brock and Nolan also teamed for the follow-up anthology, The Devil's Coattails: More Dispatches from the Dark Frontier.

Brock's films include the highly-regarded documentaries Charles Beaumont: The Short Life of Twilight Zone's Magic Man; The AckerMonster Chronicles (about legendary agent and editor Forrest J Ackerman), and the forthcoming Image, Reflection, Shadow: Artists of the Fantastic.

A health nut and gadget freak, he lives in the Portland, OR area, and loves his wife Sunni, their family of reptiles/amphibians, and practicing vegan/vegetarianism. Visit his website at:

http://www.JaSunni.com.

Christopher Hawkins lives in the Chicago area, where he co-edits the One Buck Horror anthology series. His previous works of short fiction have been published in Sinister Tales, Murky Depths, and The Harrow, as well as in the anthologies Read By Dawn vol 2, Shadow Regions, and The Big Book of New Short Horror. For more information about his life and his work, visit:

www.christopher-hawkins.com.

Ken Goldman is a former English and Film Studies teacher at George Washington High in Philadelphia. An affiliate member of the Horror Writers Association, Ken has homes on the Main Line in Pennsylvania and at the Jersey shore depending on his mood and the track of the sun. His stories appear in over 600 independent press publications in the U.S., Canada, the UK, and Australia with over twenty more due for publication in 2012. He has written two books; a book of short stories, *You Had Me At ARRGH!!* (Sam's Dot Publishers) and a novella, *Desiree* (Damnation Books).

G. K. Hayes was Managing Editor of the science fiction magazine Critical Mass, and is a multi-award winner for his short fiction. His most recent stories, *You always Hurt the One You Love* can be found stumbling about in Zombiesque from DAW books; and *Papa Doc and the Ugly Black Mambo* hides beneath the covers of Zombies from Dark Moon Books. G.K. Hayes, himself, resides at: www.gkhayes.com.

Gregory Bastianelli is a New Hampshire native and graduated

238

from the University of New Hampshire. He worked for nearly two decades at a daily newspaper where the highlights of his career were interviewing shock rocker Alice Cooper and B-movie icon Bruce Campbell. His stories have appeared in the magazines Black Ink Horror, Sinister Tales and Beyond Centauri; the magazine anthologies Cover of Darkness and Encounters; the online magazines Absent Willow Review and Down in the Cellar; and the pulp anthologies Men of Mystery Vol. II and Dan Fowler, G-Man. His horror novel, Jokers Club was released in November by JournalStone.

AJ Brown is a story teller who pens emotionally charged/character driven stories that often include a touch of dark paranormal. His work has received such honors as a Pushcart nomination, and his story 'Picket Fences' was the editor's choice for issue 12 of Necrotic Tissue. Bards and Sages Quarterly, Liquid Imagination, and SNM Horror are a few of the literary zines where his stories can be found. If you'd like to learn more about AJ Brown's life and work, visit his blog: AJ Type Negative.

David Bischoff is a New York Times bestselling writer of horror, fantasy and science fiction. He is also a script writer with screen credits that include *Star Trek: The Next Generation*. Books beginning to become available as ebooks include : *The Destiny Dice, Tin Woodman* and *The Infinite Battle*. As an editor, his efforts include the recently released *Broadwalk Empire* and *The Storie Of Margie Harris, Vol. One*. He lives in Eugene OR.

Danny Rhode's debut novel, *Asboville,* was published in October 2006. Well received by critics it was selected as a Waterstones Booksellers Paperback of the Year. It has been adapted for BBC Films by the dramatist Nick Leather. His second novel, *Soldier Boy*, was published in February 2009. He is currently working on his third novel. Danny's speculative short stories have appeared regularly in publications on both sides of the Atlantic. His first venture into e-publishing, a collection of previously published short stories entitled *The Knowledge and other stories*, is available now from Amazon Kindle. Visit his website at:
www.dannyrhodes.net.

Bob Macumber writes out of Brandon, Manitoba, Canada. He is a die hard fan of the horror genre and keeps a special place in his twisted, little heart for creature features. He will continue to weave tales of the gruesome and macabre, so if you enjoyed A Cat Named Mittens, stay tuned horror fans. When not writing, you can catch Bob stepping in the cage and competing in Mixed Martial Arts.

Nicky Peacock is an English author living in the UK. She runs a local writers' group and had been published in the US by: Dead Avenue Press, Wicked East Press, Dark Moon Books, Static Movement, Seven Archons Press, Pill Hill Press, Escape Collective Publishing, Post Mortem Press and of course, Blood Bound Books. In the UK by the British Libraries and Walker Books. For further information on her and her work please see: www.creativemindswriting.co.uk/page18.htm

Matthew S. Dent is a writer of dark fiction, based in a small village in rural Berkshire, in the United Kingdom. He writes to keep the demons off his back, and when he doesn't have a pen in his hand he can usually be found neck-deep in politics. Matthew's stories have been published in a number of anthologies and magazines, and he can be found on Twitter at @MatthewSDent or at: http://matthewsdent.wordpress.com

Lawrence Conquest lives in Bristol, England. His previous stories for Blood Bound Books are: "The Face in the Sand' (published in *Night Terrors*, honorable mention Best Horror of the Year 2010), 'Beneath the Trees' (*Seasons in the Abyss*) and 'Life to the Lifeless' (*Steamy Screams*). Novella 'Feeding Ambition' is forthcoming from the same publisher. More info can be found at: www.lawrence-conquest.blogspot.com

Angela Bodine currently lives in West Virginia with her husband and three children. She spends her spare time writing about things she's always wanted to see . . . and the dark places no one wants to go.

Mike Tager hails from Baltimore, Maryland. He is currently applying to Master's Programs in Writing. His work can be found if you look for it.

Justin Gustainis is a college professor living in upstate New York. In addition to a number of short stories, he is the author of the Morris and Chastain Investigations series of novels (Black Magic Woman, Evil Ways, and Sympathy for the Devil), as well as the "Haunted Scranton" series (Hard Spell and the forthcoming Evil Dark). He is also editor of the anthology Those Who Fight Monsters: Tales of Occult Detectives. Mister Gustainis is a graduate of the Odyssey Writing Workshop.

Dominic E. Lacasse writes mainly horror and considers H.P. Lovecraft and Edgar Allen Poe his main influences in this field. He currently lives in Halifax, Nova Scotia, Canada, where he is pursuing a Master's degree in Classics. He finds in fiction a means for the expression of his interests, in ancient languages and in all things old and unknown—or in true Lovecraftian language, things 'better left unknown.' He is originally from Calais, a small town in Maine near the Canadian border, and he remembers with fondness gawking at Stephen King's house as a child.

Richard Farren Barber was born in Nottingham in July 1970. After studying in London he returned to the East Midlands. He lives with his wife and son and works as a Development Services Manager for a local university.
He has had short stories published in Alt Fiction, Blood Oranges, Derby Scribes Anthology, Derby Telegraph, Murky Depths, Midnight Echo, Midnight Street, Morpheus Tales, The House of Horror, Trembles, broadcast on BBC Radio Derby and performed at the World Horror Convention. For 2010/11 Richard was sponsored by Writing East Midlands in the development of his novel "Bloodie Bones."
His website can be found here: www.richardfarrenbarber.co.uk

John Morgan has been a member of the Ghost Story Society and a familiar face at meetings of the Birmingham Sci Fi Group, listening to authors such as Terry Pratchett, Iain M Banks and Harry Harrison talk about their work. To date, he has had twenty-or-so short stories published in various small press magazines and anthologies, and is currently having a nervous breakdown trying to get to grips with the first draft of a novel.

Made in the USA
Middletown, DE
31 December 2017